Silent Sky

*To Kent,
Happy Reading,
Happy Flying,
Enjoy!
Cate McGhee*

Cate Mighell

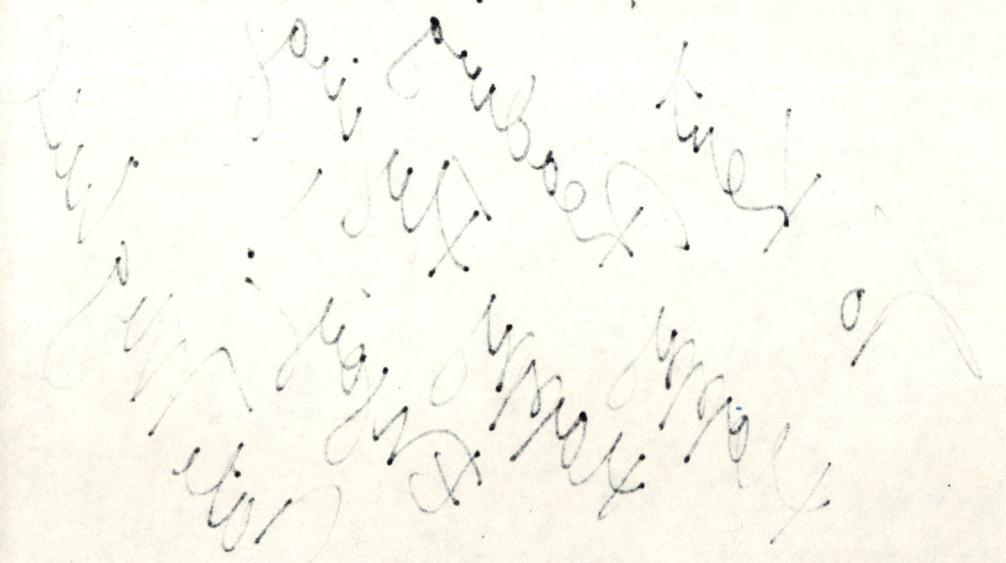

Silent Sky

A Reina Dessiner Mystery

Cate Mighell

One Sky Publishing

Cate Mighell

Copyright 2013 by Cate Mighell.

All rights reserved. No part of this publication may be reproduced or transmitted in any form or by any means (electronic, mechanical, or otherwise) without prior written permission from the author.

ISBN: 978-0-9888908-0-0

Requests for permission to copy or reproduce this work should be submitted to the author at
cjmighell@gmail.com
or One Sky Publishing at
requests@oneskypublishing.com

Printed in the United States of America
by Mira Digital Publishing
1010 Hanley Industrial Ct.
Brentwood, MO 6314

Silent Sky

Acknowledgment

This story is dedicated to my children.
- to Bryce for reading, reading, and reading *again* the early versions and providing constructive feedback.
- to John for reading the first few chapters and giving me exactly the encouragement I needed by saying he couldn't wait to find out what happens.
- to Kennan who always believed in me and understood the dreamer behind the mom machine.

This story is also dedicated to the many instructors and friends who encouraged me when I began flying and who supported me in my business and writing endeavors.

The quote below kept me going. It was stenciled big on my flight school wall:

Whatever you can do,
or dream you can do,
Begin it!
Boldness has genius, power, and magic in it.

~Goethe

Cate Mighell

Disclaimer

Although every writer draws from their personal experiences,
please be assured that there is no character in this book
that represents a real person.
Any similarities to people or places you may know are
entirely coincidental and unintentional.
Every character in this book is purely fictitious.

Enjoy!

Silent Sky

Cate Mighell

Prologue

Maria lay stretched on the floor, arms extended perpendicular from her body. She had lain there so long that her muscles no longer cramped, having either relaxed or gone numb. The first time she prostrated herself, some months ago, her tears had soaked the carpet, each drop disappearing silently into the soft, hand-woven, Persian rug. Now, the tears were gone. Only the daily face down, heart down, body down embrace of the ground remained. A total release into its hardness.

She knew Peter would be home soon. Rising slowly, muscles and joints creaking at the transition from horizontal to vertical gravity loads, she doubled over at a sudden pain in her side, as if she had been stabbed. When she could finally stand straight, she turned to the long mirror in the corner. Staring without recognition, she whispered, "Why do you look for the living among the dead?"

She shook her head violently as if to clear it, straightened her skirt, and reached for a brush. Seeing that her left cheek carried indentations from the carpet - a long line, crossed by a shorter line - she patted and rubbed the marks away. But what did it matter? Peter would never notice.

Entering the kitchen, she surveyed its tidiness. The table was set, napkins folded and ready for laps, water glasses filled and ready for lips. But it was for appearances only. She knew he wouldn't eat. She furrowed her eyebrows in surprise at the homey curtains and the little knickknacks on the windowsill. Although chosen by her, they seemed foreign, placed there by a stranger. Gazing at the large crucifix on the wall above the knife block, she noticed a splash of red on it. She took a sponge from the sink and wiped it off. Tomato sauce from last night's pasta.

Disoriented, she glanced at the wall calendar for the date, then turned away without remembering it, one day the same as another. Going to the oven, she pulled out the rice casserole and placed it on the black and blue trivet, one of the few items from her mother's kitchen. She stared at the steaming dish, knowing it would cool and congeal and then she would dump it, untouched, into the garbage.

Maria heard the click of the front door in the silent house. She stared sightlessly out the window into the gray of the day as her ears followed his footsteps down the hardwood-floor hallway and into the bedroom. She heard the thump of his body as it fell like a dead weight onto the mattress, and the *oof* of a weary exhalation.

She turned to the refrigerator, then walked slowly and silently down the hallway to the bedroom. She sat down gently next to her husband, her weight barely indenting the edge of the bed, and smoothed the hair from his brow. Damp, sticky, hot. Bending to kiss his forehead, she tasted salt on her lips. She knew he was dying, regardless of what the doctor said.

"Maria . . . ."

"Yes, Peter."

"I'm so thirsty . . . ."

"I know. I brought you some orange juice. Here, drink." She held the cup to his lips.

His head fell back on the pillow. "You're too good to me," he murmured, eyes closed.

"Yes," she whispered back. "Yes, Peter."

Cate Mighell

Six Weeks Later

Cate Mighell

Chapter 1

In a month's worth of jail visits, Reina's client had not spoken a single word. Evidence proved the woman could speak; her verbal confession was on record, but she'd remained silent since the day of her arrest. She had no more story to give. She'd willingly forfeited her constitutional rights, refusing to post bail, refusing to hire an attorney, refusing to make an attempt at self defense.

As Maria's assigned public defender, Reina Dessiner sat looking at her client in frustration. Day after day, she tried to get a rise out of the gray and lifeless woman, hoping to find a way through the curtain of silence. A less determined attorney might have given up, but Reina didn't quit easily. There was something about this woman that both irritated her and stirred her compassion. Plus that, she didn't like to lose.

"Maria, as you know, we pleaded 'standing mute' at the arraignment, *best damn use of that plea I've ever used, too,* but ultimately the finding is going to be guilty or not-guilty. I'd like it to be not-guilty."

No reaction from Maria.

"I had hoped we could get your confession tossed out because you offered it so quickly that the police officers who took you to the station failed to read you your rights. *That was clever of you.* You are familiar with the Miranda Law, aren't you Maria?"

No answer.

"Maria?"

Maria's eyes remained on her lap.

"Well, Judge Takahashi didn't see it our way. She said your words appear to have been offered without 'undue custodial or interrogative influences.' She denied our pretrial motion to suppress the confession. Do you know what that means?"

Silence.

"I'll tell you what it means. It means I'm running out of options or ideas on how to win freedom for you. It means I really need your assistance now to understand how I can help you."

Maria sat, unmoving, a shriveled shell of a woman. Reina waited, as she waited each morning during their visits, hopeful for a response. But she waited in vain. It was like she'd been given a book to read that, when opened, was completely blank. No words, no voice, no story. Reina sat for a few moments longer, listening to the sound of nothing. With a sigh, she stood, nodded to the guard, and headed to her office.

Chapter 2

Reina awoke in a sweat from the falling dream. Always the falling dream. But this time it was different. Eyes closed, she recalled being dragged through the air by two large birds-of-prey who pecked and fought over her, each trying to wrest her from the other bird. As the dark bird yanked her free from the larger, lighter bird, her arm severed at the elbow and she dropped toward a sea of flames. Falling backwards, she could see the dark bird circling overhead with her bent and broken arm in its beak.

With some effort, she forced herself to open her eyes, shaking off the lingering tendrils of the nightmare. She turned onto her side to cuddle into Sam, snoring on the pillow next to her. Scooching close, her breasts pressed against his arm, she inhaled his scent, a combination of mint bodywash and sweat. After five nights together, she really only "knew" him in the biblical sense, but right now it was nice to have someone with whom she could snuggle.

As the frightening dream receded, her physical needs emerged. She arched her neck to reach up and nibble gently on his ear, her tongue making little circles around the grooves and knobs of his earlobe. He stirred and mumbled something incoherent, which she took as approval. She breathed lightly into his ear and continued her kisses down his neck, nipping a little on his shoulder and emitting a low growl as her fingertip traced lightly up his arm and across his chest. She brushed his nipple with her traveling hand, back and forth, then rolled it between her thumb and finger. He moaned lightly, his body awakening to her touch. Moving slowly, her wandering fingers continued south to his warm, flat belly, stroking and tapping and teasing, then on through the patch of soft hair. She wrapped a fist around him and said, "Looks like I found some meat."

Completely awake now, Sam opened his eyes and flipped over on top of Reina, pinning her arms to the bed. "You know what happens when you awaken the sleeping lion?" he whispered.

"No, what?" she breathed back, her eyes wide, heart thumping in anticipation.

"He'll eat you alive," and he proceeded to do just that, dropping his lips to hers and forcing her mouth open with his tongue. As his mouth worked over hers, one hand reached down and twisted her hips to the side. With a quick motion, he slapped her hard on the ass.

Reina arched her back with a deep moan. Rolling over again on top, she lowered herself on to him and whispered, "It's the lioness that does the hunting."

Placing his hands on her hips, he moved her up and down slowly, then faster and faster until they both found their release, with a purr and a roar. She collapsed on top of him, then rolled to his side, resting her head on his chest. As her breathing returned to normal, she heard him snoring again. *That didn't take long.* Her brain started humming, "a wimoweh, a wimoweh, the lion sleeps tonight . . . ." She closed her eyes and slept.

Reina awoke a minute before her alarm. She turned to reach for Sam, but the adjacent pillow was empty. Rising to an elbow, she saw the note: "Didn't want to wake you - I'll call."

And instead of awaiting his call, she reached for the phone, her voice still husky from sleep, "Come back."

"I can't."

"Yes, you can. Just hop on the elevator."

"I'm not dressed."

"Perfect. Come just as you are . . . ."

When he refused, with the excuse that he had ironing to do, she knew it was over.

Rolling over in bed and stretching, Reina wondered if she should feel bad about giving her body to someone with his priorities in such a . . . wrinkle. Running her hands lightly over her smooth skin, along the flatness of her belly, she inhaled the lingering scent of sex. God, what a night. For a brief moment, she contemplated whether she regretted it. *Hell no.* She enjoyed their nightly trysts as much as he did. Apparently more, in fact, she admitted, looking again at the note from Sam on her pillow. She crumpled it and tossed it on to the night stand. Damn. Passed over for laundry. Definitely not a good start to the day.

After showering, arming herself in a conservative black suit, and strapping on her four-inch Jimmy Choos, she thought, there's nothing like a pair of sexy, spike-heeled pumps and a shitload of work to help forget an *affaire d'amour* or an *affaire de lust* anyway. There's a reason we women love shoes, she reasoned. They never leave us or outgrow us. They're always happy to go out with us, even when we've gained a few pounds. Tipping her toe onto the floor, she glanced backward, down the length of her leg, at the pencil-thin heel on the sleek shoes. *And you never have other things to do, especially not ironing!*

Turning toward the mirror, she completed her understated look by pulling her long dark hair back into a clip and slipping on a pair of unobtrusive garnet earrings. Before leaving, a quick glance at King 5 News gave her the Seattle weather for the day. *Maybe.* She wondered how they could be wrong so often and still keep their jobs. The meteorologists in the Northwest frequently explained how "The Convergence Zone," the geographical phenomenon that resulted from coastal air detouring around the Olympic Mountains and colliding again over the Puget Sound, made accurate forecasts very difficult in the greater Seattle area. What that meant to Seattleites? Carry both umbrella and sunscreen at all times.

Flipping through the channels, she came across a piece on the mob gathering in front of the courthouse. Clearly, the forces were amassing in support of Peter Stone, popular televangelist *and* the alleged victim of her client. Crap. She'd better allow extra time today.

It just doesn't get better than this, she thought, heading out to her car. A high-publicity, losing case with a mute client, a hostile judge, and a glory-seeking prosecutor. No deals. Not that Maria would have agreed to a deal anyway. The woman appeared resigned to life in prison. *And if she can't frickin' stand up for herself, maybe that's where she belongs.* It didn't seem fair that, just because her client was too lame to speak up, her attorney should have to go down with her.

Reina knew people were lining the dock to see her sink and she suspected she'd been assigned this case *because* it was a sure loss. Although she had little tolerance for victim mentality, in herself or others, she couldn't help but feel a twinge of it now. It's just not fair, she thought. Immediately, her inner realist shot the complaint back in her face. *Not fair? Whoever said life's fair? Get over it. And, jeez, everybody loses sometimes.* Still, Reina felt a slight nausea at the thought of public failure. Not something she did well.

She pulled out of her condo parking lot and headed down the hill toward Lake Union. As she merged into the morning traffic on Westside, her phone rang. Breaking the law, she answered it, putting it on speaker to keep her right hand free for shifting.

Trey, her assistant, gave her the news, "He's out."

She searched her mental register for people she'd helped put in prison, with few results. Her specialty was defending not incarcerating.

"Stone," Trey added helpfully.

"What? You're kidding."

"Nope. They released him this morning."

"*Diablo*!" Reina exclaimed, reverting to her favorite childhood expression. "Last I heard, he was still in ICU. What happened?"

"I don't know," Trey replied, "and I'm not sure the doctors do either. All I know is he walked out on his own two feet, about fifteen minutes ago. I have a friend at the hospital who called me right away."

"Good work." Reina smiled at yet another example of Trey's extensive circle-of-friends network. After considering for a moment the ramifications of Stone's unexpected recovery, she started thinking aloud to Trey, "Well, this changes everything. It means the charge will remain attempted murder. Of course, you and I both know the courts consider an attempted murder as good as the real thing. But who knows, maybe realizing he's alive will loosen up Maria's tongue." Reina felt a spurt of hope at the thought, then continued, "In any case, I want to talk to him, so get the notice out today so we can schedule a meeting for next week."

"Will do." With a laugh, Trey added, "Oh, and I guess at least one of the doctors is touting it as a 'miracle recovery.'"

"Oh yeah, I don't doubt that. I'm sure that'll be the buzz all over the media now. I don't need to tell you this, I know, but if he - or his people - make any public comments, I want to know about them immediately. Oh, and thanks for the update, Trey. Keep me posted if anything new comes up."

Pulling into an empty parking space some distance from the Courthouse, Reina turned off the engine, and relocked the doors that unlocked when she removed the key. She glanced in both directions to make sure some overly-zealous journalist wasn't bearing down on her. No mics heading her way. She had a minute to think.

She pulled out her notes and reviewed what she knew of Reverend Peter Stone's decline. After suffering back-to-back colds, with chest congestion, runny nose, and weepy eyes, Stone had visited his doctor complaining of the "flu" with painful abdominal cramps, vomiting, and bloating. Telling him "it's just a virus," the doctor sent him home to his wife's tender care. A week later, Stone returned to the clinic with symptoms of increased vomiting. The doctor's notes stated "the patient presents symptoms of difficulty breathing, uncontrolled muscle spasms and extreme lethargy." His body was, in fact, teetering on the verge of total shutdown.

A visit to the lab revealed low blood cell counts. The doctor admitted him immediately to emergency. An MRI showed dangerously enlarged organs – heart, kidneys, liver, brain - all swollen and extremely stressed. Further blood tests and a liver biopsy revealed toxic quantities of Atrazine, a pesticide most commonly used for weed control, notably around crops like corn and Christmas trees. When asked about recent exposure to such farming enterprises, he mumbled something about his wife's friend owning a Christmas tree farm, then fell unconscious. The doctors performed hemodialysis on him and placed him in an induced coma. He'd hovered on the edge of death for weeks, with his devoted congregation praying for him day and night.

And now, he'd simply risen up and walked out, in what appeared to be a miracle recovery. Maybe all those prayers had helped, or he'd "healed" himself as he had "healed" so many others on primetime television.

Reina could feel her brain switch into high, her thoughts sharpening like a knife being honed. Despite occasionally longing for a job with less accountability and less visibility, she loved the mental adrenalin of criminal law practice. If her client wouldn't talk, maybe the victim would. She felt the discouragement she'd struggled with earlier slip away as she pulled on her dark sunglasses, slung her black case over her shoulder, and headed to battle.

***

The remote, upper-floor men's room of the courthouse was known as a quiet place, where one could take care of business. Sitting in the farthest stall, trouser legs pooled around his ankles, Jerry unrolled a large ball of paper to wipe his hands. He'd been quiet; he was always quiet. He didn't need any paraphernalia, didn't need any dirty magazines, to get the job done. He'd learned years ago to alleviate the stress of court with his own private form of relief. Lately, though, it had become a daily routine, particularly when he went up against Reina Dessiner. At least she made this part of his day quick and easy. *She thinks she's so hot, Miss Harvard Law School. Big Fucking Deal. I've got her this time.* He smiled as he buttoned his trousers and exited the stall, glancing in the mirror to smooth what was left of his hair. *I've got her right where I want her, in the palm of my hand.* Glancing down at his hands, he grabbed the door handle and walked out of the restroom without washing, laughing at his little joke.

***

Reina sliced her way through the first hostile front of the day, the throng of Reverend Stone's devoted fans aggressively waving signs near the courthouse entrance. She grimaced at one that read, "Vengeance is mine sayeth the Lord" complete with images of flames licking at the words.

One of the women in the crowd, in a salmon-colored sweat suit, leaned in as Reina passed and shouted, "No defense for evil!"

Reina glanced at the woman's face, twisted in hate. *Ah, the irony.* Continuing on to the entrance, she met the second attack - the news dogs - outside the door.

"What does Maria say now?" asked one of the journalists, shoving a huge microphone at her face.

"Now that Reverend Stone has recovered, is Maria talking?" another called out.

Several others shouted questions, excited about the recent news of Stone's release, "How will Reverend Stone's revival change your defense?"

Reina half-smiled at her friend Liam, the tallest of the media hounds, who didn't even try to push his microphone at her. For that kindness, she'd give him a private statement later. She lifted her hand just enough so he'd see a subtle "call me" signal.

To the rest of the crowd, she simply replied, "No Comment."

Entering the courtroom, she felt the third hostile wave pulsing through the room. A full house in the audience gallery. She knew, if the room were divided into "bride" and "groom" like at a wedding, all the spectators would be on one side of the aisle. And it wasn't her side. No need to look around - she could feel the angry arrows directed at her back as she walked toward the defense table. *If looks could kill, I'd be dead meat.* Despite the noble theory of innocent until proven guilty, "we the people" generally created their own verdict, prematurely. What's more, they often chose to hate not only the "murderer" but his or her legal representative as well. It was a tough job.

***

Jerry, seated at the prosecutor's table, heard the clicking of heels on the parquet and rolled his eyes to his assistant. "I wonder what color her hair is today?" he sniggered, remembering the redhead he had faced off against last time. He turned in his chair to watch the tall striking woman pass through the partition surrounding the audience section of the courtroom. Still brunette. All in black, from hair to toe. Everything except her strange green eyes. He caught a twinkle of red earrings and wondered for a moment whether she'd matched her jewelry with red polished toenails. His mind wandered further to the thought of other red possibilities. Panties? Bra? He felt his dick stir in his pants. Turning back to face the bench, he reminded himself with satisfaction that he'd be the one to break the cocky bitch's uninterrupted winning streak. Rumor had it that her success in the courtroom could be attributed to her abilities in other areas. Everyone suspected the Chief Public Defender had a particular interest in the hot young attorney that went well beyond professional regard and Jerry had no doubt she'd been awarded easy cases in return for other favors. She'd only recently prevailed in her very first murder case. *You got lucky once, but you're playing with the big boys now.*

    Reina greeted Jerry with a friendly, "Good morning."

    Jerry stood and extended his hand, a custom of his toward opposing counsel. "Wearing black to your own funeral, I see."

    Her hands full, Reina sat down without shaking his outstretched hand and replied with a saccharin smile, "Reports of my demise are a little premature, I think."

    "You've gotta be the only one who believes that," he said with a curl of his lip. Turning back to his seat, he thought, go ahead and feign cheerfulness. Your client doesn't have a leg to stand on. And the media is gonna love ol' Jerry for saving our good God-fearing public from crazy, jealous, murdering wives. His thoughts turned to *The Time*'s morning coverage of the upcoming trial. It wouldn't even be a story if not for the big-name recognition of Reverend Peter Stone. And then, the writer had to make it into some mystery about "Silent Maria." The final line of the article had really galled him: "If anyone can get to the truth, it's Reina Dessiner." *What a load of crap. She probably spreads her legs for a journalist boyfriend, too, so he'll write whatever bullshit she tells him*. He cleared his mind of the vision of her with legs spread. It was getting harder to concentrate these days. He felt his tension rise as he thought of the success of her first murder case. Sure, she'd rocked the foundations of the Seattle Police Department with that exposé of officers on the dole, but this case was different, he reminded himself. Cut and dried. There was nothing mysterious about "I did it." He smiled smugly to himself. The press would be eating their words when he slam-dunked sweet little Maria straight into the can. He rubbed his forefinger and thumb across his moustache thinking of the pleasure it would bring to lick cocky Reina Dessiner.

As he sat relishing his *prima facie* victory, his assistant leaned over and whispered in his ear, "They just released him."

"Who?" It took Jerry a minute to comprehend. "Not Stone? I thought he was as good as dead."

"Apparently, either modern medicine or good old-fashioned miracle won out. The doctors let him go this morning."

Jerry closed his eyes, removed his glasses, and pinched the bridge of his nose. *Shit*. Things just got a whole lot more complicated. He whispered back, "Well attempted murder is as good as the real thing and this should amp up the media coverage, which is just fine with me. Get him on the phone. I want to talk to him. Today."

***

The court stood as the judge entered the room. Reina self-consciously smoothed her conservative black skirt and jacket as she returned to her seat. She suspected "Hashi," as some of the attorneys nicknamed the judge, despised her. Every time Reina had the misfortune to be in her courtroom, the judge picked her apart, and not for her legal abilities. Either her hair was too messy or her shoes made too much noise or her scarf was unprofessional or the paperwork was wrinkled or there was a water stain on a document. Hashi always found something to criticize in Reina. Now in her seventies, Judge Takahashi had clearly earned her chops, so Reina made every effort to show proper deference and respect, despite what felt like unjustified personal attacks. But she had no illusions about getting the judge to lean favorably toward her case. Today, Judge Takahashi simply looked with withering scorn at Reina's spiky shoes setting under the defense table as she announced that she expected jury selection to be done by the end of the day so counsel had best be quick and sharp about it.

Reina pulled out her notes and a list of questions. She knew Jerry, who had a lot riding on this case, would continue to push hard on the jurors. She leaned back in her seat and settled in for another long day.

Chapter 3

Emerging finally from the dim halls of justice, Reina observed with pleasure that the weatherman's prediction of late afternoon drizzle had proven completely erroneous. Starting up her silver Mercedes, she took a moment to rotate her head and shoulders, loosening up the day's tension as the Roadster's convertible top retracted. A gorgeous clear sky stretched overhead with high, stratus cloud wisps snaking across it like silky white ribbons. The expanse of blue, from horizon to horizon, beckoned her to come play.

Turning off Pike street onto her favorite entry ramp for the I-5 express lanes north out of Seattle, Reina gunned her car a little, enjoying the momentary burst of speed up the tunnel-like ramp. After all, nobody said how *long* it should take you to get to freeway speed. And chances were, she'd soon be slowed to a crawl anyway in the daily rush hour. Fortunately, the express lanes were clear. Emerging from the dark, covered section of freeway, she saw the main I-5 lanes were gridlocked. Good choice.

She knew most of her colleagues could be found right now at their favorite Belltown watering hole, The Gavel, with double martinis in hand. Although not opposed to unwinding one olive at a time, she had other plans today - plans admittedly altered by her now *ex-beau's* load of linen.

After a reasonably quick trip up I-5, she arrived at her destination. Pulling into Wayward Airfield, she parked in the dusty grass behind True Blue Aviation, scooped her flight bag from the miniscule trunk of her car, and walked toward the old hangar building, smiling in anticipation.

As she passed Hawk's old Willys Jeep in the parking area, she glanced into the open-top vehicle and saw a jumbo can of spinach on the passenger seat. Hawk worked as True Blue's primary Certified Flight Instructor, or CFI, in aviation lingo, and he had some peculiar habits. The can of spinach brought to mind Hawk's unusual name for his vehicle - Eugene. She recalled their bizarre conversation, some years ago, over the name.

"So, why do you call your Jeep 'Eugene'?"
"It's because of my love for Olive Oyl."
"Your love for Olive Oil?"
"Yes."
"I don't get it."

Hawk just laughed. At the time, Reina wondered whether she was stupid or he was crazy. A few months later, she overheard a lunchroom conversation in which the speaker made reference to his partner's resemblance to Popeye's girlfriend, Olive Oyl. Remembering Hawk's comment, she googled Popeye. Apparently, in the popular '60s cartoon series, Olive Oyl had owned a Willys Jeep, named Eugene, given to her by her Uncle Ben. This Uncle Ben could appear and disappear at will, tell the future, and even travel in the fourth dimension. Ah, Reina had thought, it all makes sense. Sort of. She smiled, *so that's where Hawk gets his powers . . . .*

Opening the door to the flight school, she saw Hawk seated next to an older man who was bent over, studying a navigation chart. Hawk silently acknowledged her entrance with a raised eyebrow and a half-smile. She felt a flutter in her stomach and tried not to check out of the corner of her eyes to see if he watched her cross the room. Hawk's lab-retriever mutt, Bravo, greeted her with a yelp, as usual, as he skittered across the wood laminate floor to show her his affection.

"Yeah, I know you like me," she nudged his nose away from her crotch. "It doesn't mean you have to molest me."

She glanced over to see Hawk smirking at Bravo's uninhibited friendliness. She stuck her tongue out at him and he laughed. Hawk had wandered into the hangar on the first day Reina's mom, Caite, opened up her flight school. Caite signed him up on the spot and he'd worked there ever since. He'd proven himself an excellent and reliable instructor, except for the occasional weeks when he would vanish, not telling anyone his destination, just that he'd be back. Caite and Reina jokingly called his periodic disappearances, "Going to visit Uncle Ben."

In his early fifties and still ruggedly handsome, Hawk wore his dark hair long and tied back in a ponytail. His vibrant blue eyes, the color of sky in summer, smiled from deep within. The flip-flops he wore any time he wasn't flying added testimony to his easy-going ways. On this hot summer day, he wore a short-sleeved shirt that revealed some of the raised scar on his upper biceps. When Reina once asked him about the scar, he told her, "My parents moved to Australia just before my teenage years. The scars are a reminder of my coming-of-age days there." She had pressed for more details, but he'd been vague, saying they'd have to spend several nights under the moon together for him to tell the story. Now, for the hundredth time, she wondered if perhaps it was his aura of mystery that caused that inexplicable sensation she felt in his presence.

Reina stopped at the front desk to say hi to Julianna. Julianna's wavy, dark locks reached half way down her back and her big blue eyes, framed in ridiculously long lashes, looked deceptively innocent. Julianna's charms extended to a generous sharing of both her easy laugh and her reinforced cleavage. All very important characteristics, considering the vast majority of True Blue's clients were of the male variety.

"Who's the new student with Hawk?" Reina asked.

"I can't remember his name," Julianna admitted in a whisper.

Reina had always suspected Julianna's office skills were not on par with her customer flirting skills. And yet, she seemed to hold things together at the busy little flight school, albeit with a fair amount of intervention and assistance from Caite.

"He's here for a flight review," Julianna continued, adding with a grin, "When I can't remember their names, I just call 'em Mike and figure I'll have a thirty percent chance of being right."

Reina laughed, "That's true. It does seem like a disproportionate number of aviators are named Mike. By the way, I like the rearranged furniture. Did you do it?"

"No. You know your mom, she likes to shake things up regularly."

Reina turned to survey the warm and welcoming pilot's lounge, attractively decorated with framed aviation posters, potted plants, burgundy leather sofas, and a sky-blue painted ceiling dotted with white clouds. "Well, I love it."

Heading to the restroom, Reina quickly changed into her jeans, tank top, and Arche ballet flats with the solid but flexible soles, perfect for feeling the rudder when she flew. She pulled her hair back into a ponytail and carelessly folded her expensive suit, stuffing it onto the shelf of the broom closet. Thank God for dry cleaners, she thought as she headed for the hangar.

Hawk, refilling his cup of tea in the small kitchen that doubled as an espresso bar, whispered playfully, as she passed, "Nice."

She laughed at his vague compliment asking, "Where's Mom?"

"Who knows?" he replied. "You know no one keeps tabs on that woman. It would be easier to wire a whirlwind, I think."

Reina laughed at the truth of his statement. Although her mom exuded a gentle calm and peace, she also possessed a quiet force that drove her relentlessly forward, sometimes in unorthodox ways. When hell-bent on moving in a certain direction, there was not much that could stop her. Six years ago, when she'd decided to start up a flight school, virtually everyone had warned her against it, indicating she would be crazy to enter such a difficult industry. They told her the best way to make a million in aviation was to start out with three. Listening to her instincts, she'd persevered and made the little aviation business a profitable enterprise.

"Well, if she returns, tell her I decided to take the Yak out today after all."

"Hmmm, too bad there's not two seats in that thing." Hawk had a way of making perfectly plain words sound incredibly sexy and suggestive. Reina again felt that tension deep in her core and her breath caught slightly in her throat. She looked at his hands with the strong lean fingers holding the cup, and his lips pursing to take a sip of tea, and decided she had best get going.

"You better get back to your student," she laughed. "You don't want to keep him waiting." She smiled over her shoulder at him as she headed out to the airplane hangar area.

In the cool, dark shop area, at the back of the big old building, sat the school's more expensive aircraft - a Cessna P210 and a Yak 55M, as well as the inexpensive little Aeronca Champ with the fabric skin that needed protection from the elements. The training workhorses, the Cessna 172s, lived outside most of the time for ease of access by students and instructors. After unhooking the door clasps and removed the stabilizing pins on the old sliding hangar doors, Reina heaved on the ancient metal slabs with all her might to open them. They creaked and groaned like a roomful of rheumatics. Customers regularly complained to Caite about the difficulty of getting the doors open. If her mother could afford it, she'd probably replace the doors but, in an odd way, Reina relished the battle of human versus steel. Every few feet, one of the overhead rollers jammed and she had to lean back on her heels and yank on the stubborn old metal with every bit of her hard-earned muscle. She knew Julianna hated closing them at the end of the day, grousing about how they always cost one of her colorful long acrylic fingernails. Reina didn't have fancy fingernails worth worrying about. But fortunately, she did have the arms from swimming laps and the legs from running regularly to give her the strength to prevail against the rusty old clunkers. Finally open, they vibrated in the wind as Reina brushed her hands together in victory.

Ha! She could hear her mother's familiar voice in her mind, "You see, dear, you can do anything you set your mind to."

Except, apparently, compete with ironing. Reina shook her head as if to physically eject the humbling thought, a lurking vestige of the morning's conversation with Sam.

Reina's heart lightened in anticipation of going flying. Getting airborne cured nearly every problem in her world, it seemed. She'd learned, in her teenage days, how strapping herself into a metal or fabric tube with wings offered an escape from the mental and emotional anguishes of life on earth. Today was not the first time she would take to the sky to heal her heart.

Her mind started to focus in on the ritual of pre-flighting the aircraft. Fuel: wing tanks full and sumped for any water droplets. Oil: nine quarts. Prop: no nicks. Cowling: tight. Fuselage, ailerons, horizontal stabilizer, rudder, gear, tires, air gauge. Everything looked good. She attached the tail dolly to leverage up the small rear wheel and pushed the heavy black and red bird out into the sun, rotating the tail to the side to prevent blowing out the hangar with her prop wash when she started the engine.

Reina nearly quit her day job when her mom brought home the Yak to live at True Blue Aviation. An impractical response to an impractical airplane. One couldn't just spend their days flying around, could they? Could they? As a flight school acquisition, it made even less sense. Only a handful of people were even checked out to fly it, including herself, Caite, Hawk, and a couple of experienced aerobatic pilots on the field. Although it produced far more expenses than revenues for the small business, her mother never expressed any regret over the purchase. Caite had claimed she'd gotten a good deal in some sort of trade, the details of which Reina sensed she'd rather not know.

"Anyway, it was either the Yak or new hangar doors," Caite had explained, adding with a laugh, "And hangar doors are a bitch to fly."

Reina stepped on the peg attached to the landing gear of the big aircraft, grabbed the hand hold on the cowling, and hoisted herself up over the leading edge onto the sturdy wing. Bending to get the parachute off the seat, she strapped it on, tightening the straps and reaching her right hand across her chest to feel for the D-ring that would deploy the chute. She'd never had to use it and, frankly, the thought of struggling out of a spinning or diving aircraft and jumping to safety sounded highly dubious. But if the moment ever came, there would be no time to think about where to pull to deploy. It needed to be automatic.

    She climbed into the cockpit, holding the side rails to lower herself into the single seat, and slid the canopy to the closed and locked position. After a quick review of the pre-start checklist, she hit the start button, heard the high pitched whine of the airstarter as it pumped air into the cylinders, and then the powerful radial engine roared to life. She immediately felt the power of the engine course through the rigid airframe and directly into her body. Unlike any other aircraft she'd flown, flying the Yak was a primal experience. She felt like she'd climbed into the heart of a jaguar. She couldn't wait to get airborne and put the constraining earthly bounds behind her.

    A mental checklist through the simple Russian instrument panel assured her that all systems were a "go." After taxiing clear of the row of hangars, a quick glance at the windsock, with its long tail fluttering gently toward the southeast, indicated she should turn to the left for runway 34. She taxied to the run-up area, making s-turns for visibility over the high aircraft nose. After completing her pre-takeoff checklists, she announced her departure over the local frequency, taxied to the centerline of the runway, added power, and held the stick neutral. As the muscular airplane gathered speed, it practically leapt off the ground into the sky, a flying jaguar.

Ah, this felt good. Like in the courtroom, she felt herself completely focus on the task at hand. Unlike the legal world, however, flying revitalized her, almost as if the experience of being airborne replenished the energy that drained out through the long day on solid ground. And, unlike after a night at The Gavel, there would be no hangover the next day to deal with.

Climbing to the north through 2500 feet, she rolled inverted for a safety check. Yep, the seat harness seemed to hold her in and nothing flew loose in the cockpit. She remembered the time her cell phone popped out of her pocket and banged around the cockpit until she rolled inverted again to grab it as it floated free.

She warmed up with a couple of aileron rolls. Then, at a level 180 knots, she pulled firmly on the stick, bringing the nose toward vertical. Her body compressed back into the seat, arms heavy as lead, the six g's turning her 130 pound frame into nearly 800 pounds of weight. Turning her head, now heavy as a bowling ball, to verify the left wing was perpendicular to the horizon, she tightened her abs to reduce the flow of blood trying to drain from her upper extremities. The light headedness faded as she climbed vertical, engine roaring. When the airframe shuddered gently, saying it was done flying, she kicked hard right rudder, into the hammerhead. Her body now felt light with the zero G's as she floated over the top of the maneuver. A glance to the right to follow the nose through the horizon, then straight down, thundering down, with the ground rising quickly toward her. Finally, she pulled firmly on the stick, bringing the beast back to level flight. Perfect exhilaration.

She did another hammerhead, rejoicing in the raw power and the three dimensional motion, then performed a couple of easy loops, snap rolling at the top of the last one. She finished her practice with a graceful Cuban Eight maneuver. It felt great to fly, great to be alive, great to be alone in the blue sky with nothing but a few silent clouds as companions. Flying liberated Reina in a way nothing else ever could. For just these moments in time, her fast-moving mind let go of everything else. Gone were the thoughts of Sam, the trial, and the items on her to-do list. They would eventually come back, but during the time she flew, she truly felt relief from all of life's daily burdens. It's kind of primitive, she thought, as she pointed the nose back to the airport. In a way, her only priority was to stay alive or to *be* alive, and all else disappeared. She felt as refreshed as she might after a good nap or a long shower.

Reina listened for other airplanes in the area as she approached the airport. She entered the downwind for runway 34, turned left to base, left again for final approach, then performed a soft three-point landing. Taxiing off the runway and back to the hangar, she waved to her mother and Hawk, who stood on the patio in front of True Blue's office, shading their eyes against the late afternoon sun.

As Reina taxied up to the open hangar, True Blue's mechanic came out and indicated to tie down on the outside grass. Exiting the aircraft, she saw Carl, the school's A & P, walking toward her.

"I've just finished with Joe's Aerostar and need the ramp clear to pull it out. He's anxious to be on his way to Montana. Just leave the Yak here and I'll pull her in later."

"Okay. Thanks, Carl." As Reina shrugged out of her chute, she saw Carl make a circuit around her steel jaguar. "Don't worry, I didn't bend any metal."

"Oh, I don't worry about that with you," Carl grinned. "I was just eyeballing the grease streaks to see how many quarts of oil I need to fetch for the refill."

"You know," Reina said as she swung herself down off the wing, "some people use a dipstick to check these things."

Carl snorted, "Novices."

Although only in his forties, Carl knew airplanes like old aviators from the war days knew airplanes. He was the trailing edge of a generation of guys who lived and breathed motors and wings, many having learned the hard way, in dogfights over foreign lands with unreliable piston engines. Wayward Field had its share of these old relics, but they were a dying breed, and their stories were going with them. As for A & Ps, Reina had heard Carl talk about how every mechanic he knew took their freshly minted Airframe & Powerplant license and went straight to commercial aviation. A fellow could make a living at a place like Boeing, but not so much in the world of general aviation.

Carl headed back to his sacred domain, the maintenance hangar, shaking his head, "Dipsticks!"

Reina laughed and went to join her mother and Hawk on the patio.

"Hawk was just asking me where you got those long legs," Reina's mom said as she approached.

"Oh, he was, was he?" Reina raised her eyebrows at Hawk, giving him a little of his own, with a challenging half-smile.

"I was just saying that it's hard to believe those long legs and powerful stride came from this little thing." Hawk draped his arm over Caite's shoulders.

"Oh, I see." Reina treated him to a mock huff. "Now, I'm a gangly man-walker."

Hawk laughed, "Hardly that, I think."

"She came by them honestly," Caite interjected. "Her dad had the same intentional way of walking. When he wasn't lounging on the beach with a cigarette and a gin and tonic, that is."

"Gin and tonic has a way of taking the intensity out of anyone," Hawk agreed.

"Speaking of, what does a girl have to do around her to get a beer?" Reina asked.

"I'll join you for that," her mom agreed. "Hawk?"

"Sorry, I've gotta run. I'll see you tomorrow." He waved and headed toward the parking area.

While her mom went in to retrieve the liquid refreshment, Reina watched Hawk walk away. *I'll bet he's not going home to iron.* Her nostrils flared a bit as she admired the slinky lion's gait of his hips in motion. As he disappeared around the corner, she leaned back in the patio chair and closed her eyes.

When Reina heard the clink of bottles being set on the wrought-iron table, she opened her eyes and asked, "Where was Hawk off to?"

"Don't know."

"Hopefully not to visit Uncle Ben."

Caite laughed, "I'm just appreciative whenever he returns. He's been like a guardian angel for me here, helping me build this business."

"Do you believe in guardian angels?" Reina raised her eyebrows in surprise.

"Yeah, actually I do," her mom smiled. "I even believe they sometimes walk on earth with us. Many times, I've had someone appear in my life just when I needed them."

"Hmmm," Reina pondered the idea.

"So how'd today go?" her mother asked.

"Which? The case, or the flight?"

"Well, both, and in whichever order you like. The plane looks re-useable and your chute appeared to be still packed, so I guess the flight went well. How's our girl running?"

"Great! Did you see my maneuvers? How'd I look?"

"You looked good. Your vertical lines were straight and your loops round." A pause, a smile, and then, "Mostly."

"Ah, perfection eludes me as always. Well, it just means I need to practice more," Reina concluded good-naturedly. "When did you fly her last?"

"Last week. Carl just made some adjustments to the rudder and I wanted to try her out."

"Sounds like as good an excuse as any to go fly."

Caite laughed. "Yeah, sometimes I get so wrapped up in running the business, I do have to make an excuse to fly. I occasionally forget I started up a flight school so I could fly whenever I wanted. It doesn't always work out that way."

"I know. Damn life always getting in the way." Reina laughed, still buzzing from the exuberance of the flight. "Where's Julianna?"

"She left early as usual. If she weren't so darn charming, I'd probably let her go. But what she lacks for in skills and punctuality, she makes up for in personality. I've heard her come right out and tell customers that, although they have to pay for the merchandise and the lessons, the attitude is thrown in for free. The guys love her."

"Well, you have to admit, she's shown a lot of dedication by sticking around for five years."

"True, and each year I have to correct less errors from her paperwork, so that's a bonus."

"What's your plan for tonight?"

"I'm heading out in about an hour for a little get-together, but until then, I'm all yours."

"Really, where are you going?"

"Oh, just hanging out with some friends, maybe dinner." Typically vague about her personal life, Caite continued, "So anyway, tell me about your day."

"Well, today we finally concluded *Voir Dire*. It was a particularly difficult group of jurors and there were a lot of challenges and strikes, but overall, I think the jury selection went pretty well. There are a couple of wild cards in the lot and that's just fine with me. The big news is that Peter Stone walked out of the hospital today. That was totally unexpected - by everyone, doctors included. But it should be good for our side." Reina paused for a minute before continuing, "Not that an attempted murder charge is a breeze, but if he died, it would have induced way too much public wailing and gnashing of teeth."

"Yeah, I can see that. I can't say I'm a Peter Stone fan, but just because he rips off little old ladies in the name of God doesn't mean he deserves to die. The media is eating this up. No surprise, I guess. That was quite a crowd chanting outside the courtroom this morning."

"Yeah, he seems to have his share of groupies."

"So, were those 'REPENT' signs the crowd was waving directed at the public or meant specifically for your client, do you think?"

"Oh, I've no doubt they were meant for Maria. And me, too, I suppose. I'm sure a double crucifixion would please the crowd."

"So, who's prosecuting?"

"I'm up against that creep, Jerry. I know he hates me, but really, it's not my fault he's always left holding the short end of the stick. I mean, his picture should be on the cover of one of those joke books about sleazy lawyers. He looks it, he acts it, and the jurors sense it. And what can I say, they like me," Reina added with a big smile. "I just wish he wouldn't leer at me every time I walk down the courtroom aisle. I feel like he's undressing me in his mind which, I suppose, is part of his effort to put me off my game. But then," she finished with a laugh, "he doesn't know I spent half my youth buck-naked and am perfectly comfortable with it."

"Yes, well, I didn't know you'd be thanking me for that some day, but you're welcome," laughed her mother. "You were a cute little naked imp, too, I might add."

"I still am," Reina assured her mother. After a pause, she added, "Although apparently not everyone thinks so," and relayed the morning's phone conversation with Sam.

"Will you miss him?" her mother asked, as if to ascertain whether this was a guy who mattered.

Pursing her lips thoughtfully, Reina stared at her reflection in her mom's mirrored aviator sunglasses. *Jesus, I need to get a tan. That scar stands out like a red stamp.* She pulled out her ponytail and ran her fingers through her hair to loosen it around her face, touching the tri-blade propeller scar on her temple lightly. "Well, I don't think I knew him long enough to really miss him. But he had some fine attributes," she finally answered with a shrug of her shoulders.

The quick smile confirmed that the pique of rejection hurt more than true heartache. Her mother had, on occasion, pointed out how she always dropped a guy the minute he liked her too much or showed a hint of not liking her enough. Reina knew a psychologist would say that, having spent her formative years without a father figure, she was destined to eternally seek that love from various men. Frankly, Reina didn't give a damn about psychologists. And having a father wasn't a panacea, either. Her mom had once confided that her own father had trained her to submission, something she'd had to unlearn and from which she'd been determined to spare her daughter.

Mother and daughter sat in silence for a few minutes, then Reina asked about Ruthie, one of her favorite flight students, and inquired about the girl's upcoming sixteenth birthday.

"Weather is usually pretty decent through October, so hopefully that won't be an issue," her mom replied. "Hawk is confident she'll be ready to solo."

Aware that a pilot's first solo remained forever a major life milestone, they planned to make the day extra special for Ruthie. Glancing at her watch, Reina said, "Well, I better get going. I'll wait for you to lock up if you like."

While her mom turned off the lights and closed the blinds, Reina thought more about gutsy little Ruthie. Ruthie had walked into the flight school earlier that year, at the age of 15, asking what she needed to do to learn to fly. Caite gave her a job washing airplanes and agreed to exchange flying time for washes at a very generous rate. Reina took the girl up flying several times over the summer, wanting to encourage her in any way she could to follow her dreams. On one flight, Ruthie had confided to Reina her mother's concerns about the flight lessons.

"She's terrified," said Ruthie. "She says if my stepdad finds out, he'll wring both our necks." Ruthie paused for a minute, a mulish look staring out between the big mounds of the aviation headset. "But since I'm paying for the lessons myself, I don't care what he thinks.

I'm pretty sure my mom won't say anything to him, though. She's too scared to ever stand up to him."

The girl's frustration with her stepdad had triggered memories of Reina's own adopted French father, who had not only encouraged her to fly, but taught her aerobatics as well. *Merci, Papa.*

Locking the door behind her, Caite said, "I'm ready. Will you be coming back out tomorrow?"

"Yes, if I get a chance. I really want to take advantage of this nice weather while it lasts. Maybe I'll see you then."

As mother and daughter walked around the building toward the parking area, they saw red tail lights at the end of the driveway. "That's strange," said Caite. "I thought everybody left a long time ago."

Suddenly, the "Vengeance is mine" sign she'd been confronted with that morning popped into Reina's mind. She recognized the tendency to get paranoid while working a case with threatening bystanders, and quickly shook off the unfounded fear, although she did try to get a glimpse of the license number on the dark vehicle. Too distant. "Probably just someone who took a wrong turn," Reina replied. As they approached her mom's car, she asked, "How's your Deux Chevaux running?"

"*Fantastique*! Jean-Pierre gave it a thorough tune-up before sending it off."

"I still can't believe you shipped it over from France. It brings back such memories of our years there."

"When Jean-Pierre told me, last year, he planned to sell it, I just knew I wanted it. I loved that car when we were in France, and I couldn't stand the thought of it going to a stranger."

"*Bien sur*. I totally agree. I mean, I learned to drive in that car." Reina laughed and added, "much to the dismay of *les pauvres Français*. But it must be hard to find a mechanic in this area to work on it? There aren't too many of these around here."

"I found a guy in north Seattle, off Aurora, who specializes in European cars. He takes good care of it for me."

Reina and Caite exchanged the two-cheek kiss of the French, a habit they'd developed years ago, and waved each other off. Reina, who'd left the top down on her car, was startled to see a white piece of paper on the driver's seat. Picking it up, she read in bold, black ink a single word: REPENT. Crumpling it, she shoved it into her purse in disgust. After starting her car and initiating the top to electronically advance, she dialed one of her two best friends.

"What's up girlfriend?" answered Getta.

"I'm going home to take a hot bath, then I'm making margaritas and nachos. Wanna join me?"

"For the bath or the nachos?"

"Haha, I love you, but not that much. How about in an hour for drinks? If you have any of that Tarantula Tequila left, bring it along."

"Sounds good, see you then."

Chapter 4

Forty minutes later, Reina was settled deep into her soaker tub with a glass of Pinot Grigio at one elbow and a three-branch candelabra at the other. As the last faint glimmer of daylight faded and the shadows of the candlelight lengthened, she felt her muscles relax and her mind empty. *God this feels good*.

She'd purchased this condo, partially, for the large, tiled bathroom with its huge tub - unusual for an older unit. In addition, its location, on the hillside above Lake Union, provided gorgeous views to the east. When the realtor unlocked the door and led her into the front room for the first time, nearly a year ago, Reina had stood, mesmerized, in front of the wall-sized windows, watching a float plane arcing in for a graceful landing between white, bobbing sailboats on the lake. She knew immediately it was the place for her. Between the view and the huge bath, she'd been able to overlook the outdated kitchen appliances, worn carpet, and tiny second bedroom. Furthermore, there was no balcony. Although some people might consider that omission a demerit for the place, it suited Reina perfectly.

Her purchase offer accepted, she had moved her few belongings into her very first home. After all the childhood years of moving from place to place, and the college years of dorm and apartment living, she adored having her own space. In addition to the activity of planes and boats coming and going on the sparkling blue water, she loved the view of the morning sunrises over the Cascade Mountains and the city lights at night. And, if she pressed her left cheek hard against the glass, she could even see the Space Needle standing tall at the end of the lake.

Half-asleep in the warm bubbles and soft light, she drifted to thoughts of her biological father. Although Reina had never really known him, he'd helped make this hillside haven possible for her. Reina recalled how, half way through graduate school, her mother had called her with an unusual question, "Can you take a break from class?"

"Not easily," Reina had replied to the inquiry. "Why?"

"Your father wants to meet you."

"My father?" Reina set down the book she'd been studying. "What do you mean?"

"He is dying and wants to meet you."

A year after their one and only meeting, Reina had received a letter from his solicitors stating he left her a small trust. She had used some of the funds from the trust for the down payment on this condo.

The hustle of the city had settled into the quiet of evening now – no planes landing, no pleasure boats buzzing on the still water, no delivery trucks beeping as they backed up for unloading, only the mournful wail of a distant siren. The faint background noise of cars and people go ing about their city lives hummed gently in the hushed air. Although she kept a small stereo by the bathtub, she seldom used it, preferring the peaceful emptiness of air without words. Half asleep, she drifted in a haze of sweet silence.

Reina heard the front door open downstairs and smiled. It would be great to see Getta. "I'll be down in a few," she called out through the bathroom door, which she'd left slightly ajar. She lay back again against the tub rim, *Ah, just a couple more minutes of this bliss . . . .* A moment later she heard the quiet shush the bathroom door made as it rubbed against the plush rug in front of the sink. Reina laughed and said, "Hey, Getta, joining me for the bath after all?"

Turning her head to greet her friend, she caught a brief glimpse of a black figure rushing across the floor. Her reflexes kicked into high and she reached for the side of the tub as a hand grabbed her by the hair and shoved her below the water. She had barely a second to snatch a gulp of air as her face went under. Scraping at the hands that held her head and shoulder under water, she flailed out, kicking and squirming to escape her captor's grasp, but to no avail. She could feel her lungs about to burst. Forcing her body to stop struggling, she went completely limp and still.

Suddenly, her assailant released the pressure on her shoulder, and reached in to fondle a floating breast. The change of position, accompanied by a slight slackening of pressure on her scalp, gave her just enough room to twist over a little in the tub. Her left hand shot out, reaching for the heavy old candelabra alongside the tub.

She grabbed the stem, and swung it hard. Her assailant flung back as the hot wax splashed his face, giving her just enough room to come up for air. Taking a huge gasp, she grasped the candelabra stem tightly and heaved it with all her might, smashing the heavy iron against his face. He stumbled back, slipping on the wet tile and clawing at his burned and bleeding face. She lunged out of the tub to follow him as he lurched from the bathroom, growling in pain. Her feet slipped and she collapsed on the wet floor, gasping to fill her lungs. Heaving for air, she heard a scream downstairs, a loud crash, and then footsteps running up the stairs. She stumbled to her feet, grabbed the candelabra tightly with both hands, planted her feet widely, and prepared to level him with it when he re-entered the room.

A wide-eyed Getta burst through the door and skidded to a halt at the sight of her naked, dripping, candelabra-wielding friend. "Oh my God, what happened?" Getta cried.

Reina lowered the candelabra and crumpled on to the rug. Breathing in painful gasps, she asked, "Did you see him?"

"What the fuck? The crazy asshole nearly knocked me down as I came in the front door. God damn it! He elbowed me hard as he ran past." Getta rubbed her side. "Jesus Christ! Who the hell was that?"

Suddenly Getta stopped her ranting and moved to help Reina up off the wet floor. "Holy shit, what did he do to you?" she asked. "Here, let me get a towel. Jesus, you're shaking like a leaf. And you're bleeding, too. That asshole! I need to call 911 and get you to a hospital."

"I don't need to go to the hospital. I have a scratched boob, bruised knees, and a torqued neck, that's all. The blood must be from the broken wine glass all over the floor. I think I have some glass in my knee and my foot. Just hand me that towel, will you?" Reina reached into the top drawer and pulled out a tweezers. "And help me get this glass out, too. It's killing me."

After drying off, Reina wrapped herself in the thick terrycloth robe Getta handed her. She grimaced as her friend extricated the shards of wine goblet from her skin, then bandaged the multiple lacerations. While Getta cleaned up the glass, wine, and water from the floor, Reina pulled on some flannel pajama pants, a T-shirt, and a pair of big comfy socks. Even when completely warm and dry, Reina felt her whole body shudder violently again. She couldn't tell if it was fear, or anger, or just a wrung-out lung spasm.

While emptying out the tub, Getta continued her expletive-laden commentary. "I should have hopped on my bike and followed that son-of-a-bitch. If I'd known you were okay, I would've run the bastard down. What the fuck was he doing here anyway? Are you sure you're okay? What an asshole!"

Getta could swear like a longshoreman and this skill always surfaced when she became excited. Reina called it her yin and yang balance – mild-mannered school teacher by day, crazy, cussing motorcyclist by night. She could almost see Getta chasing down the guy on her crotch-rocket bike just like in the movies, *à la* Angelina Jolie.

They made their way downstairs to find the door wide open and a shattered bottle of tequila lying next to Getta's motorcycle helmet on the doorsill. "Shit!" Getta picked up her helmet, dripping with Tequila, and inspected it for scratches. "I sure as hell hope I don't get pulled over anytime soon. A cop'll be able to smell my head from twenty feet."

"Speaking of cops," Reina said as she pointed to the liquor cabinet in the corner. "Why don't you make us those margaritas, while I call the police."

Chapter 5

The patrol car arrived with siren blasting.

"Thanks for coming quietly," Reina greeted the officers at the door with friendly sarcasm.

"Sorry about that, Reina," said Franco. "My new partner here likes to drive fast and loud. He just transferred from New York. We'll civilize him to Seattle ways before too long," he grinned.

"Yeah, good luck wi' that." his partner responded, extending his hand to Reina, then Getta. "Hey. I'm Jomar. Nice ta meet cha." He smiled at Getta then turned back to Reina, "I hear you an' Franco go way back."

"Well, as far back as law school and as far away as Boston." She smiled up at Franco. "I think he followed me to Seattle."

"You got me there," laughed Franco, looking warmly down at Reina.

"Crap," Jomar said, "I didn't know I was riding with an attorney."

"You're not," Franco frowned. Turning away, he asked, "What happened here?"

As Reina watched Getta show Franco and Jomar the Tequila-soaked helmet and describe how the intruder had shoved her aside, she recalled how Franco, her pizza and beer buddy, had described his disillusionment with law school several years ago in Boston.

"I just don't think I can adequately represent someone I know is guilty," he had anguished aloud. "Sure, I know it's their right to get a fair trial and all that, but if someone's a criminal, they're a criminal. I can't see myself trying to get them off, through circumstantial evidence or some other legal trick. That goes too strongly against my innate sense of justice." He looked at her and added, "No offense, of course. If you can see straight to do it, go for it."

Reina knew Franco's sense of right and wrong was outlined in bold black markers. You break the law, he'd told her many times, you go to jail. It's that simple.

"No offense taken," she assured him. "So you *are* gonna transfer to the Police Academy?"

"I think so," Franco replied after a long silence. "Are you disappointed in me?"

"Of course not," she promised him. "I'll just miss seeing you around. But the most important thing to do is to follow the path that's right for *you*. Following someone else's path just gets you . . . " she paused, searching for the right words, "well, it just gets you somewhere other than where you're meant to be." She finished her impromptu wisdom with a shrug and a smile.

"Anyway," Franco smiled, "I like the idea of being a patrol officer, out on the streets and all that. Back to my roots, you know. Where I came from."

As Reina expected, Franco excelled at the Academy and could have his choice of cities in which to build his career. Seattle topped the list, for some reason. After three years on the force, he'd earned respect in his precinct, with a reputation for hard work, integrity, and a finely-tuned instinct.

The officers returning to her side brought Reina back to the present. She asked how they had gotten in to the building. Theoretically, a security code protected the front door, but it didn't seem to be deterring anyone tonight.

Franco answered. "A couple was just leaving and they held the door for us. Russian sounding, didn't speak much English, had a baby in their arms," he described them to Reina.

"A baby," Reina couldn't help exclaiming flippantly. "That thing is a monster. He was almost thirteen pounds at birth. I expect him to be sporting a moustache any day. And does he have lungs! They're on the second floor, but I can hear him crying all the way up here on the fifth."

"I was a twelve pound baby myself," Franco replied, somewhat defensively.

"Twelve pounds. Holy shit. When did *you* start shaving?" Jomar joked.

Franco frowned again at his new partner's levity, then turned to Reina, his face serious as he returned to business, "But this isn't a social visit. What else can you tell us?"

Reina relayed details of the bath attack to the officers and they all trooped up to the bathroom to view the scene of the crime. She described the little bit she'd seen of the assailant, but not being in the mood to provide evidence, she omitted the part about the breast grope.

"Do you have any idea how he may have gotten in?" Franco asked.

"Well, usually it's Mrs. Jensen who holds the street door open for people who want in. She lives right on the ground floor and seems anxious to help anyone fumbling for the security code. We've tried to explain to her the purpose of keeping the door secure, but it never seems to stick. She's even invited complete strangers to come in to her condo for a cup of tea. I think she's both lonely and senile. However, you might want to check and make sure she's okay. She's in 101."

"Will do." Franco jotted down her name in his notebook. "You may want to talk to your super about changing the code as well. The four numbers on the key pad are so worn off it would only take a couple of attempts to figure out the correct combination to open the door."

"Have you had a chance to look around? Is there anything damaged or stolen?" asked Jomar.

"Not that I can tell. If theft was his intent, he could have taken what he wanted and left without ever entering my bathroom. It appears he was more interested in doing me mischief than pilfering jewels or electronics."

"Are you sure it was a he?"

"Well, now that you mention it, I may be making an assumption, based on certain, um, behavior. Frankly, my view of the attacker was mostly distorted through water."

"I'm pretty sure," Getta agreed. "When he shoved up against me, I got a pretty good, um, feel, I guess you'd say. It may have been a hard-bodied, androgenous female, but I'm thinking it was a male."

"Do you know anyone who would want to harm you?"

Reina choked out something between a laugh and a snort. "I'm a public defender. I deal with criminals every day. There are plenty of people who get pissed off when I prove the innocence of someone they want to be guilty. Let's see, then there's the three police officers who were recently dethroned from their little corruption scheme. Probably their spouses hate me, too. I did get a nasty-gram from one of them recently." Reina saw Franco's look of concern, but continued on, "And then, there's that extremely hostile crowd outside the courthouse today. You probably saw them on the news?" Both officers nodded. "Well, I don't have a specific red-hot death threat to tell you about but . . . but wait, I do have this." Reina took her purse off the kitchen countertop and pulled out the crumpled "repent" notice from her car. "This was left on my car seat today. It may be nothing. But, as you can see, it's hard to narrow down the field when trying to identify those who might 'want to harm' me."

"Now don't you wish you'd been a police officer instead of an attorney?" joked Franco. "So much safer." Returning to his professional demeanor, he added, "We'll take this love note here, and I'd like you to forward me the message you received from the officer's spouse, if you would. And if you think of anything else, or recall any threats from the past, just call me - day or night. You've got my number." He looked full into her face for a long second. "I'm always here to back you up, you know," he added quietly.

"I know," Reina replied with a grateful return smile.

After checking the bedroom and bathroom for potential evidence, the officers headed toward the door. As the girls thanked them, Jomar said over his shoulder, "And next time, ladies, lock the door will ya? This may not be the Big Apple, but there's plenty of maggots around here, too."

Clicking the door's deadbolt on the heels of the departing officers, they sat down to finish their margaritas. Within seconds, Reina began blinking hard, struggling to keep her eyelids open. With her brain fuzzed from Tequila and the aftermath of adrenalin, she leaned her head back and closed her eyes, letting gravity suck her into the chair.

She barely noticed Getta help her out of the chair and up the stairs.

In what seemed like a voice from the end of a long tunnel, her friend said, "I'll sleep in the spare bedroom. I need to let my helmet dry anyway."

"Thanks," mumbled Reina as she fell into bed, pulling the covers close around her neck. "Glad to have you here."

Chapter 6

After a short but uneventful sleep, Reina arrived bright and early at the jail for a pre-trial visit with her client. Reina's hopes of finally inspiring some conversation out of Maria appeared to be unfounded. "How do you feel about Peter's release from the hospital?" she asked.

Nothing.

"It may seem like this will make your life easier, but we still have to fight attempted murder, which the State takes very seriously. Anything you can tell me will really help."

Nothing.

"I'll be talking with Peter next week. Is there anything you'd like to tell me first?"

Nothing.

Dispirited by the continued, unbreakable silence, Reina sat drumming her fingers on the tabletop. Her thoughts turned to her own problems. As she typically did during their sessions, she began small-talking in an effort to get Maria to engage. "Well, I had an exciting night last night. You're not going to believe what happened to me, Maria. I went home to take a bath and someone broke into my house. Not a robber, apparently, since he didn't take anything. He seemed more intent on doing me harm than anything else."

Maria's downcast gray eyes turned up to meet Reina's. Encouraged by this sign of life, Reina continued rambling on. "Yeah, the nutcase attacked me in my tub. It's a good thing I can hold my breath for a long time or I might've been a goner." Reina waited for a moment hoping for a response from her companion, whose eyes were still fixed on her.

After listening to the clock tick for several minutes, she continued with her small talk. "I dunno. Maybe he was on drugs or something." Pausing in contemplation of this possibility, Reina stared off into the distance. She eventually continued, "You know, that could be it. His eyes were really weird. They looked almost gold, or red, like they were on fire. And the pupils were huge." She remained lost in thought for several minutes, trying to recall details from the intense few moments of the attack. "Hmmm . . . . Yeah, I suppose that was it. Some crazy on drugs."

Reina suppressed a shudder as she relived the moment. "Anyway," she continued with a shake of her head to clear the memory, "I think I beaned him pretty hard in the face with my candelabra. That's funny, too, because I just got that thing at a garage sale last month. What a fortunate coincidence. I mean slapping him with my wet hand certainly wouldn't have stopped him." Reina didn't care to think of what might have happened if she hadn't knocked him down. She shook her head again to shake off the frightening thought.

She continued talking aloud, almost forgetting Maria's presence as she worked her way mentally through the experience. "He had a weird, strong smell, too. I could smell it all through the house. My friend noticed it too. Kind of like --"

"Curry." The answer, coming from Maria, practically knocked Reina off her chair.

"Yes! That's it! What . . . I mean . . . how did you know? How could you possibly know that?"

"It was my husband's friend."

"What?" gulped Reina. "What do you mean your 'husband's friend?' Good grief, for thirty-some days you've not said a thing, and now this?"

"My husband has some very special friends." Maria's flat, emotionless voice hung in the air for a moment.

"Why would your 'husband's friend' attack me? What else can you tell me?"

"He needed to die."

And she would say no more.

Chapter 7

After the morning's bombshell from Maria regarding her husband's "friend," the day in court seemed anticlimactic. Jerry's opening statement, overly long as usual, told the jurors they would see "irrefutable evidence" of how the defendant had, in "cold blood," administered poisonous orange juice to her husband, ruthlessly watching him sicken before her eyes as she fed him his death drink. Jerry guaranteed the State would prove the defendant's (stabbing an incriminating finger at Maria) Attempted Murder beyond a reasonable doubt.

Although Jerry made good points in his statement, he had an annoying habit of rephrasing each point three times to really drive it home. Personally, Reina preferred the punch-punch effect of brevity. Watching the jurors, she tried to get a sense of their reactions. Did they stare at Maria in judgment or look at her out of the corner of their eyes? She glanced frequently at the jury chart, trying to get to know them so she could address them as a friend. Bottom line: people tend to agree with people they like and to whom they have an affinity. She needed them to like her and she hoped to help them feel an affinity for Maria.

Reina did not like to defer her opening statement, leaving the jury with Jerry's words in their minds, but in this case she did so. She rose. "Defense defers to the second half." Prosecution had deluged her in Discovery with a witness list that appeared to include everybody who knew, or ever *had* known the Stones. She wanted to see how the State's witnesses lined up before presenting her statement.

Of course, the jury would have access to Maria's confession, and it was pretty damning. But Reina only needed one of them to see it her way, and she had high hopes for one particular juror who took a contrary stance to every question posed to her during the jury selection. Reina had expected Jerry to use one of his peremptory challenges to exclude the woman, but he'd let her pass. Perhaps he feared Reina would counter with a Batson Challenge, claiming his strike was based on gender. As in a game of chess, Reina tried to anticipate her opponent's move, but be equally ready for unanticipated maneuvers. Although winning the game was part of the thrill, the real satisfaction for Reina was watching her clients regain their freedom. That was the passion that kept her up late at night reviewing notes and planning strategies.

To Reina's surprise, Judge Takahashi recessed court after opening statements, saying the witness' testimonies could wait until next week. Looking over at Jerry, Reina could see he was equally astounded, and a little pissed off, by this unusual behavior from Hashi. As she gathered up her papers, Reina was surprised to look up and see Jerry leaning over her table. Before she knew what he was doing, he placed one damp hand on hers, sending a feeling of revulsion through her, and said, "Well, you get a nice little reprieve, Dessiner, but come Monday, you're mine."

Reina withdrew her hand and said with a sweet smile, "Dream on, Jerry. I'll never be yours." She grabbed her stuff and headed to the door, detouring to the ladies' room to wash her hands. What was it about that man that was so creepy?

Back at the office, Reina expressed her amazement about the early recess to her supervisor, Carson Fain, whom she found in the break room, refilling his coffee cup. "I've never seen Judge Takahashi leave early or cut the day short before. She's usually like a cattle herder, driving us hard all day. I wonder if she's ill?" Reina poured herself a cup of coffee as she talked, spiking it with a few drops of cream.

"I believe she has family in town," Carson replied, leaning back against the counter top and crossing his long legs in front of him while he sipped his coffee. Tall and slender, Carson wore his Armani suit like a birthright. Reina secretly wondered how he always managed to appear so cool and wrinkle-free. *He probably never gets any criticisms from Hashi.*

"What?" Reina widened her eyes in feigned astonishment. "It's hard to imagine her with family. I kind of envisioned her living alone on some craggy peak somewhere."

Carson raised one elegantly arched eyebrow, saying gently, "Well, she has precious little family. Most of them died or disappeared during the Japanese internment.

I know she herself came out of the camp as a penniless orphan."

"Oh," Reina replied, feeling like a heel for her snarky comment. "Did she ever marry? Does she have any children?"

"No," Carson answered. "She was too busy clawing her way to the top of that craggy peak." He paused for just a moment to let Reina squirm from her careless words. Then, continuing on thoughtfully, he added, "It is not common knowledge, and not something that needs broadcasting, but I do know she was very sick when they rescued her from the internment camp at the age of six. Sick with gonorrhea. Complications from the disease destroyed her ability to bear children. The family she is meeting today is her adopted son, an abused orphan himself."

"Oh my god," exclaimed Reina. "I had no idea."

"I know you didn't. I only tell you because of the tension between you two. She would be the last person to ask for compassion from anyone, but it may, nonetheless, be warranted. Again, this is not something to be repeated to others."

"Of course."

"Perhaps now you understand why justice is her passion. Especially when it comes to those who prey upon the weak and defenseless of society." The two colleagues sipped coffee in silence for a moment before Carson nodded her a good day and headed off to his office.

Reina spent an hour working on some of her other caseload items, including forwarding to Franco the emails from the angry spouse of the police officer she'd help put behind bars. The woman had emailed her seven times in the last twenty-four hours, accusing Reina of "ruining her life" and "destroying a good man." She also hinted at some sort of vague retribution on the "nosy attorney" who "stuck her nose in where it didn't belong." Hopefully Franco could sort it out. In the meantime, she'd be watching her back.

Packing up her black bag with weekend work, she waved goodbye to Trey, who was on the phone. He gestured frantically to her not to leave, and she waited while he concluded his phone call. Placing the phone back in the cradle, he said to her, "Remember Markus Pratt?"

"The guy whose number you got from Maria's cell phone records?"

"Yeah, the only person she called regularly."

"Yeah. Did you get a hold of him?"

"Well, as you recall, his cell phone number was disconnected, but I had tracked him down to Stone Kingdom, where he apparently worked in the graphics department."

"Right. And we had to wait for him to return from his vacation in Taiwan since you, uncharacteristically, had no 'boots on the ground' there."

"I know," Trey shook his head dejectedly. "A sad failing on my part. In any case, he was expected back two days ago. But, according to my new friend at Stone Kingdom, he was a no-show."

"Do we know if he ever went on his trip?"

"Glad you asked. One of my old college roommates works as a flight attendant. He snuck into the system and found out Markus was a no-show for his flight, too."

"Did you try his home?"

"Does a bird fly? Of course I tried his home. Moved out. Apartment for rent."

"So, no show at his job, no show for his flight, no show at his apartment?"

Trey nodded in confirmation.

"*Diablo*!" Reina cursed, "Either he's hiding something, or someone else got to him first. Did your new friend at Stone Kingdom have anything else to say about him?"

"She mentioned she had seen Maria with him several times over the past couple of years - walking, talking, having lunch, that sort of thing."

"So the one person who might be able to shed a little light on Maria is gone missing. This just keeps getting better." Reina stood for a moment, tugging her lower lip. "Alright, thanks Trey. Let me know if anything new comes up."

Another mysterious friend, Reina thought, as she walked to her car. Maybe this is the "husband's friend" Maria had referenced? Reina shook her head. Too many shadows. She phoned Trey, "Did you do a background check on Pratt?"

"Of course."

"Any criminal record?"

"Nope."

"'kay, thanks."

"Yep."

Setting aside work issues, she decided to enjoy the unexpected freedom of the shortened day. Her mind slipped again, however, to thoughts of the stern judge. She tried without success to picture Hashi laughing and joking over drinks now with a beloved son. Humanizing the craggy Asian Eagle caricature she'd developed around the harsh and ruthless judge turned out to be quite difficult, despite what she now knew about the woman's tragic childhood.

With a few hours to kill, Reina headed into town for some shopping. At Nordstroms, she snagged a deal on a pair of jungle-print, platform Christian Louboutin's with sexy black cutouts. *These'll get me a Hashi rash, but what the hell.* Feeling victorious from the successful retail therapy, she phoned her friend Liz, then made a quick call to her mom to say she wouldn't be out to fly after all. A short drive to Pioneer Square brought her to Liz's art gallery.

Liz rose from behind her desk when Reina walked in and flipped the closed sign in the window. After a quick cheek kiss, Liz smiled, "Wonderful to see you dahling. I'm quite ready to go. Absolutely famished, in fact. Just have a look around, whilst I freshen up."

"I love this new stuff," said Reina, when Liz returned. "Is this a local artist?" Reina knew Liz tried to support the local art community as much as she could. She had opened the gallery nearly two years ago and worked hard to develop its reputation. Well-placed, on one of the old, brick, cobblestone roads in the tourist area of town, it attracted plenty of visits, just not a lot of big spenders. Liz loved her job, which was just as well as she certainly wasn't going to get rich doing it.

"Yeah," replied Liz, "he lives up on Camano Island and does the quirkiest things with old furniture and egg tempera paintings and magnetic, moveable art. He's quite a character. It really comes out in his work."

"Some of it seems impressionist, some surrealist, and some just plain bizarre. Egg paintings? Really?"

"Yes, apparently it is some lost way of mixing colors that he uses. Some of his stuff even glows in the dark. Quite brilliant, I think."

"Hmmm. I'll have to keep an eye on this guy."

"He's a bit cheeky, but a dear sweet just the same. He wears spectacles without any lenses, which is a bit distracting, and his hair always looks like he just traveled cross-country in a ragtop." Liz laughed, "He's so daft, yet so talented. I'll introduce you one day. As a matter of fact, they do an art studio tour of the island each year on Mother's Day. Perhaps we can take your mum up there?"

"I'm sure she'd love it."

"So, where shall we go for tea, luv? We're spoiled for choices, really, but my most recent discovery is a brilliant little place on Post Alley with the best crab cakes in town." Liz's baby blue eyes lit up as she described the crab cakes, right down to the lemon, garlic, aioli sauce. Pretty Liz loved to eat and each day she fought anew the supreme battle between food and figure. Her long blonde hair hid the roundness of her shoulders and the roundness of the rest of her drew plenty of admiring glances wherever they went. And as if that weren't enough, thought Reina as she waited for her other best friend to turn out the lights and lock the door to her gallery, her British accent conquers the remainder of the male species.

"Sounds great," said Reina. "I suppose you have a favorite waiter already eating out of your hand? I'll be lucky to get him to even take my order with you at the table."

Liz giggled and accused her of exaggerating which, of course, they both knew was not the case.

They drove separately as neither wanted to leave their cars on the street for too long. In the evening, when the tourist shops closed down, Seattle's large homeless population roamed more freely. Once, Reina left her car on the outskirts of Pioneer Square for a long evening and returned to find a bum draped over the hood, passed out drunk. She didn't care to reenact that scene.

They found parking across from the piers along the Seattle waterfront, under the Alaskan Way Viaduct. Reina pulled into the first available slot, hoping Liz would find something not too distant. Parking could be pretty tough here. As she locked her car door and reached for her phone to call Liz, she saw her friend walking toward her, from a parking spot about two blocks away. She waved and walked to meet her.

Crowds of people still milled about the waterfront. Once an important part of Seattle's shipping trade, the colorful piers now primarily supported the bustling tourist activity with a variety of shops and restaurants. Reina and Liz crossed the trolley tracks - installed for tourists mainly, but reminiscent of Seattle's working trolley of old - and proceeded to the base of the Hillclimb. This set of huge, steep stairs led from the waterfront to the area around the Pike Place Market, which included their destination of Post Alley. More tourist shops, coffee shops, and the occasional guitar player strumming for dollars lined the Hillclimb. They made only one quick stop for Reina to pick up a fresh supply of African Red Bush Tea and some *Herbs de Provence* at her favorite spice shop.

    Continuing on to the home of the fabled crab cakes, they turned to enjoy the expansive water view to the west. Giant orange shipping cranes dotted the shoreline to the south that lined Seattle's working flank, and the busy Alaskan Way Viaduct in front of them flowed with a never-ending stream of traffic. Beyond that, the setting sun shone brilliantly upon the waters of Elliot Bay. One of Seattle's iconic ferryboats could be seen pulling in to Pier 52, and another proceeded slowly outbound through the sparkling blue bay, on its way to Bainbridge Island. The big, green and white, flat-bottomed boats carried hundreds of passengers and cars daily across the Puget Sound and through the Strait of Juan de Fuca waters to various islands and destinations on the Olympic Peninsula, making up the most extensive ferry system in the United States. Further west, the Olympic Mountains lined the horizon, glowing under the descending sun's huge orange globe. Reina and Liz stopped to witness the sun's disappearance as it dipped behind the snow-capped peaks. They stood for a few moments watching the tiered layers of clouds, stacked over the mountains, begin to tint orange, gold, and pink.

"On days like this, there's no prettier place in the world," said Reina.

"Yeah, for a moment it's easy to forget the 294 other days in the year when you can't see past your umbrella," replied Liz. After watching for a few moments more, as the hazy clouds intensified in color, they turned for their dinner destination.

Although several other couples awaited seating at the busy little restaurant, the girls were led, without delay, to a cozy table in the corner. Eating out with Liz was always a pleasure, reflected Reina. She seemed to have permanent "reservations" wherever a good-looking waiter could be found. Liz started to sit, then stepped around the table so Reina could slip into the chair with its back against the wall. Reina smiled in appreciation of old friends who understood your neuroses and accommodated them without question.

Within seconds, a handsome waiter, with eyes the color of deep chocolate, arrived at their table, welcoming them with a heavy Spanish accent and a soulful gaze for Liz. Somehow, Liz managed to order drinks and flirt shamelessly with him in one breath. Reina wondered if the crab cakes really were the reason Liz adored this place, and if Rob knew. Rob, the most easy-going guy on the planet, had been Liz's steady beau since college days. Almost as indolent and pretty as Liz, the two went together like cream and sugar. Reina couldn't really imagine him being bothered by anything Liz did, or vice versa.

Contrary to Reina's expectations, the waiter did indeed glance away from Liz for just a short moment to take Reina's order. After Liz appreciatively watched the good-looking Spaniard walk away from the table, she turned to Reina and said, "So, dahling, I hear you're crusading for truth again?"

"Oh, *The Times* got carried away with that, didn't they?" answered Reina. "Somehow, they found out my client hasn't spoken for over a month and now it's become a great mystery." After a pause, she added, "Although I wouldn't admit it publicly, I'm beginning to think they're right. I'm going to do a little investigating to see where it leads." She unconsciously rubbed her sore shoulder as she spoke.

"What's up with your shoulder?" asked Liz. "I know a great masseur if you need one. He's hot. Really. I mean it. Four stars." It hadn't taken Liz more than a few months after her arrival in the city to have the greater Seattle area mapped out with the essential resources for everything a girl might need. Like a Thai restaurant, she rated them all on a hotness scale of one to five.

Reina laughed. "No, I think I'll be okay. As long as I don't get attacked again."

"What? What do you mean attacked? What happened?" Liz leaned forward in shock.

Reina relayed the details of the bath attack. When Liz asked if she had any idea why the man would want to harm her, she claimed ignorance.

"It may have just been some nut on drugs."

"I would have been terrified," breathed Liz, wide-eyed.

"Well, it wasn't what I would call just part of the evening fun, but it made me more angry than frightened." Changing the subject, Reina asked, "So, how are your parents?"

"Oh, still prattling on about getting out of New York. They've been hinting at moving to California for some time now, but I doubt it will ever happen."

"Is your father still practicing?"

"Yes, he claims he'll never retire."

"Do give them my love when you talk to them next," requested Reina, fondly recalling visits to Liz's family during her Boston days. Like Reina and her mother, Liz's family moved to the United States when their daughter decided to attend college in Colorado. Her father, the Honourable Gilbert Michael Heyer, arranged a transfer from the London office of his law firm to its New York branch and his wife, Anne, had delighted at the opportunity to conquer a whole new world of high society. Apparently, the conquest of New York must have been achieved if they were now looking to move to California. Probably, Reina suspected, with the intent of immersing Anne into the fame and flash of Hollywood.

The crab cakes arrived, along with some delicious smoked salmon bruschetta served gratis by their devoted waiter. Reina smiled up at him, but with his eyes on Liz, he didn't notice her gesture of appreciation. *Well, at least I get free food when I go out with her.* Reina shook her head in amusement.

Over the last of their bottle of Columbia Valley Chardonnay, Liz remembered to ask about Sam. Surprised, Reina realized that, other than the text she'd ignored from him that morning, she'd not given him a single thought,

"He decided he had more *pressing* matters," quipped Reina, describing their last conversation to her friend.

"Ha, I guess that's not what you meant when you said you were looking for an Ironman," Liz joked.

"Yeah, more like an Iron*ing*man," Reina fired back with a laugh.

They paid their bill, with a generous tip for Mr. Handsome, and started the long walk back to their cars. The skies had darkened and the old gas lights were burning, reflecting dimly on the glistening cobblestones of Post Alley. "You see," said Liz, "today is one of our 294 drizzle days after all. It never fails to amaze me how quickly the weather can turn around here. Well! We've no umbrella, so we'll just have to get wet."

They linked arms as they walked, huddling together to stay dry. As they rounded the narrow bend near the Market, Reina heard the sound of an engine approaching. Turning to look just in time, she saw a vehicle heading straight for them. Grabbing Liz's arm, they jumped back into a dark doorway, nearly stumbling on the figure of a passed-out drunk taking cover from the night. The big black Hummer roared past them with a splash.

"Bloody 'ell!" shouted Liz, waving an angry hand at the receding vehicle. "Watch where you're going you effin' nutter! Good God! People need to learn how to drive around here."

Reina's eyes narrowed speculatively. "Let's get out of here and back to our cars. I've had a long day and I'm wiped." Taking a ten dollar bill out of her purse, she slipped it under the hand of the sleeping bum. Stepping over him, they looked cautiously both ways for traffic, then continued on their way. As Reina thought about the dark road under the viaduct, she began to wish they'd parked somewhere closer, or better lit.

About fifty feet ahead, they could hear loud music blaring from a bar, its door standing open to the road. As the girls passed into the rectangle of light streaming out the bar's entry onto the cobblestones, they - literally - bumped hard into Hawk, at that moment exiting the crowded room backwards while he called a last goodbye to friends.

"Whoa!" Hawk pulled back from the human collision with eyebrows raised in surprise. "Look what the cat dragged in." He gave Liz's wet figure an appreciative glance. "What are you two ladies doing out on this soggy night?"

"Same thing as you, probably, enjoying a little city life," Reina replied, then continued with introductions. "Hawk, this is my friend Liz. Liz, Hawk is the chief flight instructor at my mom's flight school."

"Nice to meet you," Liz said, with the flutter of her eyelashes that was part of her DNA-deep response to any interaction with the opposite sex.

"The pleasure's all mine," replied Hawk and he looked like he meant it. "I'd be happy to escort you ladies to your vehicle, if you'd like?" Without waiting for a reply, he extended his left elbow and invitingly drew Liz's arm through it. He then crooked the other elbow for Reina, smiling a half-smile that seemed to offer both a challenge and an invitation.

"Why not?" Reina replied, raising an eyebrow and placing her fingers lightly inside his elbow. Their eyes met at the electric shock that zipped between her fingers and his forearm. "Must be some static electricity in the air from the storm."

"Indeed," agreed Hawk, mouth serious, but blue eyes crinkling at the corner in a smile of their own. "Well, where to, my fair companions?"

"We're down under the viaduct."

"Excellent. Then down the Hillclimb it is. Good thing I came along to help you down those dark, slippery steps," he declared gallantly.

Liz giggled and Reina rolled her eyes, thinking, he's really getting into this knight-in-shining-armor thing. Aloud, she said, "Yes, if only you'd brought your white charger and sword, the rescue would be complete. You don't have a sword in there do you?" She peeked around his elbow at his torso.

Hawk raised his eyebrows, tilted his head sideways toward her a bit, and smirked at the question, saying, "I *have* been known to carry a sword . . . and ride a charger, too, for that matter."

Liz giggled again and Reina shook her head slightly at her inadvertent sexual innuendo. I mean come on, she thought, he's your mom's employee. Her hand, resting on the contours of his muscular forearm, tingled lightly and she had to exercise conscious restraint to keep from tracing her fingertips the rest of the way up his arm. The heat from his skin seemed to spread all the way down her body. *Shit, what is it that makes me feral around him?*

Liz was telling Hawk about the crazy driver they'd narrowly escaped. She added, "You Americans have no respect for pedestrians. I can't tell you how many times I've been nearly run down in crosswalks here. British drivers are much more conscientious. Only once did I fail to stop for a pedestrian, and the old woman in the crossing wagged her finger at me so violently, I felt guilty for days."

Hawk laughed, then turned to look down at Reina with unreadable night-sky eyes. "You okay?" he asked quietly.

For perhaps the first time in her adult life, Reina felt the urge to be protected in a man's arms. She nodded and looked away, afraid the darkness wouldn't hide from Hawk the naked longing in her eyes.

The trio made the dark walk down the now wet and deserted stairs of the Hillclimb without incident. At the bottom Reina pointed to her car, not far down the lane. Hawk and Liz deposited Reina in front of her Roadster, she with a hug and a kiss, and he with his half-smile. They waited while she got in and locked the doors, then continued on to Liz's car. Reina backed out and drove down the one-way road behind them, observing Hawk and Liz talking and laughing with each other like old friends. She rolled down her window and leaned out as her car coasted up to their position, "Hey, Hawk, do you need a ride to your car?"

Hawk replied, "No. No, I'll manage just fine. Don't worry about me. Thanks, though."

Reina shrugged and called out, "Okay, then. Goodnight." Driving off with a wave, she watched in her rear view mirror as the two stopped and talked in front of Liz's car for several minutes. Hmm, she thought, it looks like Mr. CFI likes blondes. Suddenly, she felt uncharacteristically cranky, for absolutely no reason at all.

She turned on her radio and headed home to bed to dream of crab cakes with big brown eyes and running for her life from dark strangers.

Chapter 8

Friday morning dawned fresh and clear after the night's storm. As court was in recess, Reina spent the morning viewing back copies of Peter Stone's weekly, televised, revivalist service. Over the last ten years, Reverend Peter Stone had become a household name to Seattleites. Whether you subscribed to his style of religion or not, you could hardly ignore the regular mentions of him, and his increasingly vast empire, in the daily news. His popular Friday night show, *The Rock,* broadcast his religious rhapsodies nationwide and he had a reportedly vast international following.

Reina started with archives from the show dated six months ago, well before the alleged poisoning began. The recording started with the typical lead-up of music and prayer and trolling for dollars. When Stone entered the stage, his energy reverberated palpably through the crowd. Robust and vigorous, he shouted out for the Lord, healing everyone in sight. People came forward with all kinds of ailments, from "I have the demon of lust," to "I have arthritis in my knee," to "I've been blind for years."

He prayed over them and placed his hands on their bowed heads, asking for their repentance and renewed commitment to the Lord. Then he placed his palm on their forehead and, well, healed them. At least, that's what it looked like. With each healing, the music swelled and the crowd went wild. There was dancing in the aisles, waving of hands, and crying out in the incomprehensible language they called "speaking in tongues." The scene reminded Reina a little of her childhood in the Caribbean, where she had witnessed natives become entranced when dancing to their traditional Soca music, with its compelling percussion beat. As with Soca, Stone's "show" incorporated powerful, pulsing rhythm with lilting, soulful voices for a mesmerizing effect.

    The cornerstone of the show, of course, rested squarely on Peter Stone himself. Short in stature with a muscular build, his incredibly intense blue eyes emphasized his undeniable charisma. He seemed to really know how to work the crowd into a frenzy with the perfect combination of gloriosa and guilt. Reina found his regular stage entourage fascinating. Two strikingly beautiful and voluptuous women swayed and sang behind Peter in every episode and a group of angelic-looking young male singers formed a boys' choir. Like a matched set of small dark birds, the purity of their innocent voices added to the impression of the heavens erupting in song. Finally, an odd assortment of other people - they may have been assistants or invitees - gathered on the stage with the performers. Or perhaps they were the recently healed? As Reina fast-forwarded through several episodes she recognized some of the same faces – the man who had the "demon of lust" removed from him and the woman who had repented of "sins of unfaithfulness," for example, appeared to have become regulars.

In each of the tapes, Maria sat impassively in the background with her head bowed and her hands folded in her lap, the sedate, demure wife of the minister. She did not enter into the religious frenzy with the crowd. Occasionally, she raised her head and watched her husband with those dull gray eyes, but for the most part, she sat as quietly as the proverbial church mouse.

Periodically, the action would cut to the close-up shots of sincere-looking church members sitting by the phone waiting for YOU to call in with your contribution to this important godly movement called the Church of Peter Stone. Reina knew that devout believers across the country contributed generously to the coffers of Stone and company.

At the end of each week's show, Peter Stone would close the evangelical session by kneeling on the stage, raising his hands to the heavens, and calling out, "Thank you, Lord, for making me your chosen one. Thank you, Lord, for working your great power through me. I am the Stone this church is built on. Amen."

As she fast-forwarded to more recent sessions, Reina saw a gradual change in Stone as the alleged poison began to take effect: Pale skin, weakened voice, a markedly diminished energy. If Jerry decided to show this progression to the jury, and he undoubtedly would, it would surely heighten the jurors' sympathy for Stone. The tapes from the most recent month were considerably less interesting, with no centerpiece of Stone, just the concerned congregation praying fervently for his recovery.

Tonight would be his comeback, she had heard. And she planned to be there to see it.

Reina stood and stretched after the long morning of televangelism. Religion by TV wasn't her cup of tea, but Stone certainly had plenty of charisma and vitality to carry the program. She vaguely recalled that the word "charisma" originally meant having the divinely conferred ability to tap into the spiritual world. The modern definition, of being attractive and appealing (regardless of spiritual connections) evolved, as most words do, through years of misuse.

Well, she didn't completely buy into the whole healing thing, but Stone's unexpected recovery definitely defied explanation. Although she had disciplined her mind through legal training to look for facts, her childhood had exposed her to things that seemed to defy reason.

Born in the Caribbean to a mother with wandering toes, Reina had witnessed some strange things in the islands. A hodgepodge of cultures and languages, the Caribbean boasted several hybrid religions as a result of the mixing of its many occupants over the years. British, Dutch, Spanish, French, and Danish colonial influences had melded in the hot equatorial sun with the African traditions brought over by slaves, imported to work the sugar plantations. One of these conglomerate religions, *Santeria*, preached that the devotee must be "reborn" with new relations to the spiritual world for healing to take place. Hmmm, Reina thought, not that different from Christianity.

She knew, too, that the *Miskitu*, whose religion spread across parts of South America and a bit into some of the islands, considered illness to be related to disturbed relations with spirits. As a girl, she had witnessed a *curandero*, or folk healer, cure a girl of *grisi siknis*, an affliction supposedly caused by sorcery. Who knows, she thought, maybe Stone does possess some mysterious gift, some connection to the spirit world? And, like the *curandero* from her childhood, if he got paid well for it, so be it. *No harm, no foul,* she figured.

Reina forced her mind to return to the cause at hand: her client. She felt a sense of annoyance at Maria for being so . . . so *bland*. For a woman who tackled life head-on, Reina couldn't understand someone as lifeless as Maria. Maybe this poisoning attempt resulted simply from the insane jealousy of a woman who could no longer stand to live in the shadow of greatness. Reina hoped to get a better sense of the couple's relationship next week, if she could arrange a meeting with Reverend Stone. So far, he'd refused to agree to a time to meet and, basically, his people had told her people he had nothing to say to her.

Reina packed the tapes back in the box and hauled them to her car. She retracted the car top for the sunny drive north to Wayward Field where she had promised to have lunch with her mother at Taildraggers, the homey little diner on the airfield.

After exiting I-5, she headed east toward the airport. Suddenly, she saw the car ahead of her brake and swerve abruptly. In horror, she saw what looked like a small animal go flying off the vehicle's bumper, across the fog line, and into the ditch lining the road. The car ahead of her surged forward, continuing on its way. Reina pulled over to the side of the road. Shutting down her engine, she got out and cautiously approached the ditch. She could see something dark in the tall grass. If it were alive, and if it were wild, it might get violent if cornered. Coming closer, she saw it was a small dog. It appeared to be breathing, with short rasping sounds. As she knelt down beside it, it raised its pitiful little head and looked at her with the biggest, softest, brownest eyes she'd ever seen.

"You poor little thing," she said softly, reaching out cautiously to touch the back of its neck, ready to pull back if it snapped at her. But the puny animal just laid its head back on the ground, either too weak or too cowed to fight. Its chest rose and fell laboriously and it flinched a little at her touch, perhaps expecting something harsher from a human. Its hair was matted and filthy and she could see its ribs outlined in its chest. One ear was almost completely gone, maybe from a fight, or disease - she had no way of knowing. But she did know that this was one of the ugliest dogs she had ever seen. She walked back to her car, trying to talk herself out of what she knew she was about to do. *Surely it's enough to call the pound, or animal rescue, or someone else to deal with it?*

She gathered up her suit jacket, still flung over the passenger seat from the day before, and carried it back to the ditch, half hoping the creature would be dead and she could be on her way. It wasn't. She laid her expensive jacket down in the grass and carefully lifted the poor beast onto it, careful of the gash on its shoulder and the limply hanging leg. Carrying it to her car, she wished for a third hand with which to plug her nose. This was no one's pampered pet. Placing her jacket with the foul bundle on the floor of her passenger side, she received a little whimper and a soulful look for her efforts, followed by a concerned bark when she shut the door to walk around to the driver's side.

"Yes, tramp, I'm still here," she assured it. "But if you mess in my car, I will toss you out into oncoming traffic, so be forewarned." Putting her car into first, she pulled a u-turn, heading for the veterinarian office she'd seen in the strip mall, across from Starbucks, at the last intersection.

An hour later, she was back on her way toward the airfield. The wounded dog, whom she'd temporarily named Ditch, was in good hands. She'd given the vet assistant her credit card number and asked that the filthy creature not only be tended to medically, but be bathed and given flea and worm treatments as well. When they'd tried to remove her jacket, the dog whimpered so pitifully she insisted it stay with the little brute. It was probably ruined anyway.

Reina parked behind True Blue Aviation, next to her Mom's easily identifiable Deux Chevaux. As she walked past it, she patted the fender of the funky old car. Reina had driven it a couple times since her mom imported it from France and it was fun to see heads turn on American roads at the vehicle's unique look, with its roll-back top and afterthought headlamps. Passing through the gate and crossing the transient aircraft parking area to reach the nearby restaurant, she saw lots of airplanes tied down outside the diner, and plenty of cars in the parking lot, even now at the tail end of lunch hour. Small restaurants typically struggled to survive on airfields, but the girls who ran this place had developed a faithful clientele, both with the fly-in crowd and the local community. Fantastic food and plentiful portions drew people in and the service, always given with a big smile and a minute or two of friendly chitchat, kept them coming back. Reina knew it had become a favorite hangout with the fun-loving pilot regulars.

    The ribbon of bells tinkled as Reina entered the glass door stenciled with a big, blue and yellow biplane. The interior, adorned with various pictures of famous and infamous pilots and their amazing flying machines, felt homey and welcoming. Like Caite's flight school, the ceiling was painted sky blue with fluffy white clouds, and an assortment of remote-control aircraft models hung in corners. A friendly place, for both pilots and non-pilots. Some regulars claimed they came in, during the Northwest winter, just for the blue ceilings, so they could remember what the sky looked like around here.

    Poking her head around the corner into the kitchen, Reina called out a friendly hello to the owners, Syndie and Susie, who were busy posting orders on the turnstile in front of the cooks. Syndie waved cheerfully and Susie blew her a kiss.

    Reina made her way toward the booth where Caite sat chatting with a couple of guys standing nearby. They were laughing, and undoubtedly telling tall tales of their latest flying feats. Reina wriggled into the bench seat opposite her mother and listened to Caite finish the story she'd been telling the two men.

". . . after criticizing all my aircraft and trying to bully poor Julianna into giving him a discount, the guy seemed to finally realize I wasn't just the hired help. He came over to me and asked, in surprise, 'Are you the owner?' I told him 'Yes.' He looked slightly shocked and had the gall to ask me, 'What does your husband think?'"

The two guys laughed and rolled their eyes, asking if she'd shown him the door.

Caite replied with a chuckle, "No. I just winked at him and whispered 'He doesn't know. Please don't tell.'"

"What did he do?" the tall pilot asked.

"He just shook his head in shock and left shortly afterward. I think I turned his nineteenth century brain upside down with the whole concept. I thought I heard him muttering something about the negative effects of giving women the vote." Caite laughed and turned to perform introductions.

"Gentlemen, this is my daughter, Reina. Reina meet Mike and Jack." Reina shook hands with the two men and they said their goodbyes. As the tall one turned to go, he accidentally stepped on his friend's foot.

Reina saw the shorter one clout him on the shoulder and say, "Jesus, Jack, you're such an oaf!" They headed to the counter to pay their bill, bickering amicably.

"Well, still flirting with the guys I see," said Reina as she leaned across the table to *faire la bise* on her mother's cheeks.

"You know it's just part of my job," sighed Caite, belying the heavy sense of duty the words implied with a pleased laugh. "Most of these guys are not only customers, but also friends. *And* pilots I share the sky with. I don't know if you've met the tall one there, Jack? He moved here recently from California after retiring from the Navy. He's earned a new call sign around here." Caite laughed again. "We call him 'Bulldog' because he's constantly bumping into things, as you just saw, like a bull in a china shop. He's the clutziest guy I know, when on *terra firma*."

"I hope he's not that clumsy as a pilot," Reina replied.

"Oh no. I flew with him and it was like aerial ballet. Beautiful. Definitely at home in the sky. So, I introduced him to some of the guys from the Blackjack Squadron and I hear he flies a pretty mean dog fight."

The Blackjacks were a local flying group made up of pilots, many with military backgrounds, who flew experimental aerobatic planes called RVs. They could often be seen over Wayward Field flying in tight formations of five, nine or even fifteen ships.

Caite added, "Those guys sure won't put up with any crazy stunts from him. I've heard them debrief, and they can be brutal. But then, when you're flying with someone two feet off your wing, you can't afford sloppy mistakes or unanticipated moves."

"Hmmm . . . he's nice looking. Married?" Reina's eyes followed him out the door, wondering if he had been her mother's date the other evening. Fiercely independent, her mother hadn't hooked up seriously with any guys in the area, although Reina knew there were several interested parties waiting in the wings. Caite's petite figure and expressive hazel eyes, combined with a great sense of humor and the ability to talk airplanes like a man, made her very popular with the mostly-male clientele of Wayward Field.

    Caite just smiled and ignored the question. "So, what's this about a wounded dog?" she asked in reference to the text Reina had sent earlier.

    Before Reina could answer, Syndie came up to take their order.

    "Hey there, Sunshine, long time no see." She bent over to give Reina a friendly hug. "Where ya been, Sugar?"

    "Oh, the usual," Reina replied. "Too much work and not enough fun."

    "Well, I know how that goes." Syndie nodded her generous blonde curls vigorously. "But I guess I'd rather have too much to do than too little." She glanced around with satisfaction at all the full tables in the room. "We're just happy to have the business we have nowadays."

    When Syndie and Susie had opened the restaurant four years earlier, the building was a shabby, run-down shack that had gone through three owners in as many years. Their hard work made it into a bustling little place, but they all knew how fragile the survival of a small enterprise could be. Reina often heard her mother mention her semi-regular bonding sessions with the two women, usually over a bottle of wine, to celebrate another month, or week, or even a day of staying in business.

"Yeah, you guys seem to pack 'em in pretty well these days."

"We sure try. I hear people will fly for hours and drive for miles for a piece of Susie's delicious berry pie. So, what can I get you ladies?"

Reina and Caite ordered omelettes, even though the breakfast hour had long passed. Susie's lunch omelette, combining garden herbs and three French cheeses in a soufflé-like fluff of egg was like eating a savory cloud. Combined with a fresh salad and baguette it made a perfect summer lunch.

Syndie tucked her unmarked order pad into her apron and departed with their orders, saying, "We should just throw those omelettes on the griddle the minute we see you two walk in the door."

"I guess we're a little predictable," Caite commented.

"Only in food, I think," Reina laughed. She then relayed the ditch-dog episode to her mom.

"Well, that was unpredictable, I agree. What are you going to do with it?"

"That's a good question to which I don't have a good answer. I guess I'll see if they're even able to get him all patched up, then try to find a home for him."

While waiting for their food to arrive, they talked for a bit about flying and various pilots they knew, occasionally stopping to watch an incoming aircraft land, or to greet various people coming and going at the busy little diner. Caite, of course, was well known at Wayward Airfield, and Reina, by association, had many acquaintances there as well. Caite often said that the microcosm of an airport resembled that of a small high school, where everyone knew everyone *and* everyone else's business.

Susie placed their food on the table just as Reina, out of the corner of her eye, saw Hawk enter with an attractive, fortyish, red-headed woman. After greeting several acquaintances, he and the woman took a booth on the other side of the room. Reina pointed him out to her mother, who had been distracted with the arrival of their food order. "Hawk just came in." She nodded across the room in the direction of his table.

Caite looked over and waved at him. He returned the salute with a friendly nod. Her next words relieved Reina from having to ask the question. "That's Joni he's with, one of our new students. I originally set her up to train under Ben, but she specifically asked for Hawk."

I'll bet she did.

"Hawk says she calls him all the time with questions about stuff she's learning. She seems very excited about getting her license."

Or excited about something else, maybe?

"He says she's not the quickest learner so he's going to have to spend a lot of time with her."

Why does that not surprise me?

"But, she pays her bills, so we're happy to help her get what she wants."

Oh, I know what she wants, all right. Reina sternly silenced her internal voice, surprised at her catty reaction. *I mean, really. What do I care who he spends time with, blonde or redhead? It's a free world. I couldn't care less. I've just always been a sucker for a guy in a pony tail, that's all. Well, some guys, anyway. But for Christ's sake, he's old enough to be my dad.*

"Reina?" Caite's voice broke into Reina's reverie.

"Oh, sorry. What?"

"Oh, I just asked you twice how you're doing. You look tired."

"Well, this case is really wearing me down, in more ways than one. Aside from the bath attack and the near hit-and-run, which I've already told you about, I'm worried about being able to adequately defend my client. The few words she's said are cryptic and disturbing and she won't come clean with me. She won't help me help her. I don't think I've ever met anyone like her, so colorless and lacking in vitality. It's like she's empty inside, a blank book, a vacant room. It's almost as if she's already dead."

"Hmmm, that's an interesting description. I've known people like that." Caite chewed another bite of her omelette, gazing out the window at something far into the distance. "I'd like to meet her," she told Reina, her eyes focusing back on her daughter.

"Well, I don't know. I mean, since she refused bail, she's still in the custody of the State. I can't exactly just bring her over."

Caite looked again out the window for a long moment. "Do you have a picture of her?" she finally asked.

"No." Reina shook her head, then continued. "Oh, but you know, I do have a box of tapes with her in them — recordings of Peter Stone's show *The Rock.*"

"I'd love to check them out."

"Well, you're in luck as I just happen to have them in the trunk of my car."

Mother and daughter finished their lunch and headed to the door. Enroute, they stopped for a quick hello at Hawk's table and Hawk introduced Joni and Reina to each other.

Late forties at least, thought Reina, back in cat mode. *Hard to tell under all that makeup. And definitely not her real hair color.*

"How are you doing, Joni?" Caite asked.

"I'm fantastic!" Joni replied enthusiastically.

That's a matter of opinion.

"I just love my flight lessons with Hawk each day!"

Yeah, and who even cares about the airplane?

"I just know I'm in good hands with him." Joni cupped her chin in her left hand and smiled coyly at Hawk. Reina could see an indentation on her empty left ring finger.

Out hunting, are we?

"He's an absolute angel!"

Alright, if you gush any more, you're gonna flood the place. Shocked at her violent reaction to the woman, Reina scolded her inner voice into submission. *Stop already!*

"Well, I'm so glad things are going well. Keep up the good work. See you back at the shop." Caite said goodbye and Reina followed her mother out.

Good lord, what is it about that woman that puts my back up, even at a distance? Reina could feel Hawk's half-smile burning into her back, almost as if he could see the raised hackles there.

As they walked across the tarmac to the flight school, Caite suddenly burst into laughter.

"What's so funny?" asked Reina.

"Oh, sometimes we get some interesting dynamics around here. I just wish I could have read Hawk's mind just then. Especially when Joni called him an angel."

"I always thought you *could* read minds," Reina joked.

Caite smiled enigmatically. "Sometimes and with some people. Not so much with Hawk."

"Hmmm. Well, I'll get the tapes and meet you inside." Walking to her car, Reina grumbled to no one in particular, "You couldn't pay me to drool over a guy like that." She carried the box of tapes back to True Blue.

Entering the pilot's lounge, she found it full of students and instructors coming and going from flight lessons. Happy to see her mom's business doing so well, she watched Caite greet several regular customers with a smile and a friendly question or two about their training. She heard her mother congratulate a young man who had, just that morning, successfully completed his final FAA checkride to become a pilot. His eyes shone in excitement and he couldn't stop smiling.

"What's next?" Caite asked him.

"Well, I just want to fly for a while without having to complete any lessons or instructor reviews," he said with a big grin. "Then, I'm going on for my instrument ticket for sure. I've been practicing listening to air traffic controllers talk to aircraft coming and going at the local airports. It's cool to hear the pilots in the system, real time. Thanks for telling me about LiveATC.com."

Reina checked to see if his feet were touching the ground. She remembered the euphoria of getting signed off for that first pilot's license. A natural high that lasted for days. And she certainly understood the addictiveness of flying, and the craving for more of the freedom the skies offered.

As they continued through the crowded lounge, Reina waved to a couple of pilots she'd met at one of the flight school's regular barbeques. After her mother stopped to pick up a phone message from Julianna, they headed through the pilot shop to the large classroom, situated in the rear of the building. The pilot ground schools were held here on weeknights so the walls were lined with white boards and posters of airplane panels and wind charts and airport diagrams.

Reina powered on the audio-visual system and plugged in a recording of *The Rock* from five months ago. She forwarded past the introductory sections then pointed out Maria, seated on one of the chairs in the background area of the stage.

"She does look pretty mousy," her mother nodded. She watched for a few minutes then asked, "Do you have any older pictures of her?"

"I don't know," replied Reina, a little impatiently. "I mean, this box is full of recordings that date back ten years, but I'm not going to waste my time looking through all of them. She's probably in them too, I would guess. Why?"

"Let's take a look."

"Okaaay . . . " said Reina with obvious reluctance, not sure what the point would be. She didn't see what a younger, mousy, gray Maria would tell them. She wanted to get going, to get ready for her evening adventures. She glanced at her watch and sighed audibly, but decided to cooperate with her mother's suggestion.

Stifling her natural impatience, Reina inserted a tape from ten years ago, the very beginning of the successful run of *The Rock*.

"I'm not sure if she's in this one," said Reina, scanning the back row of chairs for the familiar gray figure.

"She's there," said Caite.

"Where?"

"There in the front." Caite pointed to the vibrant young woman standing next to Reverend Stone, dressed in white muslin with long, shining, brown hair flowing past her shoulders. Maria was smiling and clapping and dancing to the music.

"*Diablo*, that can't be her. *She* looks like the one who's been poisoned. What in God's name happened to her?"

"That, my daughter, is a very well-put question."

Chapter 9

After packing up the tapes and saying her goodbyes, Reina headed toward home. Driving along the perimeter of the airport, she had difficulty keeping her eyes on the road as a restored P-51 Mustang crossed directly ahead of her on its final approach to runway 34. Wayward Airfield, built in the '30s, had seen use during World War II as a training and support field for the Naval carrier programs in the area. Even nowadays, historic warbirds such as Mustangs or Spitfires or Migs occasionally flew in to land or perform maneuvers here. Today, there were several aircraft in the pattern, including her mom's old 1946 Aeronca Champ dressed out in Navy colors. She pulled over for a moment to watch the Champ driver do a gentle three-point landing on the adjacent grass runway. As she drove off, she glanced sideways, straight down the length of the main runway, with the afternoon sun slanting across it. Past the approach lights, the broad white stripes marked the landing area of the long strip of shimmering pavement. She wondered if every pilot got a spiritual lift, as she did, when looking down runways. They were such symbols of hopes and thrills and adventures, past and future. Unlike a mile of freeway, which could take you exactly a mile, a mile of runway could take you anywhere in the world.

She drove home quickly, watching carefully for any officers out for their monthly revenues. She knew, from experience, that even her friendship with Franco wouldn't get her off on a speeding ticket. Franco was a stickler for doing things by the book, friends or no friends.

After the recent exposure of corrupt police officers in his department, Franco had been righteously furious at his fellow law enforcers for breaching the public trust. The week after Reina's trial concluded, he had bought her dinner at the little Italian place off of Eastside, on Lake Union. Over appetizers, he personally and painfully apologized to her, saying there was no excuse for a person wearing the uniform of authority to abuse the power and honor given to him. He solemnly promised to her that the officers in question, and others like them, would come to justice.

"Even if you have to do it yourself?" teased Reina, trying to lighten his spirits.

"Of course not," he replied stiffly. "You know I'd never take the law into my own hands."

She assured him she did indeed know that and then she declared dramatically, "Between the two of us, we'll clear the streets of The Emerald City with gun and gavel." She pounded the air with her fist for effect.

"Sounds like a plan." Franco's eyes glowed a bit at her idealistic words. Reina had hammed it up a bit to lighten his mood and was happy to see him smile again.

As she parked in her assigned spot in front of her condo building, Reina put aside all thoughts of police officers, friendly or otherwise.

Mrs. Jensen stood waiting to hold the door open for her, saying, "Hello, Dearie. I could tell by the way you pulled in that you're in a bit of a rush. Well, you'll be glad to know, your friends are here already. And it looks like they brought you some goodies, too." The old lady put her fingertips together in front of her chin and looked hopefully up at Reina, saying, "Perhaps you girls could bring them down and join me for a spot of tea?"

Reina smiled, knowing Mrs. J had a fondness for "goodies." "I'm afraid we can't tonight, Mrs. J. We're going out soon. We'll have to do it some other time."

As Reina headed to the elevator, the old lady shuffled behind in worn pink slippers. "Can you girls join me for tea tonight?" she asked, already forgetting they had just discussed this idea. "I could invite that nice boy, Sam," she added, putting her fingertips in front of her mouth again, the way she did when she thought she was being clever.

"Soon, Mrs. J. We'll have tea with you soon," promised Reina as she pushed the elevator button several more times thinking to herself, and *that* is why one should *never* have a relationship with someone in their building, especially with a Mrs. Nosybody around.

"He's such a nice boy, that Sam," Mrs. J rattled on at Reina's elbow. "Always so nicely dressed, too. Not like those other sloppy, messy young men."

"Yes, Mrs. J." With an evil afterthought, Reina added, "Maybe you should invite him to tea today. I'm sure he'd like that."

Mrs. J, with fingertips actively bunched again at her lips, started muttering to herself in excitement at the idea, "Hmmm, yes, that would be lovely, wouldn't it? Mr. Jingles would like that. Don't you think Mr. Jingles would like that?" She looked at Reina for confirmation that Mr. Jingles would approve.

Just as Reina decided to escape to the stairs, the elevator bell rang and the old lady stepped back in alarm. Mrs. J had once gotten "stuck" on the elevator (she'd forgotten to push any of the buttons) and so she now refused to go onto those "evil contraptions." Reina waved goodbye to her, grateful that the fear of elevators kept the old busybody from wandering the upper floors. She chuckled to herself at the ambush she'd set up for Sam.

Her friends were waiting for her in her condo, each having been given the security code (on the off chance Mrs. J was napping) and a key to her place.

Reina entered to see Getta placing a bag from Bartell's Drug Store on the counter and Liz already plopped in the corner chair with a Starbucks Grande Latte in one hand and an espresso brownie balanced half-eaten on her knee. Getta and Liz had agreed to accompany Reina to *The Rock* tonight, but before leaving they had some alterations to do.

"Oh great, you're here already," Reina greeted each with a hug. "No unwelcome visitors this time, I trust?"

"Hey, I'm ready for them now," Getta replied as she pulled a heavy 3/8 inch ratchet from her bag.

"Good God! You're not going to carry that with you everywhere you go now?" exclaimed Liz, as Reina took the stout metal tool in her hand to feel its heft.

"No, just whenever I come over here or go out with Reina for the evening. You know Reina attracts trouble like honey draws bees. There's always some damn crazy thing buzzing around her," Getta grumbled, then added, "Who knew I was putting my life in permanent jeopardy by becoming her friend?"

"I know. I wish somebody had warned me, too," Liz joined the lament. "Actually, about both of you. I was daft to let you two troublemakers sit down at my table in Art 101. But God knows you wouldn't have passed without my help!"

Reina and Getta both laughed, without disagreeing. Liz continued, "Naively, my family thinks the world of you two. Especially Thomas," Liz added with a mischievous look out of the corner of her eye at Getta.

Liz's older twin brothers, Thomas and Michael, met Reina and Getta when the three girls were college roommates in Colorado. After graduation, Getta left for Madrid to spend two years obtaining her Masters in Spanish and Thomas somehow ended up there as well. Everyone knew there was something between the two, but nobody seemed to know exactly what – including Getta and Thomas. And they didn't seem in any big hurry to figure it out, with Getta in Seattle now and Thomas working three thousand miles away, playing his saxophone with a band in New Orleans. In the interest of promoting the relationship, Liz had mentioned to her brother a few times that there was a vibrant music scene in Seattle as well, but he didn't seem to take the sisterly hint.

Reina added to the tease, "Yeah I miss Michael and Thomas. Don't you Getta?" When Getta refused to rise to the bait, she continued on, "Anyway, let's just hope your families never find out the truth. Getta, I can almost hear your Aunt Hannah saying, 'That Reina. She seemed like such a nice girl.'"

Getta laughed. "You know damn well Aunt Hannah loves you as much as me. Hell, maybe more."

"Aunt Hannah is such a sweetheart. I just don't know how you stayed so slender growing up in her home, the way she cooks. I'd have been 200 pounds by high school."

"Well, I doubt that. Liz maybe, but not you."

"Oi!" protested Liz, her mouth full of brownie. "Speaking of which, I need to go visit Auntie Hannah. Does she still make those fabulous cinnamon rolls?"

"Yes, and she would love to see you both and have an excuse to make a batch of whatever food you request. You should all come do a pajama party with us soon. I know she misses having you around."

When Getta's parents were killed in a boating accident, leaving her orphaned at the tender age of nine, Aunt Hannah stepped in to care for her brother's child, giving her a home in her cozy little bungalow on Queen Anne Hill. After her travels for college and graduate school, Getta returned to her hometown and moved back in with her aunt, reclaiming her old childhood bedroom, complete with posters of motorcycles and teenage heartthrobs still hanging on the wall. Although Getta sometimes longed for a place of her own, she hated the thought of leaving her aging aunt to live alone now. Fortunately for their ongoing relationship, Aunt Hannah let Getta do exactly as she pleased, having completely shed the adopted mantle of watchful guardian the minute her brother's child turned eighteen. As a result, the two got along splendidly.

Reina agreed an overnight should happen soon, then turned her attention to the Bartell's shopping bag. "So, what color did you get for me this time, my pretties?"

Getta pulled out the box of hair dye and replied, "You know, it's been a long time since we've done blonde, I kinda felt the platinum thing coming on."

"Great. I'm ready for a fresh look, girlfriend. Let's do it."

"Okay, and then Liz is going to cut it, too, so we can spike it out for you."

"I'm all yours, chicas. My hair is in your hands."

"Jerry's gonna love the new look," joked Getta as she prepared the hair dye. "Didn't you say he often comments on your hair?"

"Yeah, he always makes remarks about my looks," replied Reina, "and he usually wants to shake hands or pat my shoulder or touch me in some way." She grimaced. "It's a good thing I don't critique *his* looks all the time – 'Gee Jerry, love that mousy brown hair. Too bad I can see your bald spot under the comb-over . . . but I do like the way your saggy suit matches your hair and mustache and tie. *Every day*.'"

"Not every day?" cried Liz in horror. She added as an afterthought, "And who wears moustaches nowadays anyway? Except police officers, of course."

"Yeah I know," affirmed Reina. "And perverts. Not to lump the two in the same category of course . . . . Anyway, ratty may be a better description of Jerry, all gray and brown with twitching whiskers. He's harmless - I think. But he does give me the creeps."

"I just can't like the moustache idea," Liz shook her head, her artistic senses seriously offended, "unless of course, it's like the one on that adorable barista dude at Starbucks, just a thin line with a neat goatee. Brilliant." Her eyes started to glow a little at the memory of her most recent flirtation.

Getta rolled her eyes at Reina in the mirror, "What *should* have taken five minutes for coffee turned into fifteen. I had to apologize to the people in line behind me, the two lover birds were taking so long." Getta's style of flirtation usually involved something like working out together, roller skating around Green Lake, or going dancing. Anything that involved physical activity.

Reina smiled at the latest tale of their ever-flirty friend. As Liz and Getta performed their Cut-and-Camo Special on Reina, their talk turned to the strange happenings of the past week and their plan for the coming evening. While attending Peter Stone's comeback show, they would look for whatever opportunity might arise to learn more about Stone's "special friends" and why they seemed to have an unhealthy interest in Reina.

While Getta used a blow dryer on Reina's hair to set the color, Liz made gin and tonics in Reina's favorite Wonder Woman glasses. Having won them years ago in a drunken Wally Ball contest at a college party, Reina considered them prized possessions. She took a sip of the icy, limey drink and smiled at Liz, "Delicious!"

An hour and a half later, Reina took one last look in the mirror and grinned at her now spiky, blonde hair. She put on Liz's Ray-Ban Wayfarer sunglasses, her knee-high boots, and Getta's black leather jacket. Getta donned a knit cap over her short black pixie cut and a pair of dark-rimmed hipster glasses. Liz pulled her blonde locks up into a French twist and wore a demure plain white dress that somehow didn't look demure on her figure. They were ready to go. They weren't really in disguise, but Reina, who had gained some notoriety over the last year, wished to be slightly incognito. After the last two nights, it didn't hurt to take some precautions.

Chapter 10

  Filmed live every Friday evening, Peter Stone's *The Rock* drew thousands of weekly attendees, both local fans and distant visitors, to "Stone Kingdom," the squat five-story structure just north of Seattle's downtown core, on Fifth Avenue. Stone Kingdom Enterprises, Inc., a non-profit corporate entity, owned the building. In addition to the Seattle real estate, the corporation had extensive land holdings and business investments, including a shipping company in Port Angeles, a soy farm in Iowa, a nationwide chain of Christian bookstores, and even an orphanage in Taiwan. Peter Stone's reach extended far and wide. Reina knew Stone Kingdom frequently held old-fashioned revivals in their Seattle facilities, as well as around the country. Their marketing personnel posted events nearly every week in the *Seattle Times* - either a seminar, or a speaker, or a weekend prayer fest. It was a bustling enterprise.

  A huge cross towered above the flat-roofed building, easily marking this as a "place of God." Although located in a quiet part of town, the proximity to the Space Needle and the surrounding attractions of Seattle Center made parking difficult here, especially on a Friday night. The dozens of handicap spots near the front of the building were filling up quickly as they drove past. By the time the girls parked and walked the few blocks to their destination, the queue of fans already snaked down the road. They took their place at the end of the long line and waited.

After several minutes, their conversation turned to whether Liz had any plans for her upcoming birthday. The three friends made a tradition of having a birthday dinner together on each of their special days.

"Where do you want to go, this year?" Getta asked.

"I don't know. As a child, I always wanted a summer birthday so I could have parties on the lawn. Now, I'd love to be on a deck or a boat. But not in November." Liz pouted a little. "It'll likely be cold and rainy." As she thought of options, she glanced up at Seattle's towering landmark. "I know," she cried, pointing skyward to the lighted disk hovering over them on spindly-looking legs. "Let's go to the Space Needle. I don't know if the restaurant is any good, but who cares? We'll go for the view. And I'll tell Rob to set off some fireworks from the roof of my place that we'll be able to see from the top deck." Liz clapped her hands in childish delight. "Yes. Let's go there. It's brilliant! And, anyway, after nearly two years here, it's about time I visited it."

Getta looked at Reina questioningly.

Reina looked like she might be getting a little queasy. "Uh . . . well," she hesitated. "I guess I could probably do the restaurant as long as it's enclosed. But I'm not going out on that deck," she added apologetically.

"Oh my gosh, I forgot," said Liz. She looked uncertain, then added good-naturedly, "Well, we don't have to go there. Anywhere is fine."

"No, no, if that's where you want to go, that's where we'll go," Reina insisted. "You know that's the rule. Birthday Girl's choice. I'll be fine. I think."

"I still don't get how you can fly airplanes and be afraid of heights," Getta commented, shaking her head in bemusement.

"I know, it's weird. But I've heard of other people, too, who don't like heights and are okay in an airplane. I think it has to do with being so enclosed and belted down in the cockpit."

"Well, we won't make you go out on the observation deck. You can stay inside and watch the fireworks from behind safety glass."

"Deal!" Reina replied, still not excited about it, but willing to make the effort for her friend's sake. She felt silly for having such a strong aversion to heights, but she'd never been able to shake the nausea and fear that the phobia produced in her.

A few minutes later, Liz said with a shiver, "I wish I'd brought a sweater." Although the days were still warmed by the last few weeks of summer sun, the hint of fall could be felt in the cool evening marine air.

"Well, I'm glad you didn't," remarked Reina as she nodded toward one of the large males who'd been standing authoritatively near the front of the line. "Unless I'm much mistaken, it looks like you've drawn the attention of 'Bruno' there, who might be able to help make sure we get in to the show tonight."

Liz and Getta looked in the direction of Reina's nod to see an oversized hulk with short, gelled, blond hair walking their way. His broad shoulders cut a swath through the crowd toward them, his muscled biceps swinging awkwardly alongside his pumped up chest in a gorilla-like amble. He arrived in front of them with a smile and greeted them in a seductive baritone. "Good evening. Thanks for coming to *The Rock* tonight, ladies. Is this your first visit?"

"Yes it is," smiled Reina in return. "We came over from Walla Walla especially for this evening's event. These are my sisters, Beth and Georgia," Reina quickly improvised, using a different variation of her friends' given names, Elizabeth and Georgetta. "We made the long trek here in the hope that Reverend Stone will pray for our mother to have a miraculous recovery like his."

"Is that right?" replied the human mountain, smiling down at Liz. "Well let's make sure you get in then. Come on up with me and I'll see to it you get priority seating."

"Oh, thank you," breathed Liz, fluttering her eyelashes shamelessly and folding her arms tightly under her now noticeably perky breasts. "I was getting a little chilly here in the night air."

"Yes, well, I'm happy to help," he replied with a sideways glance down at Liz's chest. "Just come with me."

The girls followed him to the entrance and stood with him under the entry awning waiting for the doors to open. The awning didn't do a whole lot to block the cold, but things certainly seemed to be warming up between Liz and Mr. Universe, whose friends, he said, called him Barry. Letting her artistic spirit run wild, Liz expanded upon Reina's improvised creation of the sickly mother, telling her new friend all about how the dear woman had cared for ten children and a drunk of a husband before falling prey to a terrible mix of Huntington's, Parkinson's, and Wilson's disease. Reina's eyebrows rose at the bizarre medical combination, but Barry was all sympathy and ears (and eyes) as Liz prattled on about the life of hardship their saintly mother endured and how she desperately needed the powerful prayers of Reverend Stone.

    When the doors finally opened, and they filed in to the auditorium, Reina leaned over and whispered in Getta's ear. "So, when do you think it might occur to our new friend to wonder why only one of us "daughters" has a British accent?"

    Getta squelched an irreverent snicker as she replied, "Somehow, I suspect he may have been hired for something other than his brilliant powers of deduction."

    Barry procured seats for them near the front of the auditorium, adjacent to the boys' choir at the left edge of the stage. Liz asked sweetly if he could point her to the ladies' room and he gallantly offered to take her there personally. Reina and Getta watched the two walk away together, with Barry's hand resting possessively on the small of Liz's back for guidance.

    Getta commented on the fortunate convenience of their large new friend. "It's wonderful that Barry has no pressing job responsibilities to tear him away from our needs."

"I'm not sure, but I suspect helping lovely ladies may actually be an important part of his job description," answered Reina. "Reverend Stone seems to have a fondness for beautiful women," she added with a nod toward the two voluptuous females from the videos she'd watched, now walking on to the stage. Both women had long, straight hair and big, heavily made-up eyes. The dark woman wore a simple white frock and the blonde wore a chocolate-colored gown. Although the dresses were of modest cut, the fabric clung to their full figures. They swayed to the music with sensual hip motions, slender arms waving like siren reeds over their heads. *Holiness in a sultry package? Why not? A sure crowd pleaser.*

Reina surveyed the packed auditorium. The *dolce* boys' choir appeared to be the opening act, with their lilting soprano voices rising in unison, like angels on high. One by one, the crowd stood and swayed, arms raised high, heads thrown back, and eyes closed. Many "spoke in tongues," the fluid sing-talk language considered a special gift from the Holy Spirit. The girls watched in fascination as men, who looked like they'd be more comfortable hunting bear than dancing, stood and let themselves go in full-body praise. A frail old lady to their right rose shakily from her wheelchair and waved one gaunt hand feebly over her head while holding for dear life to the arm of her chair with the other. Reina hoped someone had set the chair's brakes. The elderly gentleman directly in front of Liz, unable to rise from his seat, began waving his cane enthusiastically in the air. As his eyes were closed, his gestures of praise occasionally required his neighbors to duck quickly to avoid cranial damage or loss of an eye.

As Liz returned to her seat, Reina glanced sideways at her friends and nodded for them to rise. Remaining seated would make them stand out like a mustard stain on a white blouse. Tonight they wanted to blend.

Reina swayed slightly to the music as she scanned the structure of the stage. A ramp ran the front length of the three-foot-high dais, ending at the corner directly in front of them. The congregation extended out from the front and two sides of the stage while the back side remained protected by a bank of curtains from behind which the "performers" entered and exited. Standing at the edges of the stage, in front of the curtained entrance, and at strategic locations behind the crowd, close genetic relatives of their friend, Mt. Barry, stood with legs spread wide and hands folded across broad chests. Despite an undoubtedly job-required, friendly smile on their faces, these men-of-bulging-biceps looked like they'd be perfectly comfortable with an Uzi nestled in their arms.

A few doors to the left, Reina saw her courtroom nemesis, Jerry, talking with one of the bouncer doormen. She pointed him out to Getta and Liz and then watched in surprise as Jerry and the security guard chatted together. Reina saw Jerry slap the man on the back in what looked like the affection of an old friend. The burly fellow looked annoyed at the physical invasion, but merely threw Jerry a glowering look, instead of the Half Nelson he probably wanted to deal him. Jerry then moved on, attempting to ingratiate himself with several others of the security staff. Reina watched with curiosity as Jerry played up the "regular pal" role with the crew at *The Rock*. As prosecutor for the State on Peter Stone's behalf, he certainly had a reason to be here, but his familiarity seemed a little strange.

    She watched with further surprise as Jerry slipped behind the back curtain of the stage without anyone stopping him for questioning. The area behind the curtain appeared to be pretty well-guarded from the public, but Jerry apparently had unlimited access. Before disappearing behind the curtain, Jerry turned and scanned the crowd briefly. Reina hoped he'd not seen her in the mass of humanity. His eyes had not hesitated on her, and he probably wouldn't have recognized her in any case. With her new "do," she looked quite different from the attorney he'd leered at yesterday in court.

    Reina glanced up at the smoked upper windows of the viewing box built out over the auditorium, where the light and sound crew operated. The high perch would make a great vantage point over the crowd, and she wondered who else might be watching. *The Times* often reported on foreign dignitaries or people of interest visiting *The Rock*. She didn't recall seeing any news of visitors this week, but with the excitement over Stone's recent recovery, she wouldn't be surprised if there were some important supporters in the crowd, or rather above the crowd, in the protected box alcove.

    Reina turned her attention back to the enthusiastic throng of worshippers. After a few minutes, she glanced over at Getta who raised her eyebrows to indicate her amazement. With perhaps the exception of her mother, Reina didn't know anyone more down-to-earth than Getta, who seldom got carried away by emotion. Reina could see her scorn and amusement at the excess excitability of the crowd. Liz, on the other hand, had fully immersed herself in the moment, giving way to the collective effervescence of the evening with eyes half-closed (she still needed to watch for her neighbor's occasionally-errant cane) and body swaying in time to the music. Reina glanced at Barry McHuge, now standing guard at the far entrance, and saw him watching Liz with pleasure. *Hmmm, I'd prefer not to draw attention, but his interest might prove useful.*

    The music rose in tempo and volume. A palpable anticipation pulsed through the crowd, the music insistent and heart-pounding. People knelt in the aisles, some with tears streaming down their faces, crying out "Praise God" and "Hallelujah" and "Thank you Lord" for the miraculous recovery of their leader.

    Suddenly, the music stopped cold and the crowd fell silent, with only a few whispers of "Praise the Lord" still reverberating in the rafters.

    In the expectant silence, the crimson curtains parted, like the Red Sea before Moses, and Peter Stone walked on to the stage.

    The crowd went wild. Shouts of "Hallelujah" and "Thank you, Jesus" filled the auditorium. Except for the infirm, not a soul remained seated as people danced and hugged each other and volubly exalted their holy, healing, all-powerful God. The boys' choir trilled the "Gloria of

Angels" as Stone walked to the podium. Dressed in a flowing white robe, Reverend Peter Stone stood still, with his head bent, while his two voluptuous sirens sang a moving rendition of "Amazing Grace." The bell-like beauty and clarity of their voices brought chills to Reina's back and, glancing to the left, she saw tears in Liz's eyes. Reina half expected the heavens to open and Christ himself to descend upon the gathering. She could see why *The Rock* had been such an enduring success.

As the last notes of "Amazing Grace" faded into silence, Stone raised his head and Reina observed the most piercing blue eyes she'd ever seen. The recorded version she'd watched of Stone paled in comparison to the man in flesh. Stone positively exuded charisma and power, even now, thin and pale from the long hospital stay. He raised his hands to the heavens, in the now quiet room, and prayed. The girls joined the audience in bowing their heads for the prayer, although Reina continued her scan of the surroundings with eyes half-shut.

As Reverend Stone thanked the Lord for his deliverance out of the hands of sinners and praised God for his miraculous healing, various members of the audience called out "Amen" in affirmation. Stone ended his prayer with words from the Gospel of John: "And Jesus said . . . 'whoever lives and believes in me will never die.'"

He lowered his arms and started his sermon to the people, "My flock, I have come back to you from the dead. Like Noah, who suffered forty days and forty nights of rain in a humble ark to save the creatures of the world, and like Moses who spent forty days and forty nights on the mountain without eating or drinking so he could be given the holy tablets of the covenant, and like our Holy Lord Jesus who wandered in the wilderness to be tempted by the devil for forty days and forty nights, I, too, have suffered for you. For forty days and forty nights, I have fought Satan in the hell fires of Gehenna, and I have come back to you victorious. I have come back to you because my job here is not done. No, my beloved children, my job here is not done. There are still sinners who walk the face of this earth. There are still sinners who stand in this very hall. There are still sinners who will face the fires of hell." Stone paused as his piercing eyes scanned the crowd pointedly. He continued, "My job is not done until each and every one of you sees the error of your ways and personally claims the salvation of our Lord Jesus." Stone's eyes glowed and his whole body emitted an aura of luminescence.

    While Reina analyzed the effects of under-stage lighting and mentally confirmed that Stone's surprise recovery had indeed happened on the fortieth day, Peter Stone began the call for repentance. He called for all to confess their inherent sin and to come forward for forgiveness. He called for humility and sacrifice and a giving up of worldly ways. He called for each to stop "laying up treasure for himself" and for every one of God's children to give his all, personally and financially, to the mighty Church of God, so that God's Great Work could be done. And, one by one, people filed on to the stage. Men and women, children and elderly, many sobbing with streaming eyes, came down the aisles and knelt in supplication as Reverend Stone led the penitents in a prayer of forgiveness and salvation.

When the procession of sinners finally dwindled, Stone called those who needed healing to the stage. Stone's assistants announced each arrival's ailment: "She suffers from fibromyalgia," or "He is deaf in one ear." The assistants then anointed the individual with oil and prayed over them while Stone placed his hand on their forehead and declared them healed. One after the other, the souls in search of healing would rise and shout, "I'm healed!" or "I can hear!" or "I'm cured!" Despite the impressive show, Reina thought it might still be prudent to keep an eye on the man cured of kleptomania when the offering plate circulated.

Suddenly, Reina saw Mt. Barry pulling Liz from her seat. Although Liz protested mildly, he insisted she go up to the stage and have Reverend Stone pray for their ailing mother. Reina and Getta stifled their laughs as Liz looked over her shoulder at them pleadingly. Getta put the palms of her hands together in a look of reverence and Liz fluttered her eyes pitifully in response.

"From what do you suffer, my child?" asked Stone.

"It is my dear mother back home in Walla Walla," ad-libbed Liz, "she suffers terribly from Hepatitis, Parkinson's, and Wilson's Disease."

"Good thing Barry looked more than he listened," said Reina in Getta's ear, "as dear mother's condition has apparently changed since we entered." Getta bowed her head and raised her folded hands to her mouth to cover her mirth.

"This is a terrible affliction," replied Stone "and requires extensive prayer." His hands moved from her head to her shoulders and back again several times, almost caressing her, as he prayed for healing. "Go now, your mother will begin to heal." He tenderly raised her from her knees with his arm around her waist and his head bent closely to hers. Liz walked back to her seat, sat down, bent her head, and folded her hands prayerfully.

"He told me I should visit him in his office for further prayer for such a serious condition," she reported *sotto voce* to her two friends.

With the healing complete, the gorilla guys passed the offering plates. One of the stage assistants exhorted the audience to remember the life-saving work the Lord performed through the Church of Peter Stone and to remember the importance of relinquishing worldly treasures if they wanted to enter the Kingdom of God. The crowd appeared to be responding generously to this admonishment as the plates overflowed at the end of each aisle, and the large bags into which they were dumped bulged with the believers' hard-earned tokens of faith.

As Stone closed the evening with a lengthy final prayer, Reina quietly outlined her plan to her friends. From Liz's description of the outer hallways, she knew the rear entrances were heavily guarded. Reina pointed to the high end of the stage ramp directly in front of them where, under the flat landing area, an opening provided access to the sub-stage area. Assuming the subfloor to be passable, they could work their way to the back area, behind the curtain. If Reina and Getta could slip under the ramp landing, unseen, they would crawl under the stage to try to gain access to the guarded area. Liz would keep watch on the outside, waiting in the restroom or wherever possible until they had returned.

As Reina finished talking, Getta closed her eyes and shook her head.

Reina leaned in, "Are you okay?"

Getta opened her eyes and smiled at her friend. "Of course. Ready when you are," she said, her dark eyes brimming with laughter.

The girls sat silently as Stone closed with his trademark final hail to the Almighty. "Thank you, Lord, for making me your chosen one. Thank you, Lord, for working your great power through me. I am the Stone this church is built on. Amen."

People started rising, talking, laughing, gathering their coats and bags, and moving toward the exits. Liz bent over to talk to the old gentleman in front of her, distracting him with cleavage and with the offer to help wheel him out of the auditorium. She turned his chair slightly to provide cover for her friends to execute their plan. Reina and Getta slipped quickly behind her, using the chair for cover, and ducked under the large ramp platform. They quietly entered the sub-stage access hole and began crawling their way along the dusty floor to the rear. The area below the stage was a clutter of hanging pipes, crisscrossed support walls, and random construction debris.

"Ow!" Getta stifled a gasp.

"What happened?" Reina whispered back.

"I scraped my arm on a screw or something. Shit, the things I do for you, Reina."

"Ssssh...."

"Okay, but if I touch something furry that moves, I'm screaming."

It took a moment for their eyes to adjust to the darkness. Reina didn't dare use the tiny flashlight she always carried in her pocket, for fear of detection. They made their way as best they could along the filthy floor. Fortunately, tiny pinpoints of light came through in spots where drill holes pierced the floor surface. They hadn't gone far when they ran into a tee. They turned right then left at another dead end and right at another, maneuvering the labyrinthine under-stage structure with occasional can lights and bunches of wiring banging them in the head. Every once in a while, the floor would thunder and vibrate as someone walked across the stage over their heads. After numerous turns, they finally arrived at what appeared to be the back wall. Working their way along its edge, they found another access panel, this time into a deserted hallway.

"I sure hope we can get out another way," whispered Getta, "I don't think we'll ever find our way back through that."

They were brushing off dust and rubbing their sore knees when they heard voices approaching from the far end of the hallway, including what sounded like Jerry's nasally laugh. A quick glance around for a likely hiding place revealed several doors on the opposite side of the hall. They slipped quietly into the one directly across from them and crouched down so as not to be seen through the small door window. Conversation came from just outside their door.

"Thanks for the tour." Reina recognized Jerry's voice.

"Of course. Happy to show you what we're all about here at Stone Kingdom. Lisa will show you out," replied Peter Stone's deep voice.

Footsteps receded down the hallway, then the faint sound of conversation came from the adjoining room on the other side of the wall.

In the dimness of the room's emergency lighting, the girls could see they were in a large kitchen. To their right, a big walk-in refrigerator and pantry shelves filled the walls. The back wall held a huge commercial oven and stovetop with a massive range hood, and the left wall housed the sinks and dishwashing area. The equipment looked a couple of decades old, although still sturdy and serviceable. In the center, a large table surrounded by mismatched chairs and stools held a box half-full of donuts, a couple of dirty coffee mugs, a folded newspaper, and several copies of *Religion Today*. Although the room looked equipped to prepare large meals for the weekend seminars and revivals regularly held on site, it apparently served as an employee lounge as well. Above the sink area, Reina spotted gray metal ventilation grates at the top of the wall. She climbed on to the large stainless steel sink drainage area to get a better look. Unable to see through them, she discovered she could at least better hear the voices in the adjacent room. She tilted her ear as close as possible to listen.

***

Back in the auditorium, Liz returned to gather the few things she'd intentionally left behind while pushing the elderly gentleman out to the foyer in his wheelchair. She dawdled as long as she could over picking up her hairclip, Reina's sunglasses, and Getta's hat, the only "things" she had to leave on the seats. Eventually, she meandered her way toward the exterior of the hall. Just as she exited the nearly empty auditorium, planning to make for the restrooms to hide for a while, Barry Hunkster appeared close at her side.

"Hi there," he lightly stroked the back of her bare arm suggestively. "How did you like the show?"

"It was inspirational," breathed Liz dramatically, feeling her nipples go hard at the sensual caress. She hurried on in some confusion. "I am so thankful for Reverend Stone's prayers on our mother's behalf. He was so kind. I've no doubt she's doing better already. We are most anxious to get back to her of course."

Barry looked down at her in appreciation, then glanced around, "What happened to your sisters . . . uh, Georgia and . . . ?" His short forehead furrowed trying to remember the other name.

"Uh . . . Nnaancy, you mean," improvised Liz. "Um, well, they uh, they went to get the car. But we parked so far away, I . . . I'm quite certain it will take them a long while."

"Too bad," purred Barry throatily, "I guess I'll have to keep you company." He smiled with pleasure at the idea.

Liz laughed nervously.

"I'll take you to see the gift shop and the sound room, if you're interested," he offered.

"Of course I'm interested," she assured him with feigned enthusiasm. "But first," with a batting of her eyes, "I do need to use the ladies' room again, if you don't mind." *Anything to buy time.*

The women's restroom, pink and heavily perfumed, was adorned with biblical pictures and statues of happy-looking cherubic angels and plastic plants. Liz nodded politely at the one other woman inside, generously reinforcing her makeup at the big wall mirror. Locking herself into the last stall, Liz quickly texted Getta: *Where r u guys?* After a few seconds, the reply came: *in the lichen*. For a startled second she probed her childhood memory of old Church of England days. *What in God's name is a lichen?* It sounds like a garden area. Maybe this place has an interior cloister thing, she thought, like old monasteries? Liz knew Getta used the swype keyboard on her phone that auto-filled words for the writer. The results were often incorrect, or even hilarious. Liz had received plenty of bizarre text messages from Getta over the years. After some deliberation, she concluded Getta must have meant kitchen, not lichen. *Well, they better not be stopping for a snack.* Her stomach grumbled. *After all, I could use a bite to eat myself.* She tucked her phone away and returned to the lobby, content to know that her friends were okay, wherever they were.

She met up with Barry Vanderhuge just outside the ladies' room door. He took her by the hand and led her to the gift shop. Several people still wandered the aisles, searching for the perfect memento of this special evening. Dawdling there as long as she could, Liz oohed and ahhed over each item. "Oh, look at this baby Jesus, he's adorable," she gushed over the plump, plush, happy-looking toy. Then, "Ooh, I love this set of plates with the Ten Commandments - now that would certainly keep your dinner guests in line wouldn't it?" she laughed, imagining what you would serve on these dishes - *Dahling, please, I insist. You simply must have another serving of my special morality pasta!*

"Come see these angel wings," called out Barry, placing the full size wings, in white feathers and sparkles, over her shoulders. He stood back in admiration and claimed them to be a perfect fit, for a perfect angel. She laughed off the fulsome compliment and, as a diversion, suggested they go to see the sound room. Throughout their meanderings, she kept her cell phone cradled surreptitiously in the palm of her hand, waiting for the vibration that would tell her Reina and Getta were ready to go.

***

In the kitchen, Getta stood guard by the door, watching for anyone coming down the hall. Her arm still dripped blood and she kept wiping it, hoping it wasn't dripping on the floor. Reina, perched on tiptoe on the sink drain, listened intently to the sounds from the other room. Although she could only make out occasional words, the sounds between Stone and what sounded like the two dancing sirens and a couple of other male and female voices were intriguing.

She tried to record the gist of what was going on in the adjacent room with her smart-phone held up to the grate and set on video record. She knew there would be no visual, but the microphone and audio on her piece were quite good. Just as her arm, raised over her head, felt ready to fall off, she saw her screen go dead and realized that the extended video record had depleted the battery life. She lowered the phone to her hip pocket.

A moment later, she almost jumped at a man's voice saying, "I'm famished. Let's go get something to eat." He must have been standing directly under the grate in the other room for it to come across so clearly. But more importantly, in a few seconds he would be standing in the room in which they now hid.

Reina jumped off the counter without a sound and frantically indicated to Getta to move away from the door. Too late to exit to the hallway, they looked desperately for a hiding place. Crouching behind the cabinets wouldn't conceal them for long so they dashed toward the walk-in refrigerator. As she ran toward it, Getta bumped into the corner of one of the chairs. Its metal legs skidded a few feet across the floor with what sounded like a screech in the dark room. The girls ducked into the refrigerator and pulled the door behind them, leaving it just a fraction ajar. They saw the kitchen light come on through the thin door crack and heard several voices, including Stone's. After a moment of light chatter, a long silence was followed by hushed words, as though the room's occupants were whispering.

Suddenly realizing she'd left her jacket on the sink drain, Reina wondered if the sight of the jacket and the screech of the chair had given them away. She didn't know why someone from Stone's group appeared to be out to get her, but finding her hiding in their refrigerator would be extremely difficult to explain, under any circumstance. She felt an impending sense of doom.

With her ear up to the crack, Reina heard a man's voice say loudly, "Well, let's see. What would you like? How about some milk?"

The two girls froze in place. They leaned so closely together, that Reina could feel Getta's heartbeat, racing like her own.

"No?" he continued, "Maybe a slice of cheese? Some yogurt? I'm sure there's something to snack on in the fridge . . . . Shall I see what I can find in there for you?"

Footsteps approached their way.

At the last minute, the woman called her companion back, in a voice that seemed unnaturally loud. "No, no, I don't want to go to all that trouble tonight. I don't think there's anything I want in the fridge. I'll just have a donut."

The girls' tension eased a bit.

After a moment, the woman laughed again and said, "Although milk *would* go quite well with my donut."

"Well then, let me get you some. And maybe I'll make a ham sandwich while I'm there," the man laughed. "I'm pretty sure there's some interesting meat in the fridge." Again, footsteps approached.

The woman laughed again, and said, "Peter, what would you do? Milk or no milk?"

"Oh, I'd love to see what's in the fridge, but perhaps later." Peter's deep voice seemed to hold a warning. The footsteps receded again.

The girls felt like part of a cat and mouse game.

"I need to make a phone call," Peter advised. "You two wait here."

Reina and Getta hovered by the crack of light, trying to catch the whispered words of the waiting man and woman.

After minutes that felt like hours, they heard a different man's voice, with an eastern sounding accent, say, "You two can go home, I'll clean up here."

"Well, okay," the first man sounded disappointed.

The room became quiet except for some shuffling noises. Eventually, they heard the click of the hall door closing just as the light coming from the tiny crack went out.

The girls slumped back against the wall in relief and waited a few moments to give the foreign-sounding man time to make his way down the hallway. Anxious to exit, they finally pushed against the refrigerator door, but it didn't budge. They pushed again, harder, only to find it locked firmly. The click they'd heard and extinction of light wasn't the hall door and the kitchen light after all. It was the refrigerator door. Someone had closed it tight and they were trapped.

***

In the sound room, overlooking the auditorium, Barry McMuscle was showing off for Liz. He illuminated the now empty auditorium, various areas at a time, and showed her how they could control the can lights under the stage to create glowing or dramatic effects. He pointed out the seats lining the big smoked windows of the sound room. He explained how they often held important visitors and dignitaries from the United States, and other countries as well. "My boss knows a lot of powerful people from all over the world," he boasted.

He offered to let Liz play with the controls, stepping behind her to help with the motions. His brick wall of a chest pressed into her back as his arms circled hers and his huge hands covered her small ones, showing her which controls to move. He controlled her hands like a marionette, placing them on various knobs and switches, now making the curtains rise, now making the stage glow, now spotlighting the podium.

Suddenly Liz's phone vibrated and she glanced at it, lying on the tabletop directly in front of her abdomen but hidden from her new friend's view by her head under his.

Squinting to see the text message from Getta, she read, *Suck in fridge*, hell.

Crap! Interpreting the mis-texted words to be "stuck" and "help," she thought, how in heaven's name does one get stuck in a fridge? Who but Reina could manage that? Trying to deflect Barry's attention while she considered what to do, Liz commented lightly on his knowledge of the sound and lights business.

"I'm good at a lot of things," he replied huskily, the breath from his lips tickling her ear.

Liz tried to move, but found herself locked in place between his bulk and the edge of the sound and lights control panel.

She said brightly, "Thanks so much for the tour, Barry. I should probably get going. I'm sure my sisters are looking for me."

He didn't reply or step back. She could hear his deep breathing in her ear.

She felt the first hint of anxiety, but repressed it, knowing the smell of fear to be a potent stimulant to many animals. She laughed with feigned carelessness. "Oh my, I am sooo hungry," she improvised. "Shall we go get a snack?"

Mt. Barry didn't budge. His breath on her ear moved to the nape of her neck. She felt his tongue lick her lightly as he mumbled a throaty "Mmmmmmm. A snack sounds good." His hands moved to her waist and lightly stroked the curve of her hips. Liz felt his interest rising behind her. She was pretty sure he wasn't referring to the same kind of snack she was.

Trying to wriggle free, she realized they were so tightly sandwiched together that her movement only resulted in grinding her rear against his crotch. He apparently took this as encouragement, moaning and pushing his hips further into her. Her thin dress wasn't much of a shield from the shaft between his hips. His hands were moving slowly up her waist. The seed of fear started to blossom into panic.

"Really," she fought to keep her voice light. "I am absolutely famished! And I have to warn you, I get violently ill if I don't eat immediately when I get hungry. I would *hate* to do a projectile vomit over this soundboard," she added with feigned sincerity.

The thought of destroying his boss's expensive equipment apparently giving him pause, Barry stopped his fondling and stepped back just enough for Liz to wriggle under his arm and move aside, out of nuzzling reach. As she headed toward the door, she said over her shoulder, with a forced cheerfulness, "Shall we go get a snack now? Do you have a kitchen here we could raid?"

"Sure," he replied, good-naturedly accepting the change of plans. "I'll take you there."

Liz breathed a sigh of relief, cursing that fateful Art 101 class under her breath as they made their way downstairs.

***

In the refrigerator, Reina pulled out her mini maglight to scan their prison. The interior of the old-fashioned unit had no door handle or escape latch, clearly dating it to a time before modern safety measures were made mandatory. A temperature indicator built in to the door showed the walk-in's controls set to freeze. "Not only are we locked in," she informed Getta with reluctance, "but the temperature is set at minus five degrees Celsius. That's considerably below freezing." Continuing to scan the interior walls, she added, "I don't see any way to adjust the temperature from the inside, so the controls must be on the exterior." She picked up a gallon of milk and shook it – although still liquid, it already displayed the beginning formation of ice crystals. Clearly, the temperature hadn't been that low for long. Struggling with disbelief, Reina had to acknowledge that someone had intentionally locked them in, cranked down the temperature, and left them there to freeze. They wouldn't last long in this ice-box.

    Reina's phone was dead; Getta tried hers, but the signal was too weak. Sometimes, though, a text message would go through when a call wouldn't and the first text she'd shot off to Liz, before the door closed, did indicate *sent*. Getta tried sending more texts, but they kept saying "message not sent." Perhaps with the door shut, the signal couldn't penetrate the walls.

    Reina and Getta shivered in the sub-zero temperature and Reina wished for the jacket she'd foolishly left on the kitchen counter. Right now, that jacket seemed like the difference between life and death, in more ways than one. She flushed to think of the kitchen occupants playing with them like she'd seen her mom's cat, Acro, toy with a cornered mouse.

They hopped and jumped and talked to stay alert. Suddenly, in the cold darkness, they heard a click and a sliver of light showed at the door. Creeping over on stiff knees, Reina heard with relief the sound of Liz's voice, bright and loud, "You know, Barry, I'm not really that hungry after all. Let's go get a drink somewhere."

"I'd love to," he replied in his deep seductive voice. A moment later the light went out, this time without the click of the door locking into place. All was silent.

Reina shoved open the door and turned back to find Getta slumped on the floor. She pulled Getta to her feet, practically dragging her out of their icy prison. She kicked the freezer door shut, shook her head to clear it of the mental fogginess, and half-carried, half-dragged Getta over to the sink. She ran the water until warm and chafed their hands together under the stream, feeling the pins and needles as the numb fingers came back to life. Leaning their faces over the sink, they breathed in the steam, gradually reviving from the severe chill.

Reina grabbed the incriminating jacket from the countertop and threw it over Getta's shoulders. They peeked carefully out the door, down the now-deserted hallway. Exiting the kitchen, they crept quietly along several corridors, crouching past doors, guessing their way to the foyer through the dark and quiet building. After a few false turns, they finally made it to the front door. One lone guard sat at the entrance, leaning back on two legs of his chair, cowboy boots propped on the desk, and eyes half-closed. At their appearance, he slammed his feet and the legs of his chair down and looked at them in alarm, uncertain what he should do. Clearly, his job required keeping intruders OUT, not in. Reina explained to him with a friendly smile that her friend had been sick in the restroom and was just now recovered enough to move under her own power. As Getta's arm hung over Reina's shoulder and she still looked slightly green, he let them pass. Reina saw him reach for the phone as they exited the door to the street.

    Just then, Liz drove up to the curb. She leaned over, threw open the passenger door to her Mini Cooper, and called out, "Thank God you're okay! Get in and let's get out of here."

Chapter 11

Reina and Getta leaned back into the car seats with relief. Reina took Getta's hand between her two hands and chafed it. "Are you okay?"

Getta nodded. "Of course, good as new."

As Liz raced off, she explained how she'd ditched Buff Barry at the bar down the road with the ladies' room excuse. "I went to the toilet so many times, the man probably feared I had a bladder the size of a pea. I've been circling the block waiting for you two. If you didn't appear within a quarter hour, I'd have brought in the Bobbies."

Now revived, Getta leaned forward, "I'm starving. Can we stop for food?"

They decided to swing by Ivar's "Acres of Clams" on Pier 54 to pick up some warm chowder. The Seattle waterfront hummed with activity on the pleasant Friday evening. Rather than try to find parking, Liz dropped off Reina and Getta to order food-to-go while she circled around to pick them up again.

As they waited in line to place their food order, Reina noticed the dried blood on Getta's arm. "Oh, you really did get gouged. Does it still hurt?"

"Not really. That damn stage. I was dripping all over the god-damned floor in the kitchen."

Reina shook her head in disbelief. "Could we have left more clues?" she asked, disgusted at their bungling attempt at sleuthing. "Between the jacket, the chair, and the fresh blood, we might as well have just written them a note."

Getta agreed they hadn't exactly been stealthy.

As they talked, the line of people waiting to order lengthened behind them. Suddenly, they were both knocked off balance by someone lunging into them. Nerves still on edge, Reina yelled, "Hey!" and whirled around to face their attacker.

Getta pivoted, with the heavy steel ratchet from her purse raised over her head, shouting, "Eat this, fucker!"

Their "attacker" fell back, as off-balance as they were, and put his hands in the air, "Whoa, sorry dude, it was just an accident. It was those goons over there who pushed me into you." He pointed to a group of rowdy teenagers, huddled and giggling off to the side. He repeated, "Sorry though, man, I really am sorry. Are you guys okay?"

As Getta lowered her weapon, the embarrassed kid said in surprise, "Ms. James?"

Looking closer at him in the dim light, Getta said "Oh, uh, hi. Trevor, is it?"

Getta taught at Nolan Dale High School in Seattle's north end. School had started a few days ago, and Reina guessed this kid must be one of her new students.

"Yeah, well you guys really should be more careful, you know." said Getta, instantly in full teacher mode.

"I know. I'm really, really, *really* sorry, Ms. James. We'll definitely be more careful from now on. I promise!" The boy nervously pulled his hair over his eyes, as if trying to hide behind it. "Are you sure you're okay?" he asked again, glancing toward his friends who had removed themselves some distance down the sidewalk.

"Yes, we're okay. I guess I'll see you on Monday then." Getta nodded to dismiss him and turned back around, saying over her shoulder to him, "And stay out of trouble."

"I will, Ms. James, I promise." He turned and slunk back to join the crowd of snickering kids.

Getta rolled her eyes at Reina and said, "Well, word will be all over school by the end of first period on Monday not to mess with Ms. James 'cause she packs a big wrench." Getta patted her purse.

"And she can tell you what to do with it, too," added Reina.

Getta laughed, "Not a bad thing to have known in a city high school."

The man ahead of them finished placing his order and the two girls advanced to the counter. Getta ordered clam strips, fries, and enough New England style chowder to feed a soup kitchen.

"You *are* hungry." Reina laughed as they walked away with their ticket for the food pick up. Getta admitted she hadn't eaten much of the snacky dinner they'd shared earlier while doing their hair and makeup. "Well, that explains why you passed out," said Reina.

"I know, right? To tell you the truth, I haven't been feeling too well lately."

Reina looked at Getta questioningly, voicing the fear that hounds every single, sexually active, young woman. "You're not pregnant are you?"

"Hell, no!" Getta snorted. "If so, it would have to be an immaculate conception. I haven't been with a guy since Lance and I broke up six months ago."

"Well, you're too skinny to hide a six month bump, that's for sure. But really, you need to twist the sheets with someone," Reina said teasingly, now more concerned over her friend's love life than her parental status.

"Oh, please," Getta snorted. "Between teaching and coaching right now, I really don't have any spare time. Or energy."

In addition to teaching Spanish, Getta coached the school's track and cross-country teams. With new classes and cross-country season in full swing, she juggled a tight schedule in the fall.

They picked up their food order and rejoined Liz for the short drive to her place. On the way, Liz commented on Reina's earlier description of her coworker.

"You were spot-on with your description of Jerry. The man needs a new tailor. And I stand by my opinion on the moustache."

"He certainly seemed to be everybody's best friend," Getta added. "What was that all about?"

"Oh, he's got his sights set on the County Prosecutor's office," Reina replied. "We've got a mid-term vacancy now, with Feyman leaving for health reasons.

Jerry's been lobbying to be chosen for the interim slot. He'll need influential friends to help him get there, though, and Stone certainly qualifies. Winning this high-profile case wouldn't hurt, either."

"That's not gonna happen," Getta said, and Liz nodded in agreement.

Reina smiled in appreciation of their support. "To be honest, I don't think he stands a chance. There's something about him that smells bad. I'm not the only one who has an aversion to the man."

Liz pulled into a parking space on Fairview. She lived in a darling but miniscule houseboat on the east side of Lake Union. From the tiny rooftop deck of her place, she could see across the lake to Reina's condo building. With binoculars, they could actually see each other's windows. The owners of the houseboat, clients of her father's New York law firm, agreed to let Liz live there with extremely favorable rental terms while her art gallery became established. The little dollhouse on the water had become something of a favorite camp for the three friends, both for its central location and the stunning view of city lights from the huge waterfront windows. Getta had left her motorbike there earlier in the day while she and Liz shopped in preparation for the evening's adventures.

"Is Rob around tonight?" Reina asked.

"No, he's in Chicago for a few days for a seminar," Liz replied. "We'll have the place to ourselves." Liz's boyfriend, Rob, didn't technically live with her, but when not traveling for his biotech business, he generally could be found at her house.

"What? No 'Beth and Bob show' tonight?" Getta asked in false dismay, referring to the taunting name one of Liz's more persistent, spurned suitors had given the devoted couple back in their college days.

Liz laughed at the old teasing tribute to her long-standing relationship with Rob. "Good God, I'd nearly forgotten that nickname," she said, adding, "The geeky guy who coined that pursued me all four years, insisting I should date him. Gary Something wasn't it? Anyway, Rob told me he read somewhere that the guy's now a multi-millionaire. Started some software business that went big."

"Damn," joked Getta. "Maybe you *should* have dated him."

"I know. Missed opportunity. If only I could get over this thing I have for Rob . . . ."

As the three friends walked down the long dock to Liz's end unit, they passed two tall guys in jeans and black leather jackets. Perhaps it was Reina's imagination, but she thought the guys looked at them strangely. As they filed into Liz's unit, Reina looked back to see the two men standing some distance down the dock, still watching them. The girls carefully locked the door behind them. Feeling somewhat paranoid after recent events, Reina suddenly realized the vulnerable and unsecure aspects of a houseboat, perched on a narrow dock, over cold water, with walls of windows. She scanned the dark waters, knowing that anyone out there could easily see into the large, well-lighted windows of the little floating house. As usual, boat traffic on the lake had virtually ceased by this hour, with only one long, thin boat trolling slowly along the opposite shore. Reina watched the fast-looking "cigarette boat" for a moment. Although she'd often seen these expensive craft off the coast of the Mediterranean, where the rich and famous liked to play, they were relatively uncommon in the waters around Seattle. In the Patagonia-clad Northwest, the rich tended to be a little more subtle.

As they devoured the chowder and shared a platter of Ivar's fresh, hot clam strips, the three girls discussed the evening's events.

Liz started with the most obvious question, "Okay, please explain to me how one gets stuck in a fridge?" As an aside, she whispered to Getta with a roll of the eyes, "Your texting is atrocious, girlfriend."

Reina explained the situation, making it very clear that being trapped in the icebox was no accident. The shutting of the door and the lowering of the temperature were clearly both intentional and malicious.

Getta then asked, "So, how did you manage with our friend Barry?"

As Liz filled them in on her adventures with the man-mountain, Reina smiled again at her good fortune to have two such amazing best friends. Just then, they heard the sound of a motor racing. Looking up, Reina saw the cigarette boat that had been idling along the lake's opposite shore screaming across the water, directly toward them. It appeared to be on a clear collision course for their houseboat. As they watched in frozen horror, the fast boat turned sharply to the right, missing the dock in front of Liz's place by what appeared to be inches and shooting a roostertail of water onto the houseboat's windows. It roared off and disappeared into the dark night.

Badly shaken, the girls debated calling the police, or removing themselves to Getta's or Reina's place for the evening. As no actual crime had been committed, and none of them wanted to walk down the dark dock again, they decided to stay put. In all likelihood, the boat prankster was long gone by now. They retired somewhat nervously to bed, with Getta and Reina taking the bunk beds in the tiny extra bedroom. Getta stashed the 3/8 inch ratchet under her pillow - just in case - and Reina thought, not for the first time, that she really should get a gun.

Saturday morning dawned clear and sunny. By the time Getta awoke for her morning run, Reina was long gone, having left a note on the toaster: "Got taxi home. Gone flying. Thanks for the help last night. See you soon."

Chapter 12

Reina finished her pre-flight inspection of the Cessna P210 and climbed aboard, buckling her shoulder harness and adjusting her headset. Even though she'd not planned on a trip this morning, Reina had been confident the aircraft would be sitting in the hangar when she arrived. Her mom kept the complicated and expensive plane for long cross-country trips more than for training. With full fuel tanks, including the wing-tip tanks, it would easily take her to her destination. She just hoped her mom wouldn't be too upset upon arriving at work to find a note from her daughter, but no airplane.

She taxied to the run-up area to do her usual *CIGARS* checklist – Controls, free and clear. Instruments, check each. Gas, on fullest tank. Attitude, set for takeoff. Run-up, mags, prop, vacuum system working. Safety, belts on. She set the flight plan on her GPS for Kalispell, Montana. At just over 300 nautical miles, she would arrive well before lunch.

With winds out of the south, she positioned on runway 16 with 10 degrees flaps. She gently advanced the throttle on the powerful turbo-charged engine to avoid over-boosting it. At 85 knots she applied a firm back pressure and the heavy bird lifted gently off the ground. Once she'd confirmed a positive rate of climb, she raised the landing gear, then the flaps, then adjusted the power and prop for cruise climb. She enjoyed flying by hand for several minutes then engaged the autopilot to follow the appropriate heading and altitude. With part of her mind watching the aircraft's systems and controls for anything out of the ordinary, she directed the rest of her mind to prepare for the upcoming meeting in Montana.

A search of public records had uncovered the Stone's marriage license and Reina had easily traced the witness on record, who happened to still live in the same small Montana town where the ceremony took place. Late yesterday, she had received an email from Heather Moss, the Maid of Honor from twenty years ago, agreeing to meet today for lunch.

Reina quickly reviewed what she knew from the limited local contacts for her client, Maria. Shari, the apparently unwitting supplier of the Atrazine Maria allegedly used to poison her husband's orange juice, appeared to be Maria's only girlfriend. Their friendship of several years didn't seem particularly close, extending only to some afternoons planting flowers together and the occasional Saturday shopping at local nurseries. In Reina's meeting with Shari over coffee several weeks ago, the woman had talked much, but said little, about the inner workings of Maria.

"She seemed like such a nice person!" Shari shook her round face, eyes widened in horror at her new awareness of fraternizing with dangerous killers. When Reina encouraged her to continue her recollections, she said, "Well, Maria was super quiet. I mean, not the type of person I normally hang out with, you know, but she was nice enough. She wasn't exactly someone I'd take to the bar with me, if you know what I mean." Shari laughed.

"How did you meet?" Reina asked, probing for more meaningful details.

"Well, let's see. I guess we met at a seminar on eco-planting at the Seattle library. Normally I wouldn't fool with such a thing, but I guess there's some grant money for farmers who plant trees. God knows I plant plenty of trees. That's what you do when you own a Christmas tree farm, you know. Anyway, it was a lot of bunk, I thought." She paused for a minute, trying to recall the question. "But anyway, yeah. I didn't know my way around the library since it was my first time there and all, so I asked a woman for directions and that turned out to be Maria. So that was how me met, you know. Then we kinda got to talkin' and she seemed interested in my farm and wanted to visit. We met a couple times at Starbucks for coffee. She always offered to pay, so that was cool."

As Shari paused, Reina asked if she would like another coffee, which Shari happily accepted.

After sitting back down with their fresh lattes, Reina inquired whether Shari ever visited Maria's house.

"Well, sorta. I guess you could say I visited her yard, but not her house. Yeah, I went over a coupla times to help weed and plant flowers and such. She never invited me in, though. She said her husband's friend lived with them and he didn't take too kindly to visitors, I guess. I seen him though, the friend that is, a few times, looking through the window. You know, he always gave me the creeps. I didn't care for the way he looked at me at all." Shari grimaced and shook her shoulders as if she'd just seen a spider. "Funny though, it surprised me she never talked about her husband. Sure, I seen him on TV, and all, but I never did get to meet him in person." Here Shari shook her head in disappointment. "I kept asking her if I could meet him because, you know, he's famous and all that, but she said he was very busy."

Reina expressed her sympathy at this sad lack of opportunity and asked, "Did Maria ever visit you at your Christmas tree farm?"

"No, she never did," Shari answered. "She said her husband didn't like her to go out too much."

When Reina asked if she could recall anything else, she added, "I remember whenever we shopped at nurseries she would watch the little kids. I always sorta thought maybe she really liked kids and I guess maybe it was hard on her to not have any." Shari's insights had been disappointingly short on substance.

Additional inquiries at Stone Kingdom had yielded no further leads. No one seemed to really know much about Maria, other than that she was Peter Stone's wife.

Reina glanced at her aircraft's panel, comparing her indicated airspeed to her ground speed on the GPS. The discrepancy between the two told her a headwind out of the southeast was slowing her down. Well, no surprise, she thought. It seemed to be Murphy's Law of Aviation that, even on same-day roundtrips, you'd get headwinds both directions of travel. Expecting winds out of the northwest in the afternoon, she resigned herself to slower travel and more gas consumption on the return trip as well. However, flying still proved a lot faster and more economical than traveling by car. Reina had analyzed many trips, comparing fuel consumption and the cost of time in the air versus in a car. She had no doubt traveling via airways made financial sense for her. Plus, it was more fun.

The GPS showed her passing over Sandpoint, Idaho. She would cross the narrow tip of the state in no time and then another 70 miles through Montana would take her to her destination. Heather Moss had agreed to drive from her home in the small town nearby to meet Reina at Kalispell City Airport, where they would have lunch at the little cafe on the field. This saved Reina having to get a rental car, and also allowed her plenty of time to return home the same day.

Reina began her descent into Kalispell. She had flown over this area last summer when she and Liz and Getta made a weekend visit to Glacier National Park. At that time, she'd been impressed by the gorgeous scenery of the area. Even now, at the end of summer, some snow remained on the rugged peaks of the Rockies. Huge Flathead Lake, lying just west of the continental divide, sparkled like a blue jewel from the air, and Reina could easily see why they called the ridge to the east of town "Castle Mountains." It was a stunning vista.

She'd not landed at Kalispell before, but her airport guide showed a 3600 foot runway facing southeast. Perfect. She made a straight-in approach to runway 13 with time enough to top off the fuel before meeting her lunch appointment.

Walking in to the restaurant, Reina observed an older couple seated near the window, as well as two guys ogling her from the counter. A lone woman in a cowboy hat sat in the far corner. Reina walked over and introduced herself.

"Nice to meet you," replied the tall, pretty brunette with a strong handshake. "I'm Heather. I came straight from the ranch, so I'm in my riding clothes." She looked down apologetically at her jeans and boots. "I hope you don't mind?"

"Not at all," replied Reina with a smile. "If anything, I'm jealous. What a gorgeous day for a ride."

"Well, it looks like you had your own horse to ride," smiled Heather. "In fact, I watched you tie her down out there. What kind of plane is that?"

Reina told her a little about the Cessna 210 and they made small talk about the countryside and weather while they reviewed the menus. Heather apologized for sitting in the back corner, but claimed that she liked to have her back to the wall.

"How funny," said Reina. "I'm exactly the same way. I have always thought I must've been a criminal in some previous life, always nervous about someone sneaking up on me."

"Well, we can't both have the corner," Heather apologized, adding with a grin, "but don't worry, I've got your back. We've had some issues with bandits around here lately, so I'm armed," she flashed her vest to display a small gun in her waistband, "and not afraid to use it either. You'll be safe with me." Heather's smile extended to her eyes, and somehow Reina felt confident that this woman could, indeed, be trusted to watch her back.

The stocky waitress finally arrived, looking as though she'd just been awakened from an afternoon nap. Reina ordered a Reuben Sandwich and iced tea with lemon, while Heather chose a Swiss Patty Melt and a diet Coke. After the waitress left, Reina asked if it would be okay to record their conversation to allow ease of recall. This was not a formal deposition, she assured Heather, she simply wanted to understand her client better and anything Heather could offer toward that end would be of great assistance.

Heather said she wanted nothing more than to help Maria and that she was happy to answer any questions, and to have the answers recorded.

"Great," said Reina, clicking on her recorder. "Let's get started then. Why don't we start by you telling me how you know Maria Shearling Stone."

"I've known Maria for basically all my life. We went to grade school together, then junior high and high school. We also went to the same church. We've been best friends since second grade."

"Okay, did you know Peter Stone, also?"

"Sure. It's a small town, so you kinda know everyone. Peter moved to town in . . . I think it was ninth grade. He had come from somewhere down South. It might have been Arkansas, or one of those states. Anyway, a new boy in high school was big news to us girls. Most of the boys we'd known since kindergarten and we remembered them picking their noses and crying on the playground when they skinned their knees." Heather laughed and added, "It's more difficult to have a crush on someone you know that well."

"So did Maria have a crush on Peter?"

"Ha! We all did. I swear every single girl in school drooled when he walked by. First of all, he was gorgeous. He wasn't that tall, so my six feet kinda towered over him, but that didn't keep me from idolizing him, just like all the other girls. I don't know whether it was by chance or by design, but he had this big wavy lock of dark hair that would fall over his forehead, making him look like some hero out of the sappy poetry we were forced to read. Then, he had these amazing, intense, blue eyes that seemed to look right into your soul. When you talked to other boys, they'd be joking with each other, or looking around at other girls, or maybe even still picking their noses, but Peter Stone would focus in on you and make you feel like you were the only person in the room that mattered. I will say that he seemed to treat everybody that way. Even if you were ugly or unpopular, it didn't matter."

"Was Maria popular?"

Heather thought for a minute. "Well, I don't know if popular is the right word. She wasn't a cheerleader, or the cutest girl in school, or any of that. But she was pretty universally well liked. She was just . . . very sweet. She was the type of person who never said an unkind word. She had a soft heart for injured dogs and scared kids and anyone who was being picked on." Heather paused for a minute, choosing her words carefully. "She had kind of a rough childhood, which may have heightened her sense of empathy."

Reina paused the recorder while their sandwiches were deposited in front of them. The waitress asked, in her just-woke-up-and-smoked-a-cigarette voice, whether they needed anything else. Reina shook her head no and waited while Heather removed her hat and ran her fingers through her long dark hair to fluff it up. Without the shadow of the large hat, Reina could see the cowgirl's eyes better, a clear, cerulean blue, like the sky at dawn. Old soul. The thought came to Reina unbidden. They dug in to their lunch.

After a few bites, Heather suggested they continue with the interview, "As long as you don't mind hearing me chew a little bit on the recorder." She smiled engagingly.

Reina professed to have recorded much worse than chewing pauses and restarted the recorder with an encouraging smile. "So, you were saying something about Maria's rough childhood?"

Heather hesitated, then said, "I'll tell you, but only off the record." She nodded to the recorder. Reina flicked it off again and Heather continued, "Her father died when we were in second grade. Although he was generally a no-good drunk, in the end he died defending her."

"Defending Maria?"

"Yeah, I don't know all the details, but apparently some transient had, um, approached Maria when she was playing in her yard and was, um, attempting to molest her, when the dad stumbled upon him." Heather closed her eyes for a minute before she could continue. "Nobody knows exactly what happened. Shots were fired and when others arrived, Maria was crying over her dying father."

Reina raised her eyebrows. "Wow. None of my searches turned up this story."

"Names were withheld, I think, to protect the family."

Reina tugged on her lower lip as she sat silently, absorbing this piece of information. *Sad, but that was a long time ago.* However, it might be worth another look at the psychologist's notes. Finally, she said, "Alright shall we continue?"

Heather nodded.

"So, how did Maria and Peter get together?"

"You know, it was strange. They just seemed to gravitate to each other. As I said, Peter could have had any girl he set his sights on." Heather chewed for a moment, appearing to be wrestling free an old memory. Suddenly she laughed, "You know, I had completely forgotten this until just now, but I remember one of the girls in our class - one of those girls with more hair than brains - actually started a fan club for Peter. Although Peter acted like he didn't like it, I thought it was pretty obvious that he *did*. In fact, I can't remember exactly how, but something the girl with all the hair said to me made me think Peter had somehow put her up to it in the first place. Even a couple of the teachers joined it. It was pretty funny."

"Anyway, I think the thing with Maria started when she talked him into going to church with her one Sunday, and from then on they were inseparable. I remember Maria saying they talked for hours afterward. She said he was a hurt little boy, whatever that means. Whatever it was, it activated her strong sense of empathy and she became his staunchest supporter."

"They dated then or, 'went steady,' I think you used to call it?"

Heather laughed. "Good job on the retro lingo. No, they didn't date at first because Maria's mom wouldn't let her date until she was sixteen. That didn't bother Maria though. The church we all attended was very fundamentalist, with some pretty strict beliefs, like very restricted courtship rules. In fact, some parents went so far as to choose their child's spouse for them." Heather shook her head in disbelief. "Anyway, Maria has always been very devout, you know. She was walking the straight and narrow long before Peter Stone," Heather laughed. "He just took to it with more flare."

"Do you still attend that church?" asked Reina curiously.

"No, I realized I don't do well with overly-legalistic rules. I'm kinda a free spirit." Heather smiled, the tan skin around her mouth and blue eyes crinkling in well-used laughter lines. Reina couldn't help but like this friendly, easy-going woman.

"I figure Maria must have been 18 when they got married. Was it a surprise? Were there any, um . . . extenuating circumstances?"

"If you mean, was she pregnant? I should think not. Although I know many a devout believer has accidentally found themselves on the wrong side of carnal desire, I think I'd have known if they'd even slept together. No, they were just two good kids who were saving themselves for marriage and they figured, why wait?" Again Heather paused, gathering her thoughts. "I remember hearing Maria talk many times about their 'mission' together. They were both pretty starry-eyed over saving the world for Jesus."

"Did you stay in touch after the wedding?"

"Oh yes, they lived in town for a few years. Peter worked as a Youth Group Leader and an Assistant Pastor and Maria stayed quite busy doting on him."

"Did they seem happy?"

"Very much so. As I say, they had a very strong vision of their mission to save the world." Heather sighed and looked like she was trying to wrestle free her thoughts. Reina waited for her to continue. "They both knew the Bible inside and out and absolutely believed in its literal truth as the Word of God." Heather shrugged and added, "I'm a free-riding Montana girl. I've roped steers with the guys and can outride most of 'em, so I never really cared for that bit in the Bible about women submitting to their husbands, and the husband being the head of the marriage and all that. But Maria and Peter definitely lived by it."

"Did it seem to bother Maria?"

"Not at all. She adored Peter and said many times that he was chosen by God for greatness. It was her . . . well, I think she felt it was her honor to support him in that greatness."

"So, when did they move out of the area?"

"About sixteen years ago. Peter joined a sort of traveling ministry group that toured the country doing tent revivals and that sort of thing. I think they even did a short mission stint abroad. Then, I don't know, maybe ten or twelve years ago they moved to Seattle and started this whole Stone Kingdom thing."

"Did they ever come back to visit?"

"I don't believe Peter has ever been back, but Maria visited several times."

Reina glanced at her notes before continuing, "And Maria's mom passed away shortly after they moved?"

"Yes." Heather hesitated for a moment then added, "I think Maria blamed herself for not being here to care for her mom. They were overseas at the time and, apparently, Peter told her they couldn't spare the money to fly her back."

"How did her mother die?"

Heather shook her head, "She was always a little, um, odd. She would wander around in the rain, and at night, with no hat or coat. She finally caught pneumonia and died from complications."

"Did you stay in touch with Maria during their travels?"

"Oh yes. Maria and I corresponded regularly."

"When did you last talk to her?"

"Five years ago."

Reina raised her eyebrows. They must have a different definition of "regularly" here in Big Sky Country.

She couldn't imagine going five years without talking with Getta or Liz.

Heather took a bite of her sandwich, chewed it slowly then continued, "Five years ago, Maria just stopped communicating. She wouldn't answer or return my calls. She wouldn't reply to emails or letters I sent." Reina could see the hurt in Heather's eyes. "I even drove to Seattle several times to knock on her door. Twice I left notes on the door. The third time, I saw the curtains move so I know she was there. But she wouldn't answer."

"Did something happen to cause a rift between you?" probed Reina gently.

"I have trotted out every pony to answer that question, but I can't think of anything. It was just like she turned off the barn lights and walked away."

Reina smiled a little at Heather's ranch-hand metaphor.

"Trust me," Heather continued, "it's ripped me up to lose such a dear friend." After a long pause, she added with some difficulty, "I guess I just came to the conclusion that maybe she was too busy or important for the old cowgirl from Montana. I mean, Peter was getting famous and they were traveling to exotic places and they seemed to be doing quite well financially." She smiled wryly, saying, "I guess it kinda proves the old saying - *A rolling 'Stone' gathers no 'Moss'*." She finished with a lackluster attempt to joke off her obvious hurt.

Reina reached over and squeezed Heather's hand in support. She waited a moment then asked, "Did you try to visit her in jail?"

"Yes. She refused to see me."

"And now she refuses to talk. Do you have any idea why she would silence her voice and forfeit her right to tell her story?"

"Well," Heather tilted her head to the side and looked at Reina with half-closed eyes, "a lot of people silence their voice and forfeit their story, now don't they?"

Hmmm, I suppose that's true. Still, Maria's case seems a little extreme. Reina continued softly, "I know this is a difficult question, but do you have any reason to think that Maria has . . . mental health issues?"

"Well, I know there's been talk of that around here recently with this whole poisoning thing and what with her mother's oddities and all. Five years ago, I would have said no way. But after having been so . . . abruptly cut off, and then watching her, um, decline on public television, and now this deal with Peter. Well, I just don't know anymore."

Chapter 13

After paying for lunch and saying her goodbyes to Heather, Reina performed the ritual of pre-flight again on her aircraft, looking for signs of bird strikes, fuel leaks, oil leaks, prop chips – anything that might have transpired during her morning flight. She well knew the importance of the pre-flight inspection and the occasional need to alter plans because of something that didn't look right. She often reminded herself of one of her instructor's sayings, "I'd rather be on the ground wishing I was in the air, than in the air wishing I was on the ground." Finding nothing amiss, she opened her flight plan with flight service and took off from Kalispell heading west. She hoped she would have the chance to meet up with Heather Moss again someday.

Other then the anticipated headwinds, the return flight passed uneventfully. Radio talk was light as she crossed high above the brown plains of Eastern Washington and the background noise of the humming engine was her only companion. She thought about Heather's comment on people forfeiting their voice and their story. Most of the people with whom she associated were hard charging, giving no quarter to anyone who dared to yank their reins. But she knew the world was full of people who ceded power to others, who allowed themselves to be victims. She saw them every day in court, in stores, in restaurants. People who willingly walked through life with imaginary prison bars pressed to their face, yielding authority over themselves to a spouse, an employer, a religion, a parent, the State. People who seemed to feel they had no choice in the matter. If she could, she'd make those prison bars disappear and tell people to step up to their lives, grab the yoke, live it. *Of course, it might put me out of a job . . . .*

The long-silent radio crackled to life, ending her reverie. She was approaching Bravo airspace around SeaTac airport.

As usual, Seattle Approach kept her at altitude to stay out of the path of incoming airliners. At ten miles from her destination, the clipped-voice controller finally told her to descend, "Five zero seven five Kilo, descend to two thousand five hundred, heading three one zero, intercept localizer."

Yeah right, thought Reina, I'll be there in two minutes; I'd have to dive 4,000 feet per minute to be on altitude. Not being the pilot of a NASA rocket, nor wanting to shock-cool her turbo-charged engine, she replied, "Approach, seven five kilo will go ahead and cancel at this time and proceed VFR."

"Five zero seven five Kilo, Squawk one two zero zero. Frequency change approved. Gooday."

"Gooday." In her contemplative mood and in no rush to land, Reina pointed the aircraft nose out toward the San Juan Islands, deciding on a sunset cruise to bleed off altitude. Watching the sun descend in glory over the

Northwest, she felt a familiar pang in her deep, deep, quiet spot at the aching loveliness surrounding her. Scattered throughout the glowing honey-red water, the islands lay like sleeping animals of blue, green, and purple below her. Along their spiny, humped skin, shadows stretched long between the low rays of the sun. The sky around her tinted pink, red, orange. She felt like she'd been swallowed by a Van Gogh painting. Immense and awe-inspiring, the beauty of her sky-world both took her breath away and left her with a strange sense of longing. She turned and headed for Wayward Field, only minutes away.

    True Blue Aviation was long closed by the time she finally taxied to a stop in front of it. Unable to maneuver the big aircraft into the hangar on her own, she tied it down at one of the parking spots in front of the flight school. She installed the control lock on the yoke, covered the pitot tube to keep bugs and dirt out, and carefully placed chocks around the aircraft's wheels. As she gathered up her things and locked the aircraft's door, the last of the setting sun dipped down on the western tree line. The full moon, already edging up over the eastern horizon, was ready to take over where the sun left off. It promised to be a beautiful night.

    She dropped the keys and dispatch book on True Blue's empty reception desk, and locked the storefront door behind her. As she stood on the patio in the dimming light, watching the battle between setting sun and rising moon, she suddenly felt achingly lonely. The airport was deserted at this hour. A light chill lay like a blanket over the old hangars. Wisps of fog were beginning to form around the mothballed DC-3 and the old PBY Catalina flying boat, and not a sound of aircraft or human spoiled the quiet air. The hustle and bustle of the busy little airport during the day lay absolutely still, like an exhausted bargirl dozing after a busy evening, waiting for tomorrow's customers and lovers to awaken her to life again.

A lover's attentions sounded pretty good tonight, Reina had to admit. There were times when she wished someone waited at home for her with dinner or drinks or even just open arms. Times when she wanted a wise listener with whom she could share the perplexities of a difficult case. Times when she wanted someone to laugh and dance with. Times when she just wanted quick sex. So far, all of those features had not yet presented themselves to her in one package.

Taking a last glance around at the sleeping airport, she headed to her car for the long drive home. Lost in driver's glaze, she thought of calling Franco, knowing, with a little encouragement, he could be hers. Not that he ever said it in so many words, but she'd seen it in his eyes. She remembered fondly all the hours they spent over salads and grinders, talking about politics, law, ambitions, life. The memories were so vivid, she could almost taste the famous proprietary Italian dressing from Fraccini's pizza place. If it were possible, she would call right now to order home delivery of a meatball grinder and house salad. But Fraccini's was 3,000 miles away and those memories many years in the past now. She didn't even know if the place still existed. And Franco was probably working anyway.

Reina made a mental note to invite Franco to dinner soon. She would be careful, of course, not to let it get romantic since she had no desire to ruin a great friendship. Only one time, years ago, had they almost gone too far. She blushed in the dark recalling how she'd impetuously - and drunkenly - pulled him down onto a park bench next to her and kissed him passionately. He had responded readily enough, plundering her mouth with his tongue and stroking her hair. When she hungrily placed his hand on her breast, he pulled back and looked around warily. His whisper that he wanted to take her somewhere safe brought her back to her senses. Safe wasn't what Reina sought. She kissed him gently and said they should both go home before things went too far. Being ever the gentleman, Franco agreed to her suggestion. Although things had been awkward for a few days, they had eventually returned to their easy-going, platonic ways.

Reina shook off her nostalgia. *Sex always complicates things, but still . . . .* Thinking for a moment about Sam, she scolded the thought away. *Absolutely not. I will not demean myself by calling to see if he might set aside domestic duties for me. Hmmmph. That low I will not go!* She turned up the radio to distract herself.

As she drove south on I-5, lost in her thoughts, she turned her head to make a lane change and noticed an old black Datsun truck in the lane directly next to her. Glancing over, she saw the small, dark-skinned driver staring intently at her. When he saw her looking at him, he hunched tightly over the steering wheel and sped away.

Weird. But then there are all kinds of weirdos in the world. Let's just hope this one isn't out to get me.

Reina pulled into her parking spot, watching carefully to be sure no black truck followed her. She let herself in to her condo, locking the door behind her. After checking each room for intruders, she dropped exhausted into bed. It had been a long day, and dinner could wait.

Chapter 14

Jerry watched Reina enter her condo and saw the lights of her unit illuminate briefly, then extinguish. He'd been waiting hours, just to watch her walk from her car. Nothing more, just watch. It was late now, and he didn't have much time left, but he didn't need much time. He drove down to First Avenue and cruised slowly, checking to see if there was anything new out tonight. New could be bad, could be a trap. But he liked to look anyway. He turned up University, pulled up to the curb and rolled down his window. She was there. He didn't know her name, or care. She opened the passenger door and climbed in.

"I didn't know if you'd make it tonight."

Jerry reached out and slapped her. "I don't pay you to talk, bitch. There's only one thing you need to do with your mouth." He pulled into an adjacent garage and parked in the corner. No attendant at this hour. He turned sideways. She leaned toward him and unzipped his pants. He grabbed her hair in a tight knot and directed her head downward, to his lap. Closing his eyes, he relaxed, in the only way he knew how.

Chapter 15

Sunday's sun rose hours before Reina, who eventually awakened to the sound of Cheap Trick music blasting from her cell phone. *Mother told me, yes she told me, I'd meet girls like you . . . .* Reaching groggily for the phone on her nightstand, she saw that, indeed, it was her mother calling. She made a mental note to change her ring tone.

She fell back on her pillow and mumbled, "Hello."

"Good morning, honey. Sorry to wake you. Late night last night?"

"Not really, I just needed a good long sleep."

"Well, hopefully 11 a.m. is adequate. I wanted to check on your flight yesterday. Did everything go okay?"

"Yeah, it was fine. Sorry about taking the 210 without any advance notice. I hope that didn't mess you up too bad?"

"No, I didn't have it scheduled yesterday so it was okay. And not to worry, Hawk refueled it for you so it's all good."

"Oh, yeah, sorry about that." For a moment, Reina resented feeling like a recalcitrant child. But *if I borrowed anyone else's airplane,* she reasoned, *I would have never returned it on empty, so I guess I deserve that.*

"Are you coming out to fly today?"

"No, I think I'm gonna get caught up on things around here. I need to be ready to go tomorrow."

"Oh, sure, I understand." After a brief pause, her mother continued, "By the way, speaking of tomorrow, I was thinking it might be a good idea to request a, um, what's it called, you know, when you get a case, um . . . postponed?"

"A continuance? Uh, okaaay . . . and on what grounds, may I ask?"

"Oh. Do you need to have grounds?"

"Well, yeah, ya kinda do. I mean, I guess I could just go in and say to Judge Takahashi that my mom said so. I'm sure she would appreciate that."

"Ah. Haha. Well, I just thought I'd really like to meet this Maria. Is there any way we could get her out of the jail and take her somewhere to talk?"

"Mom, I appreciate your effort to help," Reina replied patiently. "I really do. But unless some valid reason comes up, I'm afraid the show must go on."

"Well, okay," her mom sighed. "I just, well, I don't know. I just have a feeling I might be able to talk to her."

"I'll let you know if anything changes, Mom. I do appreciate your concern. Love you."

"Love you too, honey."

Reina ended the phone call with a roll of her eyes. *Mothers. Precious but exasperating.* She rolled out of bed and padded naked to the bathroom, thinking, if there's anyone who'd like to get Maria to talk, it's me. Who's been sitting there every morning trying to squeak a bloody word out of a stone turnip? *Well, I can't help her if she's too meek to help herself.* Reina felt that disgust for her client again, the scorn of the strong for the weak.

Opening her eyes wide at the stranger in the bathroom mirror, she ran her hands through her nearly-forgotten hairdo. She smiled at the spiky, blonde hair. One of her co-defenders was holding a birthday party tonight at The Flamboyant Pig, a lively bar on Capitol Hill, and Reina looked forward to her colleagues' reaction when she showed up with the new style.

She spent the afternoon reviewing her trial notes and planning her upcoming week. Listening again to Friday night's surreptitious phone recording from the kitchen vents at Stone Kingdom, she heard the typical exclamations of "Oh, Yes!" and "God have mercy!" and "Praise the Lord!" and such. At one point, Peter Stone's booming voice could be heard saying, "And the greatest sinners shall receive the greatest salvation." and the women's voices responding with "Amen!" and "Deliver us Lord!" It appeared to be just a passionate, fundamentalist prayer session, in which case Reina regretted getting locked up in a refrigerator for it. She had hoped to stumble on to a clue that might explain why someone seemed determined to remove her from the picture and, by extension, might also explain Maria's actions.

Although she personally found televangelism slightly offensive, Reina realized that being a big phony certainly wasn't a capital crime. And clearly Maria had supported her husband for this long, so why would she suddenly turn against him? Reina could find no logical basis for her client's alleged behavior.

At four p.m. she packed up her notes, as ready as she could be for court the next day. She spent ten minutes doing floor Pilates, ending with a hundred abdomen crunches. Aerobatic flying, with its physically demanding changes in gravitational forces, required keeping her abdominal core strong. She exercised religiously every day to stay fit for her favorite hobby. Slipping out of the shorts and t-shirt she'd been wearing during her study session, she started hot water for a shower. Just then, the hall doorbell to her condo buzzed. Although she wasn't expecting anyone, she wrapped herself in a towel and padded down the stairs on the off chance it might be one of her friends. Both Getta and Liz had been given the exterior security code and a copy of her interior door key, but an unspoken courtesy required a ring before entering each other's personal domains.

On the way down, she grabbed the heavy statuary Celtic cross that adorned her stair landing. Just in case. *Hmmm*, she analyzed the hefty implement as she wielded it in her hand like a baseball bat. *Perfect for delivering blows to the head. In fact, could work for vampires and stopping bullets, too.* She smiled with satisfaction at her handy, multipurpose, impromptu weapon.

A peek through her door peephole revealed a fisheye view of the hallway and a seedy looking middle-aged guy with long thin hair, droopy eyes, and loose jowly cheeks. He looked like a Basset Hound. Reina wondered how he got past Mrs. Jensen. Even in human form, Mrs. J was the sworn enemy of all things dog-like. Last year, a couple from the fourth floor dressed up as Charlie Brown and Snoopy for a Halloween party. When Mrs. J saw them in the hallway, she tried to chase "Snoopy," a full grown man, out the door with a switch broom held high. Mrs. J's hate of dogs knew no bounds. She always feared they would chase her beloved cat, Mr. Jingles. It didn't matter that Mr. Jingles had been dead for years.

Well, if not Mrs. J, then probably the building's super had welcomed the man inside. Maybe even directed him to Reina's floor. Almost as old as Mrs. J, and nearly as senile, the super willingly let strangers in based on their ability to produce the name of someone in the building, regardless of the fact that all tenants' names were clearly visible on the front mailboxes. "Security" seemed to have a somewhat unique definition in this condo building.

Enjoying, for a moment, her secret view of the canine-looking visitor, Reina watched in fascination as his loose jowls swung back and forth in time to the beat emanating from the music source in his pocket. Plugged into earbuds, and chewing something gummy, he held his hands behind his back, out of sight. He looked harmless - maybe a magazine salesman - but Reina felt disinclined to open the door to someone she didn't know, especially while wearing nothing but a towel. She visually double-checked that the lock, deadbolt, and chain were secure, then trotted lightly back up the stairs, replacing the Celtic cross to its rightful spot on the landing. She locked the bathroom door behind her and went back to her shower, humming Elvis, "*You ain't nothin' but a hound dog.*" Time to go have some fun.

Chapter 16

When Reina arrived at The Flamboyant Pig, her co-workers from the county's public defense team already filled the room. They had taken over the bar area and Happy Hour appeared to be in full swing. Walking into the bar in her black mini skirt and spiky blonde hair inspired the good-natured catcalls she had anticipated. She smiled seductively and struck a pose for her friends' benefit, placing one stockinged and stilettoed foot high on a stool rung and throwing her head back with an alluring over-the-shoulder glance.

"Hey, come and get a drink, hot stuff," called out Ned, one of the senior defenders.

Reina laughed and joined him at the big wood bar.

"So, how's it going?" he asked.

"Great. I am *so* ready for a fun night."

"Good. Well, I wasn't sure you'd make it tonight, with your big case tomorrow. I'm sure you've been busy."

"Yeah, I have been busy, that's for sure, but I'm about as prepared as I can be under the circumstances. At this point, I could definitely use some liquid stress-relievers."

"Okay then. Let's get you a drink. What are you having?"

"A Tanqueray Martini sounds perfect."

As Ray, the Pig's handsome-but-gay bartender, mixed her martini, Reina made her way around to the other side of the bar, greeting various co-workers on the way. At the far end, she propped her elbows on the bar next to her assistant, Trey, cradled her chin in her hands, and said dreamily, "Yes, he is gorgeous isn't he?" while fluttering her eyelashes in Ray's direction.

"Oh, God, am I being that obvious?" Trey asked with a grimace.

"Yes, but I think he's used to it. At least you have a better chance of getting a wink from him than I do," she replied with a dramatic sigh.

"I don't know about that," her assistant responded dejectedly. "I've been in here half a dozen times and he doesn't even know I'm alive. I've over-tipped him every time, too."

"Well then, don't get your briefs in a bunch over him. There are plenty of other good looking dudes here on Capitol Hill to choose from." Changing the subject, she quickly updated him on her weekend activities on the Stone versus Stone case. "Hey, I finally had a chance to talk with the Maid of Honor from the Stone's wedding. I don't know that I learned a lot, but I'll get you the recording tomorrow to transcribe for me. Apparently, Maria's mother exhibited some mental instability and there are some childhood influences that may warrant we take another look at those notes from the psychological analysis."

"Sounds good. I'll pull the file for you tomorrow."

"Great. But that's for tomorrow. Tonight we forget about work and have fun. Oh, there's my martini." Reina saw Ray deposit her drink in front of Ned. "Talk to you soon." She placed her hand on Trey's shoulder in a friendly gesture and turned to make her way back to Ned's side where her ice-cold, double-olive drink awaited.

As Reina took a sip, Ned leaned toward her and said, "Hey, just let me know if you need any advice or assistance on this case. I'm sure you don't want to talk shop right now, but I'd be happy to help in any way I can."

"Thanks, Ned, that's very nice of you to offer. I can't think of anything at the moment, but I'll let you know if something comes up," she smiled. A good-looking guy in his mid-forties, Ned had gone through an unpleasant divorce about a year ago. His wife apparently fooled around on him, gender indiscriminatingly, for several years. Devastated when she finally ran off with another woman, he had pulled back from any social interactions with his colleagues. Reina enjoyed Ned's company and his intellect and was happy to see him start socializing again. They chatted for a bit, then Reina excused herself to go wish a happy birthday to Carolyn.

Already a couple of drinks into the evening, Carolyn cheerfully exhibited the usual attorney's ability to consume large quantities of alcohol and remain absolutely coherent. Her generous figure was squeezed between two of the younger male attorneys and her soft arms were slung over their shoulders. As Reina approached the table, Carolyn called out, "Girl, take a look at this. I've got myself a delicious reverse Oreo here." She sashayed her shoulders and ample chest back and forth, "MmmMmmMmmm!"

Before Reina could reply, Othello leaned in from the other side of the table and said, "Why don't you white boys move aside and let Reina squeeze in between Carolyn and myself. We'll show you an Oreo cookie done right."

They all laughed and good naturedly made room for Reina. By unspoken agreement, no discussion was allowed about cases or clients. Instead, the conversation centered around social activities.

Carolyn described how she'd been to see *Tosca* recently at the Seattle Opera where, apparently, she'd been a dead ringer for the woman performing the main character role. "People were looking at me oddly in the lobby during intermission. At first I was like, 'What, you never seen a large black woman before?' Then I realized they thought I was the star, coming out to mingle with the crowd. One little girl asked me to autograph her program."

"What did you do?" Reina asked.

"I autographed it, of course."

"As the star, or as you?"

"As me of course, baby, I *am* a star!"

They all laughed. "Well, I'm not a big opera fan," admitted Cody, one of the reverse Oreo's 'white boys,' "but I've always thought it must be depressing to be an opera singer and have to die at every performance."

"Yeah, and they never die easily," chimed in Ned, who had joined them at the table. "I went to *La Traviata* a couple of years ago, and every time I thought the heroine was dead, she'd revive and sing some more. Any sadness in her dying was tempered by the relief when she finally *did* die." Everybody laughed, but Ned suddenly looked a little sad. Reina guessed he was thinking of his wife who probably accompanied him to that opera.

"Well, it's a good thing I didn't start singing in the lobby," Carolyn jokingly filled in the awkward silence, "or the *Tosca* fans would have figured out pretty quickly I wasn't the star."

"But you are the star tonight," said Othello with a suggestive wink, "and I happen to know they have a karaoke machine here. Come on, guys, let's start the singing with 'Happy Birthday' to lovely Carolyn." The birthday celebrants formed a semi-circle around Carolyn and sang a rousing rendition of the traditional birthday song. Othello then went to the karaoke machine and crooned "My Girl" by The Temptations while gesturing soulfully at Carolyn.

After the laughter and groans died down, Carolyn stood up, rolled her eyes, and said, "Well, I think the jury's still out on that one." She bounced up to the mic and performed the perfect answer to Othello's "My Girl" with "Stop, In the Name of Love" from Diana Ross and The Supremes. Cody was next with AC/DC's "You Shook Me All Night Long."

Reina finished her second martini, stood up, and waved to the other women on the defense team to join her on stage. After a short huddle, they leaned in together at the microphone and began crooning "Oh yes, I'm the great defender, defendin' when you're not around . . ." to the tune of "The Great Pretender." The guys from the office hooted and clapped to the women's tune. Aaron, the Oreo's other 'white boy,' fell out of his chair. There was definitely some drinking going on.

As Reina returned to her seat amidst the cheers and jeers, her way was suddenly blocked by the Bassett-hound guy who'd knocked on her door earlier that day. Her initial alarm at his unexpected presence subsided when he handed her a large manila envelope and asked her to sign for it. She signed and commented on his working late. He just grinned and nodded, jowls a-flapping, before slouching off. Stifling paranoid thoughts of Anthrax, she slit open the envelope. Inside rested Prosecution's record of their interview with Stone. *Diablo! That son-of-a-bitch Jerry, what the hell is he doing sending it to me on the night before trial?* She would need to familiarize herself with its contents. Grabbing her purse, she said her goodbyes, adding with a grin that "some of us have to work for a living."

As she headed toward the door, Ned caught up with her. "Hey, I'll buy you an early breakfast if you want some company going over those," he offered. "I know a great little all-night diner down in the SoDo area."

Reina hesitated for only a moment, then accepted with a smile. "Actually, that sounds great, Ned. I'm certainly going to need some coffee, and I'd appreciate the company, too."

Ned drove them down to Manny's Diner, off of First Avenue. Manny's was a hole-in-the-wall type of place frequented by truckers, police officers, and dock workers – the guys who always knew where to find good food. They walked in and were told by the busy, busty waitress to grab any booth. Reina spotted one in the corner and planted herself with her back against the wall, wondering if maybe her last name really should be Dillinger. She ordered a pot of coffee and a Denver Omelette with crispy hash browns. Ned chose the nightly special, a smoked-salmon Eggs Benedict with caper-spiked Hollandaise sauce.

While they waited for their food, Ned summarized the little he knew about Reina's case. "So, I heard Peter Stone got out of the hospital on Wednesday, which means Jerry probably met with him sometime within the last few days. It should be interesting to see what he has to say. Is your client still maintaining silence?"

"Yes. She's spoken a few cryptic words, including 'He needed to die,' and 'My husband has some very special friends,' but otherwise nothing."

"That's kind of bizarre. What did she mean by, 'My husband has some very special friends'?"

"Who knows?" shrugged Reina, hesitant to disclose the multiple recent attacks against her to Ned. The first one, of course, was on public record with the Seattle Police Department, but the other incidents were very circumstantial and, frankly, rather embarrassing when it came down to the refrigerator escapade. Besides, she didn't want people getting all protective over her and getting in the way of her investigation.

"Are you planning to talk to Stone?" Ned asked.

"We tried to schedule a meeting, but he refuses to make time for us. I'm planning to talk to Judge Takahashi on Monday about ordering a deposition. It may be the only way he'll sit down with us." Reina leafed through the pages she'd removed from the envelope. "Well, at first glance, these documents don't show much of interest. If he has something to say, he's not saying it."

"You know, you could probably request a continuance based on late delivery of documents by Prosecution."

"Yeah, the thought came to mind. Of course, that might seem reasonable to me and to you, but remember I've got Hashi on the bench."

Their breakfasts arrived on old, faded, diner Chinet loaded high with the hot and generous portions that clearly established Manny's claim to fame with the working crowd. Realizing she was famished, Reina dug in with gusto. It felt good to soak up the gin in her stomach with something solid. As they ate, Reina relayed what she knew of Stone Kingdom's empire. Clearly, the various business ventures thrived under Stone's guidance, or perhaps they'd been blessed by his God. Either way, Reina found nothing particular in the company holdings to suggest justification for her client's alleged actions. Ned inquired about life insurance, and Reina confirmed it could be a possible motive.

"There is a large policy on Stone, but if Maria is found guilty she would be precluded, of course, from benefitting by it."

"But perhaps she didn't anticipate getting caught."

"I don't know. Apparently, she had a bag packed and ready to go in the foyer when the police arrived. And she certainly wasn't reticent about the confession. She spit it out so fast the officers didn't have time to read her her rights. Part of me wonders if that wasn't intentionally contrived with the hopes of getting off on a Miranda Warning violation. But I don't know if she's that smart. In any case, it did her no good since Hashi denied my motion to dismiss the confession." Reina chewed a bite before continuing. "Without words or facial expressions, Maria's impossible to read. It just doesn't make sense. Getting caught, or the possibility of conviction, doesn't seem to surprise, or even faze her at all. But then, she obviously holds her emotions pretty sternly in check."

"It is odd," Ned agreed. "How sound do you think the confession is?"

"Well, I'm not sure what you mean," Reina's eyebrows furrowed as she tilted her head to the side in question and ran her fingers through her hair. She noticed Ned's eyes move to the tri-blade scar on her temple. The harsh diner lights probably made it stand out like a witch's mark.

Reina continued, "I mean, I can see why someone might make up a denial, or an alibi, to cover guilt, but why would someone make up a confession to cover their innocence?"

"I've seen a lot of strange stuff over the years," Ned replied. "I once had a client who gave a full - and convincing - confession to a sensationalist race-hate crime. As it turned out, she had nothing to do with it and just wanted the publicity."

"Hmmm," Reina murmured, tugging her lower lip. "Well, I can't get her to either repeat or recant her confession to me. It certainly would be easier if she would speak."

"Or, she could be covering for someone else. What about a boyfriend?" Ned continued to explore all the possibilities.

"There is one male friend she seemed to contact regularly. However, he has dropped off the radar."

"Oh?"

"Yeah, just disappeared. Disconnected number. Quit showing up for work, missed his vacation flight, moved out - or was moved out - of his apartment. No sign of foul play, however, and no match in the morgue."

"That does seem suspicious. Maybe it was his gig and she's taking the fall."

"Or *their* gig and she's left holding the bag."

"Or he was her first victim." Ned waggled his eyebrows.

"I don't know about that. She's not exactly your standard black widow type. I have to wonder too about the other friend, the 'husband's friend.' Maybe they're in cahoots together. Or he's forcing her to do something against her will . . . or the husband's friend is also the missing friend. With Maria not willing to talk, I feel like I'm sitting in the dark surrounded by shadows I can't even see."

"Even when people talk you can't know if what you hear is true. Too often, words just confuse the issue. You think you've got someone figured out, then they do something that makes you realize you never knew them at all."

Ned looked a little glum and appeared to be alluding to his own recent experiences. What little Reina knew of his personal circumstances came from water-cooler scuttlebutt. Not being officially in his confidence, she struggled with a reply, saying simply, "Yeah, life sucks sometimes."

They ate for a moment in an awkward silence, eyes on their respective plates. As Ned dabbed up the last bit of egg yolk with a final bite of English muffin, Reina looked up and saw Franco and Jomar walk in the door. She waved to them and they made their way over to her booth.

"Hey there, little defender of the public, how's it going?" Franco greeted her with a smile.

"Not too bad," she smiled back. "Ned, I'd like you to meet the real public defenders, Franco Mancini and Jomar-- " Reina squinted at Jomar's badge trying to read the officer's last name in the glare of the diner lights.

"Jomar Green," he filled in for her.

"Thanks. Don't think we got the full introduction the other night. This is Ned Williams, a colleague of mine."

The men exchanged a polite round of "nice-to-meet-you" and shook hands. Reina invited the two police officers to sit with them and they agreed, saying they were just in for a quick cup of coffee.

"How was breakfast?" asked Franco, squeezing in next to Reina and eyeing her empty plate.

"Delicious!" replied Reina. "I'll have to remember this place for those late nights out."

"Out tearing up the town, were you?" Franco asked, looking speculatively at Ned.

Ned raised his eyebrows and jutted his chin at Franco, "We sure tried." He turned and winked at Reina, as if to demonstrate the intimacy between them.

"Just a birthday party for a fellow attorney," Reina interjected between the bristling Alpha males. "How's your shift going?"

"We've had bettah," responded Jomar.

"I'm sorry. Rough night of crime in The Emerald City?"

"Some nights are tougher than others," Franco's mouth tightened as he paused. "We recovered the body of a boy from Olympic Park tonight."

"Oh, how horrible!" exclaimed Reina. "Was it a homicide? Gang related?"

"We don't know much yet. Someone called 911 reporting a body on the beach. It looks like it may be a drowning, although there are signs of violence. He's young, maybe ten. Too young." Franco looked grim.

"It's such a travesty when someone dies so young," agreed Ned.

"Yeah, this is the second Asian boy we've found in the last month. It's possible a boat of illegals may have capsized offshore."

"Or it may be gang related." Ned shook his head. "I used to think ten a little young for some of the gang activities we see, but like you guys on the street, we get some pretty youthful offenders in our office."

"They start young, that's for sure," Jomar agreed. "Remember the eight year old that shot his mama and sister here last year? That was before I transferred from New York. I remember reading 'bout it and worrying cuz my sister lives here with her kids. They're good kids, but jeez, ya never know. And unfortunately, her husband's a crazy mothah - only half there half the time. I dunno why the *H* she keeps taking him back." He rolled his eyes and head in disgust.

Jomar must have learned pretty quickly, thought Reina, that his new partner wouldn't tolerate swearing on the job, even during a social break. Franco took the honor due his uniform very seriously, sometimes to the amusement of his fellow officers who had been on the force long enough to have their idealistic fervor sanded down a bit by the grit of the streets.

"Well, we'd better get going," said Franco, draining the last drops from his coffee mug. "Crime doesn't take coffee breaks, you know." He shook hands again with Ned, but his smile was for Reina. "It's good to see you Reina. Ned, nice to meet you. See you around."

As he stood, Franco said to Reina, "Oh, by the way, the answer to your text question is yes. Call me tomorrow. I'd like to know why you wanted to know."

"Okay," Reina agreed. So, the wife of the police officer who sent nasty-grams to her owned a black Hummer. *Hmmm.*

She and Ned waved the officers off, paid their bill, and walked in silence to Ned's car. Ned checked the window for parking tickets.

"Just in case Officer Mancini was feeling a little vindictive about someone else having midnight breakfasts with you," he grinned at Reina.

Reina laughed. *Alpha males!*

Ned drove Reina back to her car. On the way, he reached over and put his hand on her hand, which rested on her stocking-clad knee.

"You're going to do great tomorrow," he said with an encouraging squeeze.

"Thanks," she replied brightly, turning her hand over to give his fingers a quick reply squeeze, then busying herself by opening her purse to search for keys. "You're a great friend, Ned. And advisor."

"I'll wait for you to get your car started."

Reina unlocked her car, started it up, and pulled onto Broadway, with a wave out the window for Ned. *Quite the gentleman. Very sweet.* She chuckled a little at the memory of Franco and Ned squaring off to each other at the diner. A little of that now and then was good for a girl's ego. Especially for one who'd recently been passed over for laundry!

Chapter 17

Reina overslept. Fortunately, her most conservative, pin-striped, gray suit hung pressed and ready to go, fresh from the cleaners. She pulled on a white silk blouse, slipped into the suit and quickly smoothed her short blonde hair back into a less sassy style than the spikes of the night before. Stepping at a half-run into a pair of conservative Kate Spade pumps, she grabbed a yogurt and three ibuprofen and made it to court on time, but barely.

Reina nodded a greeting at a smirking Jerry who said one word to her as she passed, "Nice." Somehow, he made the innocuous word sound insolent and indecent.

As Reina sat next to Maria, she smiled warmly and pressed her client's hand. She whispered to her, with more confidence than she really felt, that everything would be fine. After the court rose for Judge Takahashi's entrance, Reina made a request for a sidebar. The judge told her and Jerry to approach the bench.

"Your Honor, I would like to request a continuance, based on late delivery of relevant documents from Prosecution to Defense."

"Explain," commanded the judge.

"Your Honor, although Prosecution's meeting with Peter Stone took place Friday morning, Defense did not receive delivery of the meeting notes until late last night and requests additional time to review them."

Judge Takahashi looked at Jerry. "Can you explain why notes were so delayed in getting to Defense?"

"With all due respect, Your Honor," replied Jerry, "I believe delivery was attempted multiple times over the course of the last 72 hours. It would appear that Ms. Dessiner was unavailable to receive them Friday evening and all day Saturday and Sunday. The courier finally caught up with her late Sunday night singing karaoke at a party in a bar on Capitol Hill."

"I see," responded Judge Takahashi. After a pause, she continued, "It is not the duty of the court to defer the process of justice so counsel has adequate time for a lively social life." She looked sourly at Reina, then glanced down at her chest. "Or breakfast. Request denied."

As Reina walked back to her seat, she glanced down to see a small dribble of pink yogurt on her white blouse. Oh my God, she thought. It's going to be one of those days.

Prosecution called their first witness, an expert on poisons. Jerry's questions encouraged the witness to go into great detail about Atrazine - where it was found and how difficult it would be for a person to accidentally become exposed to enough Atrazine to cause any bodily harm. The witness also verified that the pesticide could readily be camouflaged in food or drink. Reina winced internally when the witness added, "To achieve a level of acute toxicology in a person without the person's awareness of the process would require long-term, regular and measured applications of the poison."

Reina asked only two questions in her cross-examination.

"Are you a medical doctor?"

"No, but --"

"Thank you. And could you please tell us if Atrazine is readily available to the public at large?"

"Atrazine can be found in weed-control pesticides sold at local home improvement stores."

"Thank you. No further questions."

Jerry called his next witness, Peter Stone's secretary. Reina knew Maria had helped out a few hours a week in her husband's office at Stone Kingdom, working under Leann Jones, Stone's head secretary. In her late forties and rather homely, Ms. Jones made a valiant attempt to atone for her shortage of looks with a push-up bra, big hair, heavy mascara, and bright red lipstick. She was sworn in and took her seat.

Jerry began his examination. "Could you please tell the court what you do for a living?"

"I am the lead secretary for Reverend Peter Stone of Stone Kingdom Enterprises, Incorporated."

"How long have you held this position?"

"Since Stone Kingdom first started up, ten years, six months, and three weeks ago," Leann answered with obvious pride. "I have seen Reverend Stone's divine work grow from only a handful of helpers to hundreds of employees."

"Could you please tell the court how you know the defendant, Maria Stone?"

"Maria worked a few hours a week in our office for many years."

"Did you hire the defendant?"

"Well, no, not exactly. I mean, she is the wife of our president and spiritual leader, so she can more or less do what she wants." Leann sniffed slightly in barely concealed disdain. "Reverend Stone asked me if I could find something for her to do so she could stay busy. So, I created work for her to do in the office."

"Did you find the defendant to be a good worker?"

Reina stood up. "Objection, Your Honor. Relevance."

Judge Takahashi looked at Jerry. Jerry replied, "Your Honor, this witness' evidence speaks to the character of the defendant."

After a slight pause, the judge replied, "I'll allow it. Overruled."

Reina sat down. Jerry repeated his last question and Leann answered vaguely, "As the wife of my boss, I had no choice but to find her a good worker."

Jerry continued. "Could you please tell the court about the duties assigned to the defendant?"

"Yes, she did relatively simple chores of photocopying, supply stocking, and filing."

"Did she work regular hours?"

"No, not really. As I say, she could come and go as she pleased. When she wanted to put in a few hours, she did so. But she always kind of kept to herself. After the first few years, she started coming in after regular business hours, I guess so she wouldn't have to socialize with the rest of the office. I could always tell when she had been there though because, the next morning, the supplies were stacked, the filing was done, and such like that. About seven months ago, she stopped coming in altogether, without so much as a phone call or a thank you letter to me to say she wouldn't be coming back." Ms. Jones sniffed audibly at the lack of consideration for her position. Although she didn't say the words aloud, they were clearly implied - *after all I did for her.*

Jerry, glancing at his notes, asked, "Ms. Jones, did you notice a change in the defendant over the years?"

"Yes, I did."

"What kind of change?"

"Well, she became more . . . quiet. She seemed to me to be depressed and . . . even more anti-social, I would say."

Reina stood up. "Objection! Your Honor, the witness is not qualified to evaluate the mental state of my client."

The judge nodded. "Sustained. The court will strike the witness' last comment from the record."

Jerry nodded. "No further questions, Your Honor."

Reina rose for the cross-examination. "Ms. Jones, is it true that Maria faithfully performed the tasks you assigned to her?"

"Well, yes, I suppose so."

"And is it true that Maria spent many hours reorganizing the files into a more efficient system, often staying late into the night to do so?"

"Well, yes, she did reorganize the files. Yes, that's true."

"And is it true that my client Maria . . . ." Reina turned and gestured to Maria as she spoke. Her unfinished question lingered in the air as she stared at her client. Maria, who had, for over forty days and forty nights, sat impassive and unexpressive, was now crying. Tears streamed from her eyes and she appeared to be having a hard time breathing, her chest rising and falling in silent heaves and her nostrils flaring widely as she gulped for air.

Reina dropped her gesturing arm and turned to the Judge. "Your Honor, may I approach the bench?"

Judge Takahashi, who also turned to observe Maria when Reina stopped to stare at her, said to Reina and Jerry, "Counsel, approach the bench."

"Your Honor, I respectfully again request a continuance. My client has barely spoken more than a handful of words since her arrest. She has been unresponsive to my attempts to discuss the case with her and has completely stonewalled any attempts at communication." Realizing her inadvertent play on words, Reina quickly continued on, hoping the judge did not think she intentionally made a joke. Levity in Hashi's courtroom, intended or otherwise, did not go over well. "I feel justice cannot be served if, through no fault of my own, I have had no opportunity to adequately understand my client. It appears, now, that we may have broken through my client's emotional barrier and I request time to establish a deeper understanding of the facts, if my client is indeed ready to open up and talk."

Reina held her breath as Judge Takahashi considered the request. Finally, she spoke. "Court is adjourned for one week."

And she stood and walked out of the room as the bailiff quickly called out, "All rise."

Chapter 18

Before Maria left the room, Reina quietly asked her, "Are you ready to post bail?"

Maria nodded between her sobs.

"I'll pick you up in one hour."

Maria nodded again as the bailiff led her out of the courtroom.

Reina phoned her mother as she walked to her car. Her mom didn't answer her cell phone. Reina dialed the flight school.

"True Blue Aviation." Caite answered in a friendly, business voice.

"Hi Mom. Are you working the front desk today?"

"Only just for a minute. Julianna ran to the bank. Why? What's up?"

"Well, you got your wish. Maria is posting bail and getting out today. Court has been adjourned for a week."

"So you did ask for a . . . uh . . . continuing after all? You are a wonderful daughter to humor your mother's whims."

"Yeah, well, it didn't quite happen like that, but we did get the continuance, so that's what counts. Now, I need to do something with her and see what she has to say – if anything."

"Why don't you bring her here? I have an idea of where we might be able to take her, but I need to make some calls to confirm it."

"Okay, but are you sure you want to get involved in this?"

"Oh yes. I think I need to."

"Well, okay. I'll pick her up and we'll be there as soon as we can."

"See you then."

Several hours later, Reina pulled into the unpaved area behind True Blue Aviation. She waited for the usual cloud of dust to settle, and for Maria to gather up the pile of damp Kleenex on her lap, then led the way into the building. The place was empty except for Caite and Hawk, seated across from each other on the red leather lounge sofas. They were both leaning forward, kneecaps almost touching, deep in conversation.

Caite rose immediately and approached Maria. "Welcome," she said, embracing her in a warm hug.

"Maria, meet my mom, Caite Parsons," Reina provided introductions. "And this is Hawk Weston, a friend and Chief Flight Instructor here at True Blue."

Maria nodded shyly through the tears that had not stopped since their onset in the courtroom.

"It's a pleasure to meet you, Maria," said Caite gently. "Please have a seat here for a moment while I talk with Reina. Would you like some coffee? Tea?" Maria shook her head no. Reina followed her mother into the adjoining room.

"I've arranged a place for us to go," Caite told Reina. "I have a friend who lives out on the ocean, near La Push. He has a cabin we can use for a couple of days. He'll pick us up at Quillayute Airport and drive us to the cabin. Hawk has volunteered to go with us, if only to keep the woodstove primed with firewood. There is a front moving in off the coast of British Columbia, but if we leave now, we can be there in about an hour, well ahead of the weather."

"We'll take the 210?"

"Yes."

"Well, I don't have a better suggestion, and at least we'll be away from prying eyes, murderous thugs, and the media. Sure. Let's go."

"Has Maria ever been in a small aircraft?"

"I have no idea. However, she doesn't have too many other options, so I say we just go. The way she's been crying non-stop, she probably won't be aware of what's going on anyway."

"Okay then. The plane is pre-flighted, fueled, and ready to go. Hawk has already filed his flight plan with Flight Service, so your chariot awaits, my love."

"Thanks, Mama." Reina brushed her mother's cheek with a kiss. "You're the best!"

Maria made no protest when they escorted her out to the shiny blue and white Cessna on the ramp. She climbed into the back seat next to Caite, clutching a large box of fresh Kleenex. Caite helped Maria get her headset on and showed her how to adjust it. Reina entered the single access door of the P210, slid across the pilot's seat to the co-pilot's seat, and donned her headset. Happy to leave the flying to Hawk today, she wanted to concentrate on her client and any stray words Maria might drop.

Hawk picked up his IFR clearance from Center and taxied into position for takeoff. Reina watched his smooth handling of the big aircraft with admiration. He wears airplanes like a second skin, she thought, easily and effortlessly. As Hawk gazed straight ahead through the windscreen for the climb-out, Reina covertly studied his profile. In the close confines of the cockpit, she could see the small bump in his nose and the widely flared nostrils. A strong nose. It took strong features to pull off a pony tail. His eyes were hooded, like a hawk's, and he sported a day's dark growth on his chin. When her focus moved to his lips, and how they grazed the microphone as he spoke, she quickly diverted her thoughts, aware of the delicious flutter crawl-stroking through her gut. As if feeling her eyes on him, Hawk glanced over at her with his trademark half-smile and she looked quickly down. Fidgeting with the suddenly important task of straightening the cord on her headset, she asked, "Quillayute doesn't have any instrument approaches, does it?"

"No," he replied. "I filed for Port Angeles, just in case that weather system we've been watching arrives sooner than forecast. I'm hoping we'll be able to cancel when we get close and land at Quillayute, VFR."

They turned west after takeoff and scooted quickly across Puget Sound and along the north end of the Olympic Peninsula, over the "jagged peaks of death" as Hawk liked to call the rugged Olympic Mountains.

With the weather system continuing to build to the north, they arrived in clear skies, albeit heavy winds flowing out of the southeast toward the atmospheric low created by the storm. Just as planned, Hawk cancelled his instrument flight plan with the air traffic controller and made a visual approach to Quillayute Airport. He executed an expert crosswind landing on runway 04, thankful to find the runway at the remote airport in fairly decent condition. They taxied to the deserted tie-down area. There was not another aircraft or vehicle in sight. With the towering trees moaning in the increasing winds, the dark clouds gathering on the horizon, and the dilapidated buildings with broken windows and doors hanging crooked on their hinges, the place had a mournful, almost ominous atmosphere. It felt like a ghost town.

Caite announced that she'd texted her friend, Steve, to say they'd arrived. He was on his way.

After securely tying down the aircraft and locking it up tight, they noticed a dark SUV at the far end of the airport. As there was no other vehicle in sight, Caite waved to the car, assuming it was her friend. Just then, a beat-up, old, blue van came careening around the corner and drove up to them. A tall, stooped man with a toothy grin and long, gray braids jumped out and wrapped Caite in a big bear hug. Caite introduced Steve to her flight mates and they climbed in for the quick ride to the cabin on the ocean. Glancing over to where she'd seen the SUV, Reina noticed it was gone.

Steve unlocked the rustic A-frame log structure with a hide-a-key located on a nail under the eaves. He dropped a grocery bag on the kitchen countertop. It contained a few essentials: a gallon of milk, a loaf of bread, a bag of Doritos, and a tub of fresh blueberries his sister had picked that morning. He turned on the water and hot water heater for them and showed them a wood shed full of dry firewood, informing them that the woodstove, their only source of heat, smoked like a wet campfire. "You can just wave a blanket over it if you need me," he joked. Before leaving, he pulled out a rusty old axe from his van for chopping the wood, and told them to help themselves to whatever food in the cupboards the mice hadn't already devoured. With a toss of his braids and a wave of his hand, he drove off with a promise to check on them the next day.

  Reina put the bag, with the few clothing items they'd been able to scrape together from the flight school broom closet, on the bed in the small downstairs bedroom. The only other furniture in the room, besides the homemade log bed, was a rustic log dresser with drawers that threatened to break kneecaps if opened too far. Although the drawers were empty, the room's small closet overflowed with cast-off but still serviceable clothing.

  Excellent, thought Reina, it's either that or the linen skirt and silk blouse I found stuffed in the closet at True Blue. She slipped out of her courtroom attire and pulled on a pair of baggy corduroy jeans and an extra large T-shirt with a huge wolf face on the front. Fortunately, she had already swapped out her expensive pumps for the pair of flat-soled flying shoes she always carried with her. She rejoined the others in the main room, smiling at Hawk's comment that three of her could probably fit in the borrowed clothing.

In Reina's absence, Maria had dried her eyes just long enough to climb up the stairs to the small loft. She placed her large purse on the thin mattress that covered most of the loft floor. She then lay down next to her bag, wrapping her arms around it, and curling into a fetal position. Reina climbed up to see if she could talk to her, but upon seeing her in this shell-shocked state, she simply placed another box of Kleenex next to the still-weeping woman, covered her with a blanket, and descended back down the loft ladder. Tomorrow would be soon enough.

Hawk threw his sleeping bag in the corner, to be used later, outside under the stars. He placed his duffel bag under the corner table and started to unpack the bag of food they'd scrounged from the hangar supplies. The hodgepodge of food included canned soups, hotdogs from the Barbecue last weekend, coffee, tea, mini cheese and cracker packages from the mountain flying survival backpack, and two bottles of wine from a recent aircraft roll-out party. It might not be a gourmet dinner, but they wouldn't starve.

Hawk, Caite, and Reina walked out to the front porch to gaze in appreciation at the stunning ocean view. The rhythmic crashing of the waves engulfed their silence as Hawk pointed to the dark cloud mass approaching from the northwest. Caite nodded and Reina glanced up at the moss covered roof, wondering how waterproof this old cabin might be. She suspected they were going to find out.

They went back inside and prepared a campy dinner of canned soup and cheese and crackers. Caite climbed half-way up the ladder to invite Maria down, but she came back and reported that Maria hadn't moved. "The poor thing must be exhausted from all that crying," Caite said, shaking her head. "Well, at least she'll be able to find some peace in her sleep."

Chapter 19

Maria had indeed entered a deep sleep, but the dreams that had finally arrived destroyed any hope of peacefulness. While in jail, Maria had not dreamt a single dream, almost as if her mind had gone dormant, as if all emotions and memories were locked out by the bars that locked her in. Now, the floodgates of recollections, layering one on top of the other in her head, washed that detachment away.

I have to make them go away, go away. Please go away. . . .

Oh Peter, sweet Peter, I need you by my side . . . your place is with me . . . so sick, so sick, with your puffy gray face . . . Stop looking at me! Stop talking to me! The husband is the head of the wife, the wife, the wife, Christ is the savior of the body, the body, the body. Stop it! Stop it! Stop the echoes . . . Oh little one. Sad brown-face, little Lin. I wanted to bring you home. I did. I would have carried you out of the orphanage. Sweet little thing, your arms so skinny, so skinny you don't want to let me go . . . .

Mama! I wanted to be there. I'm sorry, I'm sorry, I wanted to be there for you . . . How would you like to go with me to visit the orphanage? I'm thinking about purchasing it. You'd like that wouldn't you? Peter, I love you! Yes let's do it . . . Why are you so angry? Don't you understand my mission is to serve all of God's children, children, children . . . .

The judge is so cold. She hates me. She wants to hang me . . . Oh God, why? And the angry crowd, why do they hate me? Why does everyone hate me? There's Sarah and Rebekah, do they hate me too? And Mary standing there waiting for me to die . . . Oh, God, why have you forsaken me? Oh my God, not Wong! Please. Please don't lock the door behind me. Don't, please don't. I hate him so. I hate him. Oh Peter . . . Can you say you are without sin? Is it your place to cast judgment? It is none but the Lord God's place to judge, so be thee careful . . . And sweet little Jimmy Lai, poor thing, poor thing, poor thing . . . silly, round-faced Shari, laughing about nothing . . . Oh God, the soft feel of Simone's lips. So soft, so soft. And Leann's lips, her huge red lips . . . Back!

Leave me alone, leave me alone. Why do those doors keep slamming? I keep running, but I can't get out! I can't get out. The hallway never ends . . . My feet are stuck and the doors rush past. I can't move. I can't get out! Let me out! No!

The images flashed through her mind like a series of video clips, clear, then blurring, then spinning around her like a cyclone. She squeezed her eyes closed tighter, covered her ears and rocked her head, moaning, "No, No, No."

On the floor below, Reina and her mother, who had retired to bed, looked at each other with concern. Reina again considered the possibility of mental health issues. The psychologist who evaluated Maria had found no mental anomalies. However, psychological problems that appeared only intermittently could be difficult to identify. Reina fervently hoped Maria would open up to her inquiries tomorrow.

Chapter 20

As anticipated, the storm hit in the middle of the night. Reina awoke to the sound of gale force winds. She lay under the warm covers, next to her softly breathing mother, and listened to the trees creaking and groaning in the winds. Huge conifers, towering over 100 feet tall, surrounded the little cabin. Any one of them could demolish the tiny structure if toppled in their direction. She heard a loud crack in the distance and then a hollow thud as the winds claimed, and the earth welcomed, an evergreen victim. Reina's nerves were edgy, but more in excitement than fear. She loved the power of the wind. With the trees creaking, the wind howling and the waves crashing, she knew she wouldn't get back to sleep. Quietly edging out of bed, she pulled on an old flannel shirt and a pair of leggings from the closet of bounty, and tiptoed to the main room, closing the bedroom door quietly behind her.

    She edged her way over to the old sofa in the pitch black room, recalling that she had seen a candle and matches on the little log coffee table. She felt the edge of the sofa and sat down, jumping up with a little squeak at the muffled "oof" the bumpy sofa emitted. She found the matches and lit the candle, then turned to see Hawk grinning at her from the couch.

"Don't let me stop you," he whispered. "Have a seat. It's on me."

She made a face at him and whispered back, "I thought you were sleeping outside?"

"I was. Until this great survival sense I've cultivated over the years suggested I might want to take cover inside."

"Hmmm, I thought you were braver . . . ." She shook her head in mock disappointment.

"Brave, yes. Stupid, no. When a large tree limb impaled itself into the ground two feet from my head I decided to relocate." He showed her his forearm with a large scratch where the ragged edge of the limb's side branches had scraped him.

"*Diablo*! Did you put anything on that?" Reina asked.

"No, but I think I'll survive. What are you doing up?"

"Couldn't sleep. Wild winds always make me restless. I'm a little wired anyway, with all that's been going on. I kind of wish I had a gun, being out here in the remote woods like this."

"Got you covered," smiled Hawk, patting the stuffed bedroll he used as a pillow.

"Really? I've always wanted to learn how to shoot. Maybe tomorrow you can teach me?"

"Maybe. If you're good . . . . "

"Yeah, if you're lucky . . . . " Reina rolled her eyes. She pushed his feet aside so she could sit down. "Quillayute doesn't have a weather station, so I'm gonna check Port Angeles weather to see what they're reporting for winds." She scrolled through her cell phone's contacts, which included most of the local airport's weather reporting stations, and dialed. The automated voice said winds were still out of the south at 34 knots, gusting to 41. Strong, but hopefully not enough to overwhelm their aircraft, which they'd left securely tied down.

Reina tucked her legs, Indian style, under the oversized flannel shirt, using it like a tent to keep her warm.

"That's a fetching outfit," Hawk whispered, "but if you want to get warm, the best place to do so is in here with me." He lifted a corner of his bedroll.

Reina felt her gut contract and her heart flutter as she considered the invitation - or was it a challenge - for a moment.

"I'll just hold you, I promise." The heat in his eyes contradicted the coolness of his words.

Holding sounded good, but she wasn't sure her will-power could withstand Hawk's charm.

"As much as I'd love to take you up on that offer, I think I'd better get back to sleep. Who knows what tomorrow holds." Reina unwrapped herself from the flannel and took herself back to the safety of her own bedroom. She slipped back under the covers next to her mother, being careful not to brush her icicle toes against her mom's legs in the small space. Eventually she slept, with only her own arms to hold her.

Chapter 21

Morning brought a clear blue sky and a gentle breeze off the coast. As Reina made coffee and toast, Maria came down the loft stairs, clutching her box of Kleenex and still dripping tears, but at a somewhat reduced rate. Reina wondered if Maria would eventually become so dehydrated from crying that she'd dry up and drift away like a dead autumn leaf. It wouldn't take much of a gust to carry her away now; she was alarmingly thin and frail. Reina encouraged her to eat, but she only nibbled a little piece of dry toast and a few blueberries.

After breakfast, Caite and Hawk went out to assess the damage and clear some of the debris away from the cabin and woodshed perimeter. Reina sat down with Maria.

"Maria," she said gently, "I know it is difficult for you to talk about this, but I need you to tell me what you can about your life. If you help me understand what led you to act as you did, what reasons you had for your actions, it will help me help you. Can you do that?"

Maria nodded tearfully.

"I've read your confession, so I understand what you told the police." Reina paused as Maria nodded again. "Can you tell me now what happened to lead to the poisoning of your husband?"

The drip of tears turned back into a waterfall. Maria's lips quivered and she looked like a deer in headlights. Reina waited hopefully for a moment, then Maria inhaled one big, shuddering sob, shook her head no, and ran into the bathroom.

Reina rolled her head back and glared at the ceiling. *Patience, patience, patience. Not my strong suit.* She sat for a few minutes listening to the sounds of crows croaking outside. She suddenly had the urge to stand up and caw loudly herself. Just then, Reina heard a vehicle approaching up the gravel driveway. Opening the heavy log front door, she saw the old blue van pull to a stop near the cabin steps. As she joined Hawk and her mom outside, she whistled, "*Diablo*, look at all this stuff! That wind wreaked some serious havoc. I hope the 210 is okay?"

"Yeah, we were just talking about that," said Hawk. "I tied her down pretty well, so I think she'll be fine. As long as no trees landed on her."

"Hi!" Steve greeted them with a raised hand as he climbed out of the driver's seat. "I wanted to make sure you weren't all lying crushed under a massive cedar," he smiled broadly.

"Thanks for the gruesome visual," Hawk laughed, "but no, we're all okay. We were just clearing up some of the detritus from the storm."

Steve studied the noisy birds in the large tree above them. "It is unusual to see so many together in one place," he said.

"I see groups of crows all the time in Seattle," offered Reina. "The city variety has a harsher sound, though."

"Those would be crows, these are ravens," Steve replied. "Did you know if you see a flock of crows, you're seeing murder?"

"So, what is the difference between a crow and a raven?"

"Size, and sound, and tail feathers are different, for starters," Steve answered. "But most importantly, Crow is just a cousin to Raven, who created the world."

"Well, it never hurts to have important relatives, I suppose," Reina laughed. As an afterthought, she added, "So, if it is a *murder* of crows, what is a flock of ravens called?"

"An unkindness," Steve grinned, "probably because clever Raven is a terrible trickster."

Steve folded his hands across his chest and turned in a circle, surveying the tree bits scattered around the cabin. "Looks like we'll be set for firewood this winter." He seemed pleased with the number of large limbs downed from the storm and especially the one massive trunk lying about a hundred feet from the woodshed. Turning back to the cabin, he said, "Wow, look at that one. It's gotta be stuck three feet in the ground." Steve pointed to a long limb that stood, impaled like a spear, standing straight out of the ground.

"Yeah, that's the one that landed two feet from my head," Hawk said, glancing at Reina. "It inspired me to relocate inside."

"Close calls like that are considered a good omen to my people," Steve responded, nodding solemnly. He then added with his toothy grin, "Or a warning. Depends." Turning toward Caite, he said, "Anyway, I'm running in to PA for a few errands. Thought maybe you'd want to go with me for supplies? It's a long drive, but I try to go in once a week to stock up."

"PA?" Reina repeated.

"Port Angeles. Takes less time to say, so most of us out here abbreviate it to PA."

"Oh, well I've got a few things I'd like to do in Port Angeles. I mean PA," Reina corrected herself with a smile. "And it doesn't look like I'm going to make any headway here, so I might as well join you."

"And I'll join *you*," Hawk said to Reina, adding in a side whisper, "as your bodyguard of course." Turning to Steve he asked, "Is it okay if we swing by the airport to verify the airplane survived the storm okay?"

"No problem," said Steve. "It's on the way."

"Great," said Reina. "Just let me grab a few things and we'll get going. What about you, Mom?"

"I think I'll stay here with Maria," Caite answered. "You two go and have fun." As an afterthought she added, "Bring back some marshmallows. Maybe we'll have a campfire tonight."

Chapter 22

A quick stop at Quillayute Airport eased their concerns about the aircraft. The Cessna had weathered the storm without damage. A large log lay across the runway, but Steve and Hawk were able to roll it out of the way, while Reina worked on some of the smaller storm debris covering the taxiways. The whole time they were at the airport, Reina had the sensation of being watched. She shrugged off the feeling, attributing it to the creepy, old, dilapidated hangars. Their glassless windows and doors did look a bit like gaping black eye sockets.

As they continued into Port Angeles, Steve kept the conversation lively with stories of how they had rescued teenagers out of the woods all summer long. The popularity of the "Twilight" series put remote Forks and the Quillayute Indian Reservation on the map, at least for vampire and werewolf fans. "As you saw last night," he commented, "the weather changes rapidly around here. That, and the marine fog that can stay for days, makes it real easy to get lost. It doesn't take long, even during the summer, to die of exposure when a day venture into the woods, in shorts and t-shirts, turns into an overnight ordeal. We've had a few cases of hypothermia, but so far we haven't lost anyone to weather . . . although we may have lost a few to vampires, I dunno."

As Reina laughed and shook her head, she noticed, in the side view mirror, a dark SUV some distance behind them. It looked a lot like the one that had been at the airport after they landed. Of course, half the Northwest population drove dark SUVs, she reasoned, but she decided to keep an eye on it anyway. She thought for a concerned moment of her mom and Maria, alone at the cabin. Maybe Hawk should have stayed with them. But then again, she had no reason to believe anyone threatened Maria. So far, all the attacks had been on her. She hoped to find out more this afternoon about the people who seemed to have their sights set on her. Port Angeles was home to Stone's shipping company as well as an adoption agency he founded and one of his chain of bookstores. She planned to do a little snooping . . . .

However, for her own peace of mind, she made a quick phone call to her mother, who answered cheerfully on the first ring.

"How's everything?" asked Reina.

"Fine. Maria and I are going to take a walk on the beach."

"Oh, okay, well be careful. You know, watch for strangers and such."

"I will," her mother assured her, "and I'll carry a big stick with me to fight off any aggressors."

"Okay. Love you, Mom."

"Love you, too, honey."

Steve headed toward the waterfront area of Port Angeles. The city had served for many years as a mill town for the huge old-growth conifer trees harvested out of the

Olympic Peninsula forests. In more recent years, tourism had risen in importance, with one of the city's attractions being the *Blackball Ferry* that transported passengers and cars across the Strait of Juan de Fuca to the charming Canadian city of Victoria, on scenic Vancouver Island. Fortunately, the tourist crowds near the ferry and downtown core thinned out as Steve drove west toward Ediz Hook, the long sand spit that extended three miles out into the Strait. They easily found a parking space on a side road near the water. Port Angeles was small enough, Steve said, that most of his errands could be run on foot. He swapped cell phone numbers with Reina and Hawk and gave them an extra key to the van. "If you need to use it to get somewhere, go right ahead," he offered. "Just let me know, text or call me, and I'll do the same for you if I move it. Otherwise, we'll just meet back here at five p.m."

    Reina googled Stone's business locations and she and Hawk headed in the direction of the Peninsula Shipping Company office, just down the street on the wharf side. She could see, at a distance, a dark SUV inside the warehouse bay. As they neared, the big overhead door of the building closed, and a small, dark-haired man hurried into the adjacent office. They approached the office door just as a black Hummer passed them slowly on the road. Reina grabbed Hawk's arm nervously as the vehicle pulled abreast of their position. She saw a man and woman smile at them and a back seat full of freckly kids waved to her out the open window as the vehicle leisurely rolled past. Probably just a family on vacation, thought Reina, I am getting way too paranoid. Hawk looked down at her with his trademark half-smile and she felt an electrical current zip from his arm through her hand. She dropped her hand quickly in embarrassment and confusion.

They opened the glass front door into Peninsula Shipping's office. The room, small and slightly dingy, boasted a dark brown carpet, stained from years of work-boot traffic. Two chairs bracketed the far corner with a small glass table between them. The table looked like it could use a scrubbing. Reina saw no sign of the man who'd just entered. He must have slipped out the back door. A large, cluttered reception desk filled the rear half of the room. Behind the desk sat a heavily-jowled woman with short, spiky, brown hair and broad, powerful-looking shoulders. If a pit bull could become human, it would be her. She looked up at them suspiciously. "Can I help you?" she growled.

"I hope so," Reina responded in a crisp no-nonsense tone. "We are setting up a branch of a large import/export business in the downtown area. I'm here to research the best local options for shipping our product from overseas."

"What is the name of the company?"

"I'm sorry. I'm not at liberty to say."

Pitbull's nostrils flared. "Well then, where do most of your products originate?"

"Generally from Asia."

"And what type of products would those be?"

"Again, I am not at liberty to discuss such details at this time," Reina raised her eyebrows with just the right touch of haughtiness to squelch prying questions. "We simply wish to get a sense of the strength of the various shipping companies in the area as we could not possibly align ourselves with a less-than-solid business. My objective is to determine whether your packaging, storage, and shipping methods would be acceptable to our corporate managers. We simply cannot afford to have damaged merchandise as a result of sloppy handling. In addition, I need some assurance that you are experienced in the regulatory matters and customs issues in international transport. Long delays due to inadequate customs manifests would be entirely unacceptable."

"Hmmph, we could discuss your needs, I guess," Pitbull barked. "We have a solid track record and virtually all of our shipping business is with companies in Asia."

"Perhaps it would be possible to get a tour of your facility?" Reina glanced out the window behind Pitbull Woman as she asked the question and was stunned to see the brown-clad backside of a familiar man walking next to the small dark-haired man they'd seen slip into the office earlier. Either Jerry had a doppelganger, or opposing counsel just walked into that warehouse.

"Unfortunately, I don't have anyone available right now to provide a tour. However, I'd be happy to take your name and contact number to arrange something in the near future. Do you have a business card?"

"Yes, I do," Reina replied without offering to give it to her. She added decisively. "I'll contact you if we wish to pursue this matter further. Thank you, and good day."

Reina turned and walked briskly out the door that Hawk rushed to hold open for her.

They proceeded several steps down the street before Hawk whistled low under his breath and said, "Whew! That was really something to see you in action. I suspect that pit bull is used to being able to intimidate people a little better than she did with you."

Reina laughed. "I had an . . . unconventional childhood, you know. We moved around a lot and I often had to make up imaginary friends to play with. I guess I learned to play-act and pretend pretty well. It stands me in good stead in the courtroom too."

"Unconventional? With a mother like yours? No?" Hawk laughed, but Reina didn't respond. They walked in silence for a few steps before Hawk asked, "Well, where to next, Boss Lady?"

Reina didn't answer, her mind preoccupied with seeing Jerry in Port Angeles. He was developing a creepy habit of turning up everywhere she went.

"Reina?" Hawk repeated.

"Oh, sorry about that." She glanced at her smart phone's GPS to get her bearings. "Um, let's see, we need to go this way," and she headed up the hill away from the waterfront.

Chapter 23

The sun shone brightly upon Maria as she walked alongside Caite, down the long stretch of sandy beach. They both wore old, worn, cardigan sweaters, a few sizes too big, scrounged from the bounteous cabin closet. Maria hugged her baggy, green and brown sweater closely to her sides, only removing her hands from their death grip on the faded material to periodically loop a stray strand of wind-whipped hair out of her mouth with her forefinger. She watched the ground as she walked.

Caite's purple, striped sweater, ending just above her knee-caps, flapped loosely in the sea breeze and her arms swung freely at her sides. Lifting her face up toward the sun and seaward toward the salty air, she sighed aloud, "Ah, this feels wonderful."

They walked for some time in silence along the long, deserted stretch of hard-packed sand, passing massive piles of the sea's cast-off driftwood dance partners strewn upon the beach. The great waves had left behind heaps of huge, blackened stumps from some ancient forest fire and whole trees with roots like wild medusa hair. There were shiny red Madrona limbs, polished as smooth as glass from years of sea-dancing, and wizened, waterlogged, yellow limbs - distant travelers from a foreign land.

After walking companionably for a while, Caite pointed to a rustic lean-to of sorts. Where the firm sandy shore started to merge with the eroding bluff, someone had turned big sticks of driftwood, crisscrossed and leaning against each other, into a cozy little shelter. A small log had been placed underneath the driftwood arch, just the right size for a little seating bench. Maria followed Caite over to the make-shift beach alcove and they sat down under the sturdy structure. They sat in silence for some time. Maria's eyes were still wet, either from tears or from the salty breeze.

Finally, Caite said, "I'd like to tell you a story."

Maria lifted her downcast eyes to Caite and Caite began, with the opening words of all fairy tales.

"Once upon a time, there was a girl. A girl with stars in her eyes. She liked to write poetry and sing and dance. When she was 16, she moved to a new town. Not knowing a soul at her new high school, she felt very lonely. Then, the varsity football captain began to pursue her, telling her he adored her and introducing her to all his friends and family. He treated her like a princess.

When she was barely 18, they got married. He worked at the local food processing plant, same as his dad and mom, and he hoped to gradually work his way up the ladder to foreman. They went to football games on the weekends and watched TV on the week-nights. She made him nice dinners from scratch and kept the house clean and put on the sexy lingerie that he liked on Saturday evenings. On Sundays they went to church and had dinner with his folks.

After a couple of years, he started leaving her home alone on Fridays, saying he was going 'out with friends.' He complained she didn't make enough money at her day job at the grocery store to pay for her evening college classes. He told her to quit school; they couldn't afford it, and he didn't like her to be out at night anyway. He said he was tired of her showing off with the "fancy food" she cooked. He wanted good American meat and potatoes. Sex became less and less frequent and he began joking to friends that she must be sterile since she wasn't pregnant yet.

The more he criticized her, the harder she tried, but it seemed she couldn't do anything to please him. If she offered to help him with something, he'd caustically ask if she wanted to do it herself if she was so smart. He would complain about the way the house looked and when she tried to fix it up he'd criticize the changes she made. It seemed that whenever anything went wrong, got misplaced, or just plain didn't go his way, it was always her fault.

Little by little, she died away. At his suggestion, she stopped writing poetry because he felt it made her 'too moody.' She stopped singing because he said she sang 'off-key.' And she stopped dancing because he thought it was 'embarrassing.' He complained that she had changed, and she had. The joie de vivre that had been her brightest quality had dimmed to darkness.

One day, she gathered up what little bits of her were left and walked out the door. She never looked back.

She withdrew the $1734 in her account from her paychecks at the grocery store and bought a bus ticket to

Cleveland. In Cleveland, she bought one way airfare to Barbados and a glass of champagne at the terminal bar. In Barbados, she purchased boat fare to a small island in the Grenadines. On the island, she slept on the beach, heart and body wrung out beyond caring. The next day, she walked through the small town and just kept going. The rutted dirt road wound through papaya and palm trees. Eventually, she found herself in front of a rusty gate with a long overgrown drive that led toward the shore. At the end of the drive she found a rickety pole building where singing natives were harvesting limes from the plantation. She asked for the office and the shiny black face under the stained bandanna nodded toward a squat building off toward the edge of the sea. At the office, they gave her a job doing accounts. She made money to eat and rent a room, plus all the limes she could want. It was enough.

She ate fruit and sometimes fresh fish. And she swam in the sea. She swam and swam with nothing in her mind or her heart. She emptied her wounded soul in the sea of souls and swam away from it.

One day, she started walking and didn't stop. She climbed around huge craters in the island's dirt street, left from monsoon rains. She passed iguanas sitting like Buddhas in trees and crews of natives clearing brush with machetes and herds of cows wandering down the middle of the road. She slept under the protection of mango trees. She ended up, finally, at the end of the island, in front of a huge hotel, built like a dream on a bluff in the middle of nowhere for no one. It was deserted and she was exhausted. She slept on the porch, in a worn wicker chair.

She awoke to a cheerful British accent. "Good morning, Dahling" as though it were the most natural thing in the world for him to find her here, at the end of the world, asleep in his chair.

He fed her. He taught her how to spearfish and crack coconuts with a conch shell and weave a hammock from reeds and mix a mean gin and tonic. He asked nothing of her. Her heart and soul were as empty as the vast blue sky and her body was like the earth. In time, she opened her earth and sky to him, as natural as the seasons, and his loving gave new life to her.

Soon after, she left his vacant hotel, on a small boat rowed by a Rasta man who sang as he rowed. She ended up on a small island in a chain of small islands. Wandering in the tiny town, she found a hidden side alley lined on one side with curious stalls displaying dyed fabrics, colorful paintings, wooden bird-cages, pungent spices. Oddly, there was neither customer nor proprietor anywhere in sight. The alley was so narrow, she couldn't walk down its crooked path without ducking under the overhanging trees on the opposite side. It narrowed more as she continued past the odd vacant stalls full of curiosities, past an aviary full of colorful birds, up the hillside past several deserted bars with cracked pottery mugs and dark beaten wood stools and wild markings on the walls. And not a human soul did she pass.

She climbed the serpentine path to a raised hilltop platform with a bench carved from the root of a tree. The view out over the sea was breathtaking. Dark storm clouds approached over the horizon. She watched the black *billows race toward the harbor, spitting angry spurts of lightning. A dragonfly landed on her right shoulder. As she turned to smile at it, she saw deep steps cut into the banyan tree to the side of the platform. At the top of the steps was a raised platform with a straw roof constructed over it. On the platform she found a round mattress of straw layered with batik covers and pillows. Carved in the tree trunk at the foot of the bed, a sign read, "Welcome, all who are weary - stay as long as you care to stay."*

And so she stayed until the child was born. Her beautiful daughter, who would be queen of her own universe and master of her own destiny.

After six months, she touched the baby's feet to the ground for the first time, allowing her infant deity to become human, and she and the child left their tree home. She found an island in the archipelago that had a bar she could tend and a little hut in which they could live. They spent little money on food and even less on clothes, living in the sand and sea and sun like natives.

Eventually, they left the islands for France. In the salty marshland of the French Camargue, she found a job feeding the manadiers and gardians — the ranchers and cowboys who worked the land. She met a man there who reminded her how to sing with the wind and who taught her how to fly like a bird. It was there, by the sea, she discovered the true meaning of love, without limits or barriers.

And so every year, this woman returns to the sea to celebrate the most important lesson she ever learned: that love does not involve ownership or control or manipulation; true love is as free and grand and limitless as the sea and as uncontainable as the sky."

    Maria's tears had stopped as she listened, mesmerized by Caite's melodic voice. She sat very still as Caite ended her fairy tale story. For a long time, she sat looking out over the crashing waves to the distant horizon. Finally, she turned to Caite. "Thank you" she said quietly and gave her a gentle hug. They walked back in peaceful silence to the cabin in the woods on the edge of the boundless sea.

Chapter 24

Reina checked her phone GPS to verify the location of their next stop, the adoption agency Stone had established for the boys from their orphanage in Taiwan. They agreed to pose as man and wife, a thought that caused that quiver in Reina's belly again. She looked sideways at Hawk and saw him trying to stifle a grin.

Located just two blocks up from the waterfront, in what used to be a residential district, the adoption agency was in a row of old homes, which had long since been made over into attorney or accountant or dentist offices. The address they sought turned out to be a large, Victorian home with a discreet sign over the door that read "Stone Home, USA." They knocked on the door and then entered. A small, blonde girl greeted them in the foyer with a smile and led them into what may have been the sitting room or parlor at one time. Now transformed into an office, the room contained a single desk and a few waiting chairs. The girl sat down behind the tidy little desk, placed strategically in front of a huge map of the world that had red pins sticking out from various spots. She smiled invitingly.

Reina introduced herself and Hawk as Mr. and Mrs. Jones and announced that they were here to inquire about adopting a little boy. The cute little blonde smiled again and asked them to have a seat, pointing to the two chairs in front of her desk.

She started into her spiel, "Well, you've come to the right place. We bring boys from our orphanage, Stone Home, in Taiwan and facilitate their adoptions to families here in the US. We have found homes for boys all over the country, as you can see by the map behind me." She turned around to point at the red pins on the map, in case they had missed it. She then turned back to continue her rehearsed speech. "You may not know that many of our boys also have beautiful singing voices, having been trained for the boys' choir on *The Rock*."

Reina nodded.

"May I ask how you heard about us?" she inquired, picking up her pen and holding it poised for important notes.

"Well, we know the Stones a little, and hearing they were involved in the adoption business, we thought we might find what we were looking for here," Reina explained.

"Ah, you know the Stones . . . ." The girl looked happy, but a little confused. "Well, we could help you here, or you could go directly through the Stones themselves. They often help personal friends who are looking to adopt. Was it a Special Adoption you were looking for?"

"Um, yes, that's it," Reina replied, thinking to herself, *who would* not *want a Special one?*

"Oh, well, those types of adoptions, for Reverend Stone's particular friends, are handled directly through him and his personal assistants at Stone Kingdom."

"Oh," said Reina, fumbling a little with where to go on that piece of information. "Well, I hate to bother them, with all they're going through right now." Reina looked saddened by her supposed friends' travails. "Maybe you could tell me if there is an advantage to a Special Adoption? Is the process expedited or streamlined?"

"Well, I'm not sure exactly," the blonde confided. "I just know that some of the luckiest boys have been placed in wonderful new homes directly through the Stones themselves, not through our agency."

"Oh. Okay. Well, thank you very much for your time. I guess I'll just talk to Peter about it then."

"Oh, yes! Isn't it fabulous news about his miraculous recovery?" she gushed. "He has changed so many lives through his works, we just couldn't bear the thought of losing him!"

"Indeed, indeed," offered Hawk, speaking for the first time since their entrance into the building. "The Christian world would never be the same, that's for sure."

"Yes, that is so true," she blushed and smiled shyly at Hawk.

"Well, it was very nice to meet you. Thank you again for your time." Reina nodded politely as they headed to the door.

As they walked back toward the van, Reina asked in pseudo-exasperation, "Must you flirt with absolutely everyone?"

Hawk laughed aloud. "All I did was smile at her. But I'll admit, I felt kinda like the Wolf with Little Red Riding Hood. I could have eaten her up in one bite."

"Really?" Reina rolled her eyes at him. "Thanks loads for sharing, but that's more information than I need to know."

Hawk just laughed and put his arm around Reina's shoulder for quick squeeze. "Hey, I think I like this detective stuff. Maybe I should change careers. I could be *The Flying Detective.* There might be a little niche for me there. What do you think?"

"I think someone's looking into our van windows, that's what I think, Sherlock." Reina nodded in the direction of the van, still a block away. They watched as a tall thin man stood peering into the front window of the van, cupping his eyes with his hands to block the sun's glare. After a moment, he stepped back and looked around furtively. He apparently saw Reina and Hawk watching him, because he suddenly turned in the opposite direction and walked off at a quick pace, his hands shoved into his pockets and his head scrunched down into his shirt collar.

Reina looked at Hawk with raised eyebrows. He responded lightheartedly, "If I had a moustache, I'd twirl it right now between my fingers and say in a fake accent, 'Hmmmm, highly suspicious.' Isn't that what detectives do?"

Reina replied with a chuckle, "How about something more useful, like checking the vehicle for tampering?"

"Ah, elementary, my dear Watson," he said, as they reached the van. "I'm way ahead of you." He dropped forward onto his hands in pushup stance and lowered his belly to the sidewalk. Reina tried not to notice how nicely his jeans seemed to fit his rear. After peering for several minutes at the underside of the van, he nimbly pushed himself upright, slapped his hands together to clear them of sidewalk grit, nodded knowingly at Reina, and marched to the front of the vehicle. He popped open the hood and stared intently at the engine. "Hmmm," he said, stroking his chin thoughtfully.

"Do you know what you're looking for?" Reina asked doubtfully.

"Actually, I have no idea. But don't tell anyone. I think this is the thing that makes the car go." He pointed at the engine.

Reina tried to stifle a giggle. "Seriously. How would you know a vehicle had been tampered with?"

"Again I say, 'Elementary, dear Watson.' There would be a big black thing with a timer attached right here. It would be ticking loudly and we would both dive for cover as it exploded like fireworks over our heads."

"Okay, I'm sorry I asked," Reina replied, unable to stop the giggle this time. She shook her head, "I'm not sure about your qualifications for detective though," and added with a shrug of her shoulders, "I'm just sayin'."

"Quite right," agreed Hawk. "I definitely will need more one-on-one training." The look in his hooded eyes belied his innocent smile.

Reina's legs suddenly felt a little rubbery. "Well," she said, looking away so he wouldn't see the warmth in her cheeks, "I'd like to run the van over to check out Stone's bookstore. Do you have any concerns about it?"

"Honestly, no. From the looks of that guy, I think he was scouting out a purse or camera to steal if he could pick the lock. But if you'd like, I'll start the van and you can stand off to the side to see if it blows me to pieces."

"No, that's okay. I'm with you. He looked more like a street bum than an explosives operative. Let's go check out that bookstore. You drive and I'll text Steve to let him know we've borrowed the van. We should be back well before five."

Despite her claimed nonchalance, Reina held her breath during the engine start. After the somewhat reluctant, but harmless, engagement of the ancient motor, they drove to the east end of town and parked in the lot next to *Simone's Stories*, one of the chain of Christian bookstores that Stone Kingdom Enterprises had started up across the country. Inside the store, there were a couple women perusing the Christian Living selections and a father and son in the Young Christians section.

Hawk and Reina wandered around for a bit, then Reina approached the sales counter. "Hello." She smiled engagingly at the tall, gray-haired woman behind the register. "I'm looking for more information about Reverend Stone. I have been *so* inspired by his miraculous recovery that I'd like to learn about how he came to his spiritual leadership. Do you know anything about him and his path to greatness?"

"Well, you're in luck!" replied the woman with a big grin, snapping the fingers of her left hand as she swung it across her thin torso in an enthusiastic, you-betcha gesture. "A new book has just been published that should answer all of your questions. It's an autobiography of Reverend Stone. He wrote it himself!" The woman sounded as pleased with this accomplishment as if she had been personally responsible for it. She plucked the volume off the countertop and proudly handed it to Reina.

"Wow!" replied Reina with feigned amazement, thinking sardonically *so that's what autobiography means*. "I definitely need to buy this," she flipped through the large glossy volume with Stone's smiling face completely filling the dust jacket. "Do you know Reverend Stone yourself?" Reina asked conversationally.

"I met him once," the woman beamed. "He came in many years ago with his wife and several of the people from his show."

"You met him?" Reina responded with appropriate awe. "What was he like?"

"Oh, very handsome, just like on TV. Although he is shorter than I expected." The lanky saleswoman shook her head in slight disappointment over the great man's diminutive stature. She continued on, thrilled to share her insider's information on such important people. "His wife is very quiet but nice. The other people with him were so lively and fun. I even met the two women who sing on stage with him." She preened a bit in self-importance. "The one is named, let's see, its either Tabitha or Talitha." She screwed her face up trying to remember. "I always get it confused with that girl on *Bewitched* . . . . Yes, it's Talitha," she confirmed triumphantly. "And the other one is Simone. That's easy because it's the same as the name of our bookstore."

"So it is," exclaimed Reina. "But, that's kind of odd," she continued, slightly puzzled. "Why would he name the bookstore after his assistant?"

"That's funny! I remember his wife asking him the very same question. When they unveiled the name, you know."

Reina didn't know and looked questioningly at the woman, encouraging her to continue.

"You see," the saleslady explained, "we are the flagship store. The first one to open back in 2004. I have worked here since day one." She squared her shoulders with pride. "Anyway, as I was saying, when they came to tour before the grand opening, and the name was unveiled, his wife asked him about the name, exactly like you just did. She asked why he had named their store after one of his assistants. He told her, rather sternly I thought, that Simone was derived from Simon, which was the original name for the apostle Peter. I remember he said it means 'He who hears' and then he asked her why she was questioning him, and he said something like, 'Do you not think I am one who hears the voice of God?'"

The woman leaned her tall frame across the counter toward Reina, clearly confiding in her. "I felt kinda bad for his wife, poor little thing. Especially when Reverend Stone came right out and said, in front of everyone, that she needed to spend some time studying her Bible a little better. The little wife just said, 'Yes, Peter' and retreated to the back of the store while the rest of the group finished the tour." She shook her head in sympathetic memory. After a moment, she came back to present day. "Well, my dear, shall I ring that up for you?"

"Yes," replied Reina, "that would be great. Thanks."

As Hawk and Reina crossed the parking lot back to the van, Reina waved the hefty book in the air and said with a laugh, "Well, if nothing else, I guess I can use it as a paperweight."

As they had some time to kill before meeting up with Steve, Reina decided to run into one of the clothing stores and purchase a pair of jeans and a tank top. Although she appreciated the cabin closet's plentiful supply of baggy, mismatched clothing, she preferred something a little less musty smelling. Hawk insisted on accompanying her, even while she shopped briefly in the panties aisle, claiming he needed to stay by her side at all times as her bodyguard. She drew the line, however, at letting him join her in the dressing room, despite the somersaults her stomach made at his offer. *Tempting . . . but not a good idea.*

They made a quick stop at a nearby grocery store to pick up a few food items to take back to the cabin, then called Steve to tell him they were ready whenever he was. Steve informed them he needed to stay in town tonight as his sister required some assistance with the remodeling project on her kitchen. "You two go ahead and take the van back to the cabin," he said. "I'll pick it up later. No worries."

Reina thanked him for his generosity and ended the call. Hawk offered to drive, and within a few minutes they were back on Highway 101 heading toward the coast. They drove most of the way in companionable silence. The road was nearly deserted except for the occasional logging truck roaring along the curvy roads at eye-popping speeds. *Those drivers must really know this road*. It didn't seem to faze Hawk when a logging truck zoomed past, but Reina couldn't help cringing a little. She vividly recalled a case one of her coworkers defended where the restraints of a logging truck had come loose as the vehicle crossed a bridge. The careening logs wreaked havoc to the traffic on the bridge and on the road below as well, killing three people - just one of those freak accidents for which you cannot prepare. In both pilot training and law school, Reina learned to think ahead to potential problems and have a plan to deal with them. *But really, what could you even do, on a bridge, with huge logs rolling toward you?* Reina mentally banished her irrational worry, as she had for years, with the reminder that ultimately, if it's your time to go, it's your time to go, and worrying about it wouldn't make one bit of difference. She turned her attention to the car some distance behind them. A maroon coupe of some kind.

    They arrived back at the cabin without seeing a single dark SUV or Hummer. When Reina saw her mom smiling at them from the front door, she felt all her concerns fade and waved in relief with the requested bag of marshmallows. Tonight would be a perfect evening for a beach campfire.

Chapter 25

Jerry followed the old blue van at some distance. Driving out of Peninsula Shipping, he'd seen the familiar figure of Reina Dessiner, oddly dressed in baggy sweat pants, entering the vehicle with some tall, long-haired, pony-tail guy. Out of curiosity, he'd trailed them to a bookstore, clothing store, and grocery store. Maybe it was her dad, but the way she looked at him didn't look all that daughterly. And frankly, the guy didn't look all that fatherly, especially when he'd watched Dessiner walk to the van from the clothing store in her new tight jeans. Maybe it was another of her lovers. The thought of her slutting it up with the guy made Jerry lick his thick lips in anticipation. He liked to watch, and always carried a set of binoculars for just such a situation.

Keeping a respectable distance behind the van, he began to wish he'd filled up on gas. *Who knew they were going out into the boondocks for their tryst?* But the thought of outdoors sex kept him going, excited at the possibilities. He imagined her naked on the moss, or being rammed against a tree and almost closed his eyes in ecstasy. *Better watch the road. Goddamn crazy truck drivers!*

When the van finally pulled into a dirt driveway, he drove past the entry, then looped back to park a couple hundred feet down the road. He grabbed his binoculars and worked his way into the undergrowth of the woods that lined the driveway. The bramble of Oregon Grapes and Salmonberries clutched at his brown suit trousers, making progress slow as he tried to avoid any serious damage to his daily uniform. Coming to a clearing, he stood just behind the tree line and focused his inexpensive, but trusty, Bushnells on the small cabin and waited.

***

    While the women prepared food to take down to the beach, Hawk chopped wood for their campfire. Standing at the sink peeling carrots, Reina could hear his laptop blasting "O Sole Mio" by The Three Tenors. *How appropriate . . . the serene air after a thunderstorm.* She wondered if he knew the meaning of the beautiful lyrics. She felt as if nothing, including a fluency in Italian, would quite surprise her about Hawk. Watching him surreptitiously through the open window, she tried to remain neutral to his shirtless axe handling, but the reaction in her gut proved hard to ignore. She couldn't help noting how the muscles in his back rippled with each swing. *He looks pretty damn good for fifty-something.*
    She saw how the raised scars she'd only glimpsed before ran in a pattern across both of his upper arms and along his chest, creating a strip of aboriginal body art. Wondering again about his coming of age experience in Australia, she recalled his hint about spending several

nights "under the moon" with him to hear his story. Shaking off the pleasant image, she looked down to realize she'd peeled and sliced enough carrot sticks to feed a whole elementary school.

Glancing up, she saw her mom watching her, head tilted to the side, eyes half-closed in speculation. Reina knew how close Hawk and her mother were. She suddenly felt uncomfortable, and filled the unusual awkward silence between them with a cheerful, inane comment about the weather. "Well, I don't see any clouds out there. It looks like it's going to be a beautiful evening."

Her mom just smiled, "Indeed."

Lacking a picnic basket to carry their dinner, they loaded a box with hotdogs, whole wheat buns, cheese slices, carrot sticks, pita chips, and the two bottles of wine along with all the necessary eating implements. Knowing that the night air would get cool, they made another pile of blankets and coats scavenged from the closet. When all was ready, they carted wood, food, and clothing down the steep steps to the beach.

***

Jerry perked to attention as he saw the cabin door open. Dessiner, the guy in the pony tail, and two unidentifiable women bundled in coats and hats, exited the cabin with arms full, heading for the bluff. His stomach grumbled. *Christ. I came all this way to watch a family outing on the beach. I've got better things to do with my time.* He debated following them down to the beach, but decided it wasn't likely to provide the stimulus he needed. Shoving the binoculars in his pocket in disgust, he turned and strode down the open driveway, not bothering to conceal himself in the woods. He started up his car, wondering what kind of night life Port Angeles might offer. These kinds of places were always full of young girls wanting to escape small-town boredom and a man in a suit could do pretty well for himself. He headed for town.

Chapter 26

  The sea winds had mellowed to just a light breeze and the lowering sun glowed huge along the horizon as the foursome made their way down the steep stairs. With the rhythmic crashing of waves on rocks providing a soothing background drone, they deposited their load in a perfect little sandy clearing in the driftwood jumble.

  Hawk, who claimed to have earned his Eagle Scout Badge at the early age of 14, took charge of making the fire. He then whipped out roasting sticks he'd carved from the local bushes, quoting the Boy Scout motto, "*Always Be Prepared*," with a wink.

  They roasted their hotdogs as the sun dipped crimson below the horizon. Maria still had not said anything, but at least she was no longer crying. Reina sensed a change in her. A tiny glint of light in her eyes and her attendance to the conversation indicated she no longer wandered lost in some hopeless world of her own. She even ate two hotdogs. Perhaps tomorrow they would make some headway.

  They sat in companionable silence as the sun's last light faded gradually into total darkness. Reina leaned back to watch for the first star to appear. She pointed when she saw the bright North Star in the darkening skies. "There it is." She repeated aloud the childish poem, "Star light, star bright, first star I see tonight, I wish I may, I wish I might, have the wish I wish tonight."

Caite smiled, and Hawk laughed, asking what she had wished for.

"Can't tell," Reina answered, "or it won't come true." Maria turned to look up at the star. She looked for a long time. Reina wondered what she might be wishing for on that distant star.

They stayed for some time on the beach, listening to the rhythmic waves and gazing into the mesmerizing flames. They roasted marshmallows, groaning at the gooey, sticky sweetness.

"Where's the chocolate for s'mores?" asked Caite.

"Sorry, guess we forgot that part of the campfire ritual," Hawk replied.

"So much for 'Always Be Prepared,'" Reina teased him.

"Hey, you were the one with the shopping list." He laughed and added, "I guess we'll have to finish off the wine instead." Hawk poured the last of the wine into their extended glasses. This time Maria held out her glass, too.

"Ah," sighed Caite with satisfaction, "nothing like cheap wine in plastic glasses to complement burnt marshmallows."

"It just doesn't get better than this," Reina agreed. They sat in silence for some time, each wrapped in their own thoughts.

Reina was startled out of her reverie by a quiet, unfamiliar voice in the darkness.

"I need to tell you something." It was Maria.

No one replied. No one moved. Reina held her breath, waiting for Maria, willing Maria to speak again.

Maria continued, hesitantly, "I want to tell you a story." And then, after a long pause, she began, with the familiar phrase, the same phrase that has been used for centuries to start fairy tales. "*Once upon a time, there was a girl.*"

Maria's voice was quiet and Reina leaned forward to catch every word. The fire had died down to glowing embers, leaving Maria's face hidden in the shadows. Her sad, whispery voice continued.

"*Once upon a time there was a girl who loved the Lord. She was devoted to obeying God's word so that His will would be done in her life. In high school, she met a boy who also learned to love the Lord. They loved each other and decided to marry so that together they could devote their life to God. The boy heard the voice of God very clearly. He knew God's mission for him was to bring the message of Christ to the masses. The girl was chosen to be his helpmate, like Mary was chosen to be the mother of Jesus and Sarah the wife of Abraham.*

The work was rewarding and they were happy. The boy grew into a powerful speaker and leader and his efforts were clearly blessed. God seemed to smile upon them in all ways except one. The girl was quite sad they were never able to have children. She prayed nightly that God would see fit to bless her with a child. Her husband, who had the ear of God, frequently listened to her prayers in order to advise her on ways to be more of a Godly woman. One night, he told her to stop her ridiculous praying for children. He informed her he had gotten a vasectomy shortly after their wedding. When she began crying in disbelief, he said to her, 'The Lord has made me his vessel for salvation for the masses, to be the father of all His children, not just our own children. Your resistance to his great plan is sinfully disobedient.' She knew he was right and that she must support God's plan. Her husband insisted she spend the next week in isolation, studying the supportive women of the Bible.

A few years later the husband suggested they purchase a boys' orphanage in Taiwan. The wife was thrilled and hoped to be able to travel to Taiwan to work with the orphans. She was even more excited when she learned her husband had arranged a program to allow the children to stay in the United States under student visas. Now, she could see them on a regular basis. At first, the husband allowed her to spend time every week with the boys, but then he told her she could only visit once a month. He felt she was getting too attached and that she was not strong enough emotionally to handle their departures back to their native country or to their adoptive homes. When she asked if they could adopt one of the boys, he told her, 'My mission is to serve all God's children. God has honored you with greatness by allowing you a place by my side. It is not yours to question God's methods, but rather to submit to your God and to your husband. As it is said in Ephesians: the husband is the head of the wife, as Christ is the savior of the body, so let the wives also be subject to their own husbands in everything. Do I need to remind you of your God's words?' The woman was ashamed of her willfulness. Her husband assigned another week of isolation to study her Bible and meditate on the honor and sacrifice given to Jacob's wife, Rachel. The woman prayed hard to understand God's will.

Despite these disappointments, the woman was happy for the work performed in God's name by her husband. People were saved every week, in front of their eyes, and stories poured in of salvations made in homes across the country and on living room floors in front of the TV. The woman felt so honored to be chosen to support this epic work. She knew, as her husband often reminded her, she needed to keep her eye on the Lord and thank Him daily that he had called her to support her husband in this great mission. She rejoiced, knowing a special place in heaven would be reserved for them.

The woman needed something to keep her busy and asked her husband if she could work. Finally, he allowed her to work a few hours at the ministry headquarters' office. The highlight of her week, however, was the Friday prayer session that followed the big evening show. It was always, for her, a powerful and uplifting communion between humble man and almighty God."

Maria paused for a long moment here, then continued even more quietly.

"Until about five years ago, that is. That was when the prayer meeting . . . changed. It became . . . completely unbearable to her. She begged to be allowed to skip the Friday meeting, but her husband refused. This time, he isolated her to study the life of Sarah who demonstrated her faith by her obedience to her husband Abraham, even *when he ordered her to sleep with the Pharaoh, and with the King of Gerar. Her husband told her, 'Your only job is to support me so I can carry out the will of God and bring his lost lambs back to him. Do you not see that lives are being saved? The Bible tells us we are made alive when we are dead in transgressions and sins. My rebirth from sin to life is critical to helping others walk the same path. Do you presume to question your God or to know better than your husband, he who speaks directly with the Lord God?'*

The woman knew God works in mysterious ways and she gave in, with a broken heart, to the wishes of the Almighty. She tried hard not to question, but to accept, the mysteries of divine guidance. But finally, her lack of faith was too much for the husband to bear. Worried about her mental and emotional safety, he assigned an escort to protect her from herself. For seven months, she only left the house for the Friday night session she had come to dread. For seven months, she stayed home and studied the Bible. In the evening, the husband returned and lovingly listened to what she learned that day and gently worked with her to improve her understanding. She told him the many stories she studied, although she never talked about the story of Sisera and Jael.

The woman knew she must accept the mission that had been given to her. She knew it was her cross to bear and bear it she would. Until one day the police came and took her away."

Maria's voice faded into the dark. Everyone sat in stunned silence, shocked by the unexpected loquacity of their quiet companion. Reina tried to make sense of what she had heard. *Clearly, it's Maria's story, but what does it mean? Peter's a bossy, self-righteous jerk, with serious control issues. No big surprise there. But what else? What am I missing?*

Caite reached out and placed her hand over Maria's, which she held tightly clenched in her lap. Maria let out a little half-sob then stood up and stumbled toward the stairs. Hawk handed Caite a flashlight, saying, "Here. Make sure she gets back safely."

Reina started gathering up their things, while Hawk put out the low-burning fire with scoops of sand. They headed back to the cabin. Neither one said a word. As they climbed the stairs, Caite called to them from the top of the bluff, "Reina! Hawk! Come quick!"

"We're coming!" Reina shouted. *Oh God, what now?*

Caite yelled, "Hurry!" as she turned and ran back toward the cabin.

Within seconds, Reina and Hawk were at the top of the stairs and running from the bluff edge toward the cabin. Relieved to see, in the short distance ahead of them, both Maria and her mother standing bathed in the electric light of the open cabin door, Reina called to Hawk, "It doesn't look like anyone is hurt." Hawk, arms full of food and blankets, nodded in affirmation.

As Reina arrived at the door, Caite and Maria each stepped to a side, with a look of shock on their faces. Reina stopped on the threshold, gazing in horror at the total chaos within. The place had been ransacked from top to bottom. Pillows were slit, with feathers still floating in the air; the sofa, turned upside down, hung with disemboweled stuffing; the kitchen table lay turned on its side; bits of broken plates and dishes covered the floor. Out of the corner of her eye, Reina saw Hawk withdraw his pistol from his belt and quietly disappear into the darkness.

The women made their way through the clutter, assessing the damage. It didn't take them long to go through the small space and see that nothing had been left untouched, including their personal bags. Other than the women's wallets, taken from their purses, nothing appeared to be missing. Maria's bag lay in shreds, as though someone had viciously taken a knife to it.

"All of this for a few credit cards and a couple of bucks?" Caite said with disgust.

"Oh, I think they were looking for something - or someone - else. I'm just glad we weren't here," Reina shivered.

"Well, personally, I wish I'd been here," said Hawk grimly, walking back in the front door. "I'd have put an end to their little game of terror. However, there's no sign of anyone still in the vicinity. There are car tracks and boot tracks, but it looks like they're long gone."

"They were looking for something all right," said Maria quietly. "They were looking for these." She pulled out two clear plastic cases from the oversized Carhart Jacket she'd borrowed from the closet to wear down to the beach. "Here," she handed them to Reina, "if anyone has earplugs, I'll go to bed, and you can watch them."

Reina took the DVDs and they all watched in silence as Maria climbed the stairs to the loft.

"I have earplugs in my flight bag," offered Hawk. "I left it out in the woodshed with my laptop." When Reina looked at him in surprise, he explained, "I was listening to music earlier while I chopped wood. Good thing, too," he added, nodding at Reina's smashed laptop on the kitchen floor.

Hawk retrieved his flight bag with the supply of earplugs he carried for passengers. After Caite took a pair of earplugs up to Maria, they spent a few minutes righting the furniture, and clearing enough clutter and broken glass to allow them to move about safely. They then gathered together in front of Hawk's laptop, placing the first DVD, with PS.09.07 written on it, into the disk player. The recording showed a small group huddled together apparently in prayer. Peter Stone and Maria, along with the stage sirens Simone and Talitha, stood with their heads bowed and their arms draped around each other's shoulders. Another woman and two unknown men also formed part of the prayer group. Words like "Praise the Lord" and "Hallelujah" could be heard. It sounded a lot like the surreptitious recording Reina had made with her phone from the Stone Kingdom kitchen the other night.

As they watched, one of the women (Talitha?) turned and kissed Peter full on the mouth. Then the other one did the same with Maria. They could see Maria pull back in horror and turn to look at Peter, but fully engrossed in the kiss, he didn't notice. In fact, his hand was half way up his prayer partner's dress. Maria jumped up and ran from sight, out of camera range. They could hear a door slam, then watched further as the heavy kissing and fondling, now being participated in somewhat indiscriminately by the whole group, finally ended. Peter then led an intense session of begging forgiveness for their sins and praising God and thanking Him for His abundant love and mercy.

"Oookaaay," said Reina with a heavy exhale after the recording ended, "I guess we'll watch the other one."

Hawk placed the first disk back in its case and popped the second disk, titled PS.08.11, into his machine.

The disk started out the same as the other one, with the arms of the prayer session's participants encircled around each other in prayer. This time, no surprise or hesitation showed on anyone's face when the kissing began. The kissing quickly progressed to full-on fondling and groping being shared by all, except Maria. The preacher's wife quietly extricated herself from the group and made her way to a chair in the corner where she sat with eyes closed and body shaking gently for the duration of the recording. Reina, Caite, and Hawk sat in stunned silence as they watched various pieces of clothing being shed by the other participants. While the unknown men fondled and caressed Simone and Talitha's bare breasts, the unknown woman knelt in front of Stone and removed his belt. A full-blown sexual orgy quickly developed, with Stone having his way with each of the three women. The intense sex scene flowed seamlessly into an equally effusive orgy of forgiveness and prayer, as the sinners bent their heads together in glorious repentance. Maria, when she finally opened her eyes to leave the room, looked like an accident victim in shock.

After the DVD ended, they all sat dazed for several moments. Reina finally broke the stupefied silence. "I can't believe I just watched that," she said in a subdued voice. After a pause, she added, "I need to get back early tomorrow. I need to prepare for a different defense. An affirmative defense based on psychological and emotional abuse."

"We can finish the cleanup here pretty quickly," her mother assured her quietly. "I'll call Steve in the morning and let him know our plans and see what we can do to compensate him for this destruction." She looked around. "But I see no reason why we can't be airborne by ten a.m."

"We're in your hands, Hawk," Reina turned to him with a tired smile. "Mom and I lost our licenses - both driver's and pilot's - in tonight's robbery, so we're your passengers."

"I'll be ready to go when you are, m'ladies," Hawk replied gallantly with a half bow. "And I'll be standing guard tonight as well," he said with a tightening of his eyes and a pat of the revolver tucked into his belt. "If anyone comes within twenty feet of this place, I'll shoot first and ask questions later."

Chapter 27

Using stuffed clothing bags for pillows, they retired for the night, with Hawk sleeping guard position in his bedroll on the front porch. Reina lay quietly beside her mom in the small bed. Finally, Reina said, "I don't understand how someone could do that to another person. Why would Stone force Maria to attend those disgusting 'prayer meetings' if she refused to participate? Clearly, it was horrifying to her and she didn't want to be there."

After a moment, her mother answered softly, "Power is a strange and potent motivator. As with a bully on a playground, forcing someone to do something against their will can be perversely satisfying to some people. I imagine it is a very heady kind of omnipotence to be able to control the people around you. And in this case, I think forcing Maria's participation probably added to the sexual titillation of the experience."

"I guess," Reina admitted reluctantly. "It may have been exhilarating for Peter, but what about Maria? Why didn't she fight it? I just can't imagine how any woman could let herself get into that sort of a manipulative, controlling relationship. Or at least, why they wouldn't try to get themselves out of it."

"I think these things often start out as loving relationships and the control or abuse happens so gradually and intermittently that it is hardly noticed. It's confusing to the victim, too, because they can't tell whether their partner's "love" is precious or devious. Moments of anger or vengeance or manipulation are followed by sweet love and attention which keep her sense of reality off balance and persuade her it will never happen again. Plus that, there's always a huge helping of personal guilt that convinces her if she would only try harder, or do better, or be more understanding, it would never happen again."

"I still don't understand. But you sound like you know what you're talking about." Reina took her mother's hand and held it against her cheek for a moment, a gesture she'd used, as a child, when she felt sad or upset about something and needed comforting.

"Well, I've seen a few things in my years on this earth," her mother said in a soft whisper.

"Hmmm, you should tell me more about it sometime," Reina replied, her eyes heavy with sleep.

"I will, my dear." Smoothing the hair away from Reina's face, she kissed her gently on the forehead. "Someday, we'll go for a long walk on the beach and I'll tell you all about it."

"Okay, goodnight, Mom."

"Goodnight, my love."

Chapter 28

The next morning, after a careful cleanup and inventory of the damage wreaked by the intruders, Hawk drove them, in the old blue van, to the airport, where Steve had agreed to pick it up later in the day. On the drive, Reina turned to Maria and said gently, "I think I understand now what drove you to do what you did."

For a long moment, Maria looked Reina in the eye but didn't respond. Then finally, letting her eyes fall down to her hands clasped tightly in her lap, she said, "No." Her voice dropping to a whisper, she repeated, "No, I don't think you do."

All three pilots participated in the thorough pre-flight inspection of the Cessna 210, which had, for two days, sat all-too-vulnerable on the ramp at the small, deserted airport. Exercising every bit of caution they all felt, they scrutinized and re-scrutinized every aspect of pre-flight. The fuel - did it smell okay? Did it look normal? The engine - was there any indication of tampering? Was the oil at the same level and color as when they'd last checked? The prop, landing gear, control surfaces - were every cotter pin and screw and weight in place? After following behind each other, double and triple checking everything, they all agreed that nothing seemed to look out of place. Hawk started up the engine. They listened carefully for anything unusual as he performed a normal run-up, and checked the controls thoroughly. Everything appeared to be a "go." He taxied to runway's edge and performed a gentle, smooth takeoff to the east.

  Hawk set the GPS for their destination, and headed toward the Olympic Mountains, many of which were still clad in snow at summer's end. He climbed gently to a height adequate for ample terrain clearance and commented on the generous tailwind that would scoot them home in no time.

  At 11,500 feet, he leveled off the aircraft and adjusted the throttle, prop, and mixture controls for cruise. Reina, engrossed in planning her upcoming defense strategy, dispassionately watched the scenery below pass by. Suddenly, she jolted alert at the sound of the engine sputtering. She took her eyes off the jagged peaks below them to look questioningly at Hawk. The engine was beginning to sound quite rough and she watched as Hawk fiddled with the mixture control. She knew the importance of reducing the flow of gas to match the thinner air available at higher altitudes. Probably the mixture knob had been pulled out a bit too far and just needed enriching. As Hawk tried to adjust the mixture control, she was stupefied to see the red vernier handle come off in his hand. She could feel the blood drain from her face as momentary panic set in. Having the mixture adjusted too far out would eventually starve the engine of fuel and result in a complete engine stoppage. Through sheer willpower, she forced the paralyzing sense of fear to the back of her consciousness. Knowing the importance of reacting calmly, clearly and quickly, she reached for the emergency checklist and began reciting the items to Hawk so that he could focus on his job which, right now, was to maintain control of the airplane. The engine sounded rougher and rougher by the minute.

She read aloud the checklist procedures for Engine Failure in Flight.

"Best glide, 85."

He repeated, "Best glide, 85."

"Auxiliary fuel pump on."

"Auxiliary fuel pump on."

As she continued to read off each emergency checklist item, he performed, and orally confirmed them. Meanwhile, she reached for the Garmin 430 GPS in the aircraft's panel and fiddled with the controls to find the nearest airport. Hawk had already begun to turn the aircraft to the northeast, roughly in the direction of the Port Angeles airport. He had rightly sensed that there was no going back to where they'd come from and Port Angeles was their only hope. If they didn't make it to Port Angeles, it would mean an off-airport landing and the terrain around the Olympic Mountains didn't offer a lot of good options.

Reina obtained the magnetic heading for Port Angeles on the GPS and Hawk adjusted the aircraft's heading to match the desired track. The GPS indicated Port Angeles to be 15.3 miles away. "If we can maintain even minimal power, we'll make the field easily," said Reina with forced cheerfulness. Just as the words left her mouth, the engine sputtered once, sputtered twice, then quit altogether. Hawk quickly tried to restart with the fuel pump, but without success. The broken mixture control had caused fuel starvation, resulting in a complete and total engine failure. The silence was deafening. No engine, no static, no talk. Just an eerie quiet.

Reina forced the mind-numbing panic aside. It's just an engine failure, she told herself, we practice and train for this all the time. No problem. We're now a glider, instead of a powered aircraft, that's all. She said, in a voice that sounded surprisingly calm and matter-of-fact, "We should have a glide ratio of about 9 to 1."

Hawk replied, "Let's figure 8 to 1."

"Right," Reina replied. "Well, we've got about two miles to descend, so we should be able to glide 16 miles." The GPS now read 14.5 miles to Port Angeles. "We can make it," she said aloud, as she thought to herself, unless the wind changes or we get downdrafts on the leeward side of the mountains.

"The tailwind will help our glide distance," said Hawk, "but I'll have to take what I get for landing. I may not have time to position for an optimal approach. Shouldn't be a problem to land this big bird even with a stiff tailwind."

Reina dialed in the frequency for Seattle Center on the com radio, and Hawk announced to the controller that they had a mixture malfunction resulting in fuel exhaustion and total engine failure.

The air traffic controller asked back, "Do you want to declare an emergency?"

As Reina thought, *Isn't that obvious,* Hawk replied calmly, "Yes, we are declaring an emergency and request emergency vehicles to stand by at KCLM, Fairchild Airport." Reina glanced back at her mom and Maria in the back seat. Her mother looked very calm, almost unconcerned. Maria was white as a ghost.

As they continued northeast toward their hoped-for landing spot, both Hawk and Reina carefully monitored all systems. At ten miles from the airport, they still had over 6,000 feet altitude, but the mountains were closing in on either side. Hawk had to turn a bit left and right to steer clear of the peaks along the Elwha River Valley. The small turning banks cost the aircraft a little in altitude and the mountain peaks began to tower over them out the side windows. The absolute silence in the cockpit underscored the intensity of each minute, and time seemed to waver like spider silk in the wind. Both pilots focused every bit of planning and aeronautical decision-making skill they'd accumulated over years of training to produce a positive outcome for this flight. But ultimately, gravity and winds would determine the result.

Hawk held the glide speed to a perfect 85 knots the whole way, but the ground speed on the GPS was clocking in at 95 knots. *No problem*, Reina thought, starting to relax a bit, *thanks to the tailwind we'll make the field with plenty to spare.*

As they began to clear out of the Elwha Valley, between the last of the big peaks, the ground speed, as registered on the GPS, suddenly dropped to 75 knots. The headwinds coming off the Strait of Juan de Fuca were going to slow them down too much. They could see the airport in the distance, but it was no longer a sure thing they would make it. Reina could feel the tension in every muscle in her body. She knew, from flying this heavy aircraft, how quickly it could sink without power, especially with a full load.

While Hawk focused on flying the aircraft, she announced to both the controllers at Whidbey Naval Base and the local Port Angeles air traffic that they were making an emergency landing on or near William Fairchild Airport. They were close enough now she could see the fire trucks, lights flashing, waiting for them to come in with a bang. She reminded the back seat passengers to tighten their seat belts, and to prepare for a potentially rough landing by protecting their heads. She turned off the fuel tanks and saw Hawk crack the door ajar so, hopefully, they would not be trapped in a pile of burning aircraft debris. They were as ready as they could be.

As Hawk banked ever so gently to the right to line up for runway 08, they picked up the vestiges of that western wind and got a gentle little push toward their goal. Reina held her breath. About 300 feet from the runway threshold, with barely enough altitude to make the asphalt, Hawk finally lowered the landing gear. Reina felt the familiar tug of the aircraft, as the drag of the gear slowed them down. *We're going to land in the approach lights!* Hawk raised the aircraft nose delicately, almost imperceptibly, millimeter by millimeter, to extend the glide without stalling the aircraft. At the last second, he lowered the flaps, ballooning the aircraft with just enough extra lift to clear the runway end lights. Time stilled for a moment until the complete silence was pierced by the high-pitched squeal of the stall horn and a tiny squeak of the tires as they touched down just inches past the edge of the runway threshold. It was the most perfect deadstick landing Reina had ever seen. She exhaled and slumped in her seat, realizing she'd been holding her breath for much too long. She turned to smile at her mom, who smiled serenely back, as though she hadn't a care in the world.

They slowly coasted to a halt. The fire trucks came roaring up, and the emergency crew hopped out, clearly torn between the satisfaction of nobody getting hurt and the disappointment of no horrific accident upon which to prove their mettle. There would be no big story to tell around the dinner table this evening, but then there would be no nightmares, either, to fend away in the middle of the night.

Hawk climbed out of the aircraft's single door and held it open for Reina to follow. As soon as Reina exited, she rushed to the edge of the runway, leaned over, and vomited violently. Hawk, helping the ladies out from the back seat, turned to look at her in alarm.

"Now, that surprises me," Reina heard him say to her mom. "I didn't think anything fazed Reina. She must have been really shook up."

Caite replied matter-of-factly, "Yes, I think her fear of heights kicked in. Surprisingly, she's not normally bothered by it when she flies, but perhaps the silence of the engine failure and the sense of uncontrolled falling reawakened the fear in her."

"Reina is afraid of heights?" Hawk exclaimed. "Hell, I would have never guessed. Has she always been that way?"

"I'm afraid it stems from a childhood experience that terrified her. Ask her about it sometime." As Reina rejoined them, her mom continued, "But right now, I think we need to give some statements to the fireman there." She nodded to the waiting emergency crew.

Hawk answered the necessary questions while the plane was towed to the maintenance facility on the field. The women left Hawk to look over their aircraft with the mechanic on staff while they went over to the terminal for something cool to drink and use of the facilities. When they returned to the maintenance shop, Reina could see Hawk and the mechanic squatting under the cowling of the aircraft. Hawk's face, as he stood erect, looked grim.

"Did you discover the problem?" she asked.

"Yes," he replied. "It appears the cotter pin on the mixture cable somehow went missing. And the castellated nut seems to have been loosened just enough so it wouldn't be apparent during the preflight, but would definitely work its way off during the vibrations of flight." He paused for a long moment, then added with a tightening of his lips, "Someone very much wanted us to not survive this flight."

Reina thought of the many recent attempts on her life, or at least the solid attempts to scare her, and she now knew the people they were up against were playing for keeps. At this point, however, precious little of the "accidents" could be proven in court. She felt it best to simply continue on their way. "Can they repair the plane so we can finish our flight home today?"

"Yes, they'll fix the aircraft for us here," Hawk paused, "but I'm not leaving until I take care of some unfinished business here in Port Angeles." And he turned and walked from the shop.

Chapter 29

Reina ran to catch up with Hawk, now half-way to the terminal building. Her mother and Maria lagged some distance behind. "What are you thinking?" Reina tried to keep up with his long stride.

He looked at her with those piercing blue eyes the color of sky, or maybe glacial ice. "I'm thinking I'd like to know a little bit more about the people who ransacked my belongings, tampered with my plane, and threatened the lives of people I care about."

"What are you going to do? Go storming in and demand to see them?"

Hawk looked at her with raised eyebrows. Reina could feel the power of his tightly controlled fury emanating from him. "Did I ever tell you I was Special Ops in the Marines?"

Reina was silent for a moment. "Whatever you're planning, I want to be there."

"I don't think that's a good idea."

"Nevertheless, I'm coming along."

Hawk shrugged, "Suit yourself."

Hawk and Reina explained to Caite and Maria they had an errand to run in Port Angeles. They suggested the two ladies enjoy a nice lunch at the restaurant while awaiting their return. Caite looked at them with that all-knowing look of hers, as if she could read their brain waves. Then she smiled gently and nodded her agreement.

Upon inquiring about rental cars, Reina learned the flight school adjacent to the terminal building could let the pilots borrow their loaner "courtesy car." Free courtesy cars at local airports were one of the great traditions of American general aviation. Reina had enjoyed this kindness in small-town airports from coast to coast. As she accepted the keys to the old white pickup truck from the friendly guy in work coveralls, she thanked him with a warm smile and promised to have it back before the end of the day. The young mechanic shyly tugged his cap down lower on his forehead, blushed, and told her she could keep it for as long as she needed.

As they drove west toward the waterfront, Hawk spelled out his expectations. "I want you to stay close behind me and do exactly what I tell you. I don't know that we'll even find anybody there, but if we do – or if they find us – we'll be unwanted guests on hostile territory. Anything may happen, but stick by my side, trust me, and I'll make sure we get out okay. Got it?"

"Got it," repeated Reina with a pit of excitement in her stomach.

Hawk parked the white truck on a side street off of Marine Drive. They had bought a couple of logo baseball caps from the flight school at the airport, and they each pulled these down low over their foreheads now. Reina tucked the loose ends of her hair under the edge of the cap. She hoped the logo's words, "Right Stuff," emblazoned on her headgear would prove to be true.

They walked quickly toward the offices of Peninsula Shipping, this time approaching it from the back side. The office which they'd visited – was it just yesterday? – faced the road some 400 feet ahead of them. The warehouses of the shipping company were grouped behind the office, to the north and west, and a six-foot-high, chain-link fence surrounded the whole compound. Angling up and toward the inside, from the top of the fencing, another foot and a half of barbed wire rows made the place appear formidable and impenetrable. Reina didn't see how they could possibly get into the facility.

"This place is more secure than some prisons I've seen," she said in a low voice to Hawk.

She followed Hawk as he skirted the west side of the fenced area. He assessed the perimeter, looking for options. As they reached the water's edge, the fencing tapered down at an angle all the way into the bay. Calm and mud-colored, the body of water between Port Angeles and Ediz Hook reeked unpleasantly of diesel oil and rotting seaweed. A bank of green, slimy rocks led down to the edge of the murky water, which appeared to be at low tide.

Hawk bent over, removed his leather mocs, and started unbuttoning his jeans. When Reina looked at him in alarm, he whispered, "Stay here if you want."

She only paused for a moment before slipping off her Keen Loafers and Calvin Klein jeans. *Thank God I picked up some decent panties yesterday.* With a quick glance down, she thought, I can just see the headlines now

"Seattle Attorney Caught Breaking into Shipping Company in Torn Underwear" *or even worse, none at all . . . .*

They each bundled their pants and shoes under an arm and started working their way down the slippery rocks, holding on to the chain link fence for support. Reina felt her foot slide on a slimy stone and immediately Hawk's hand appeared at her waist to steady her. She followed him into the cool brown water, feeling her toes sink into the soft mud. With the low tide, the water only reached to just above their knees before they were able to straddle the last bit of fencing to reach the other side. They made their way up the slick stones on the inside of the fence barrier and quickly rinsed the mud from their toes. While Hawk slipped easily back into his faded jeans, Reina struggled and wriggled to get her snug new skinny jeans pulled up over her wet skin. She looked up to find him watching her with shameless pleasure and felt her face grow hot under his gaze. *Oh my God, I can't believe I'm blushing like a school girl.* She stuck out her tongue at him once again. He grinned and they turned toward their mission.

The backside of the compound was a sea of old, badly-cracked asphalt overgrown with tufts of grass and weeds. Discarded junk littered the ground: patches of broken glass, cast-off boat motors, scraps of metal, old paper wrappers, rusty oil barrels, and other human flotsam. Hawk and Reina quickly proceeded through the wasteland to the nearest warehouse. Hugging the back wall closely, they worked their way around the corner to the waterside of the building, seeking a door or window.

Ahead of them, they could see a long dock. Several watercraft of various sizes bobbed gently on the quiet water including a large trawler, a smaller fishing boat with overhead tackle gear, a couple of runabouts, and a long, shiny cigarette boat.

At the farthest edge of the warehouse, a large bay door stood open. They inched their way along the wall to the opening, watching carefully for any sign of human activity on the boats or from the warehouse. If someone happened to walk out the door now, there would be no place for them to take cover. Reina's nerves were on edge and every sense alert and ready for immediate action, if needed. Hawk stopped at the edge of the door, with his hand extended toward Reina for her to stop close behind him. He peered carefully around the door frame. After a couple of seconds, he waved her forward with his extended hand and they edged their way around the door and into the deserted warehouse. They quickly took cover behind a row of shelving, packed to the rafters with large boxes.

They paused, listening for voices. A murmur of distant conversation came from the front of the building. Creeping their way down the row of shelving toward the sound of voices, they could see a light coming from the window of what looked like an office partition build-out. Hawk reached the office wall and hugged it tightly as he ducked under the window and headed toward the open door. Reina crouched down and followed him closely, hoping no one could hear the thunderous pounding of her heart.

Reina recognized Stone's voice coming from the office, tight with anger, "We can't have any more accidents. This is the second time this month. If you can't exercise better control, I'll find someone who can."

Then a mumbled reply from an unknown person, "Don't worry boss, I'll make sure it never happens again. Even if it means I have to make every trip myself."

"Good. We've had enough problems with the group down in Portland. That case in April that got tracked to the Port Angeles clothing store came a little too close for comfort. And we still have to deal with Taylor who wants another one and who is getting too god-damned careless." After a pause, Stone added, "Unfortunately, he knows too much, so we're gonna have to oblige him. Who do we have that will fit the bill?"

"I'll check into it and let you know," the man replied.

"Good. You know what he likes."

"Yes, sir."

They could hear footsteps. Suddenly Stone's voice called out, "Hold on there!"

Reina stiffened, thinking he had somehow caught sight of them.

They heard the unknown man say, "Yes, boss?"

Stone replied, "And get rid of that damned leech attorney. I'm tired of him trying to rub up against me every time I turn around. Show him to his car, drive him to the airport, or dump him in the bay. I don't care. Just get him out of my hair."

"Yes sir," the man replied and again they heard footsteps headed toward the door.

Hawk flattened himself quickly against the wall throwing his arm against Reina's chest to force her to do the same. Reina was irrationally surprised to see a pistol in Hawk's other hand. She held her breath as the unknown man exited the office, head down and in a hurry. Fortunately, he looked neither left nor right and didn't notice the intruders braced against the wall. The exterior man-door creaked loudly as he yanked it open and exited. All was silent in the office.

After a minute's wait to see if anyone else might be with Stone, they heard his voice speaking again. "Senator Taylor, please," he said politely. Then a pause and, "Tell him it's Peter Stone." After another pause, he continued in a warm, kind voice, "Yes, of course I'll hold." In the interim silence, Reina could hear Stone's fingers drumming on the desk. "Samson!" Stone's friendly voice boomed out. "How are you, my friend?" A chuckle was followed by, "Yes, yes, I know. We're looking into it right now. And we certainly appreciate the generous donation. It will, of course, go toward furthering the Good Work." A pause as Stone listened to the voice on the other end of the phone line. "Of course. Yes, yes, I know. But listen, you have to promise to be more careful, old man. You know I'd never tell you how to . . . satisfy your needs, but if this one gets into the news, unsolved case or not, it'll have to be the last one." Then, after a long pause, Stone finished off the conversation, "Okay, well as long as we understand each other. We should have one coming your way soon. Have you decided on the name you want to use this time around? Clayton Wiles. Got it. Okay, you take care now." Peter laughed, then finished with "Yeah, you, too. Talk to you soon, *Clayton*." Another laugh and they heard the phone clunked down into its cradle.

Several minutes passed, then they heard Stone exclaim, "What the hell!" and his chair scraped loudly against the floor followed by footsteps stomping toward the open door.

Hawk turned, quick as a jungle cat, pulling Reina with him around the corner of the office walls, quickly crouching out of sight. They heard the squeaky warehouse door open, then Stone's voice blast out, "I told you to bring Maria and the DVDs. I don't want the others. What did you bring her here for, and what about that snoopy girl and her long-haired friend?"

Hawk and Reina had backed up so they had a visual line of sight through the corner of the office window and straight on through the open office door. Reina saw an irate Stone confronting a small, dark-skinned man who held two women in front of him with their hands bound – Maria and Caite! Even from twenty feet away, Reina smelled the strong odor of curry. *God damn it. This is the guy who tried to drown me in my own bathtub!* In the light streaming on the small group from the open office door, she could see, with some satisfaction, that he had red burn marks and a large bruise on his right cheek. As Reina caught her breath, Hawk squeezed her hand, warning her to react silently.

The small man answered Peter in an accented voice. Reina immediately recognized him as the man who'd "cleaned up" that night in Stone Kingdom's kitchen. "Nobody seems to know where ze other two went. And nobody's admitting to where ze DVDs are. Zey are not on zese two. Trust me, I searched zem good." He smiled leeringly at Caite and slapped her bottom.

Caite smiled sweetly back at him and, quickly raising both hands, swung them back firmly to elbow him hard in the ribs. He emitted a pained "oof" then, his dark face twisting in rage, slapped her hard across the face. Caite's face snapped back from the harsh slap.

A cold anger seized Reina, taking the place of the nausea-producing fear she'd been feeling. Leaning close to Hawk, she felt his shoulders tense. She could feel the fury in him as well.

"Anyway," the small man continued, "apparently she's already watched ze DVDs, so I did not tink it was wise to leave her behind to talk about zem."

"Yes, really quite interesting, those DVDs," Caite said to Stone in a conversational tone. "Was it your vanity that suggested you record all those sex-fests, or did you just want a chance to get off on them again at a later date?"

"I don't need to apologize or explain to you or anyone else what I do behind closed doors," Stone responded curtly to Caite's jeering. "It's a free country. Anything you saw was done by consenting adults. It may not meet your moral code--"

"or anyone's," inserted Caite.

"--but frankly, you don't have much say in the matter, now do you?" Stone smiled smugly at her.

He then turned to address his wife, like a parent disciplining a recalcitrant child, "Maria." He looked as if he was trying to stare her down. "This has gone on long enough. You know you are only harming yourself, your husband, and frankly, Christians throughout the world. You need to hand over those DVDs now and we'll be done with this thing."

Maria didn't say anything.

Peter repeated her name, grim and threatening, "Maria . . . ."

"She doesn't have them," Caite finally chimed in.

Maria stood paralyzed in fear.

"What do you mean, she doesn't have them?" Peter roared, turning his intense eyes on Caite.

"I had them, and I left them with a friend who has been instructed to send them to King 5 TV if we don't return by dark tonight."

"What?" Maria finally cried out, with a look of horror. "Oh dear God, please tell me you didn't do that?"

"Well, yes, dear, I did. I thought it would be best and, in fact, it looks like it was."

"No, no, you don't understand. Those things must never fall into public hands."

Caite looked at Maria in surprise.

"You don't understand," repeated Maria. "I took them as a sort of personal guaranty but, whatever happens, whatever happens, people must never know!"

Maria continued with a sob, "Oh God, have mercy," as she crumpled to the floor.

Peter turned to his "special friend" and barked out instructions. "Wong, take that woman and go retrieve the videos." He turned to Caite and said with venom, "Maria and I are going for a boat ride. If you do not lead Wong directly to the DVDs, then Maria will not be coming back." Turning back to Wong, he added, "Let me know when you have them in your possession and when you have . . . taken care of business." Peter looked hard at Wong as if to make sure he fully understood the directions issued. When Wong nodded, he smiled. "Good," he finished with a jerk of the head toward the door. "Now go."

Hawk started pulling Reina toward the door they'd entered. As they backed off, Reina heard Maria saying in a frightened voice, "Peter, I hate that cigarette boat. I don't want to go on it. It's too fast."

Her husband replied softly, in false assurance, "Don't worry my love, we're taking the fishing boat. Although, you know, it can be quite dangerous with all that heavy tackle and loose ropes and big hooks swinging around . . . ." With a distinctly ominous edge to his words, he added, "Yes, very dangerous. But you can be sure I'll take care of you, all right."

As Reina and Hawk exited, they could hear Reverend Peter Stone's mocking laughter reverberating in the emptiness.

Chapter 30

As they slipped out of the warehouse into the still, deserted shipyard, Hawk whispered to Reina, "There's no time to lose. You need to get on that boat. And here, take this." He shoved his gun into her hand. She cradled the cold barrel uneasily in her palm.

"But you never taught me how to use it."

"You've seen enough movies, you'll figure it out. I'm going after your mother." And he was gone.

Keeping her head on a swivel for any human activity, Reina dashed across to the adjacent warehouse that ran the whole length of the waterfront. She quickly slunk around the corner to the water side and ran to the farthest edge, just feet from the long dock where the boats they'd seen earlier were still bobbing peacefully side by side. Glancing back to the warehouse from which they had come, she saw no one yet approaching the dock. *Maybe they're gathering life jackets? Or weapons?* She hesitated for a moment, while every survival instinct in her body told her *not* to cross the open area between the building and the boats. Then, she remembered the little curry-scented asshole attacking her in her bath, locking her in the fridge, and slapping her mother across the face. A steely fury came to her aid. She gathered her resolve, leaped onto the dock and within seconds had rolled herself over the low stern of the fishing boat.

Reina didn't know much about boats, but she quickly perceived this craft to be a true working vehicle. No prettier on the inside than on the outside, its floorboards showed rust-colored stains in many spots, and huge coils of heavy rope lay piled high in the corners. She stumbled over the massive iron support base of the towering-high outriggers, with their dangling hooks swinging gently overhead. Ducking low, she quickly entered the cabin and searched for a hiding place. At the fore of the cabin, a raised platform with a captain's chair and a big, spoked steering wheel contained the boat's navigation equipment. Below the platform, she saw a little hatch door that, she guessed, might lead to some sort of sleeping quarters. Aft of that, a miniature galley equipped with a tiny stove and refrigerator, and directly behind the galley, a small table surrounded by built-in benches, adjoining what looked like a storage closet. On the right side, three small sling bunks were affixed to the cabin wall. Her quick survey of her surroundings noted that each of the bunks had chains attached, on one end, to the wall above it. Peering over the edge of one of the bunks, she realized that, at the other end of each chain, a small set of handcuffs rested on the thin blankets. The sight of the handcuffs made her blood run cold. Aft of the tiny bunks, a miniature room stood with door slightly ajar. A quick peek inside confirmed it to be the boat's head, with an undersized toilet and sink. Not where she wanted to hide. Reina opened the closet door to her left and slipped inside, forcing herself behind the row of hanging rain slickers and shoving her feet inside a pair of large rubber boots on the floor. She hoped the weather wouldn't turn nasty enough to require raingear for the occupants. She heard a voice from outside. Standing ramrod still inside the cramped closet, she willed her wildly racing heart to stay inside her chest and forced her breathing to stabilize somewhere below the hyperventilation stage. She quickly silenced her cell phone. Hearing her Cheap Trick ring tone blaring from the closet would surely give away her hiding place.

She heard Peter's voice approaching the boat. "Sit down and stay down!" he commanded Maria roughly as they entered the cabin. Then she heard the sound of the engine firing up. Bracing herself as the boat lurched gently forward, she listened to the low hum of the engine settling into a slow idle. She heard some indistinguishable murmuring of voices and began to wonder what she could possibly do from the closet. With the background noise of the engine, she could not distinguish any specific words, or get a sense of any action. She had no way of knowing how or when to act. For the time being, nothing could be done but wait. Carefully handling the heavy steel revolver in her pocket, she gently explored it with her fingertips to identify the safety latch that must surely be a part of its construction. She gently wrapped her hand around the butt end and barely felt for the trigger, ever so lightly. She had no desire to blow off her toes in the rubber boots.

After what seemed like an eternity, the engine suddenly cut off and she tensed, knowing she needed to be prepared to save Maria, but uncertain how. She braced her legs to balance in the now gently rolling action of the floating craft, practically jumping when she heard a voice that sounded as if it were right next to her ear.

"Now we just wait," said Peter.

She realized Peter and Maria must be sitting on the bench adjacent to the closet. The sound was crystal-clear. *It's like we're sitting at the same table.* Boat builders, like airplane companies, she thought, must use the lightest materials available. The closet walls were certainly constructed of some very thin material. Her muscles began to cramp. She waited.

***

Hawk had quickly retraced his steps to the old white loaner pickup truck. He slid behind the wheel and pulled onto Marine Drive heading in the direction of the Peninsula Shipping buildings. Approaching slowly, he saw a black SUV pull out from the shipping company's gate, turn right, and speed off directly toward him. Hawk hunched down in his seat, pulling the flight school's baseball cap closely over his eyes. He couldn't see into the dark, tinted windows of the passing vehicle, but he knew who the driver and passenger were. He quickly turned onto a side street, did a neat U-turn, and pulled back onto Marine Drive, following at some distance behind the black vehicle.

As Hawk anticipated, the SUV headed in the direction of the airport. After several minutes of driving, they arrived at the Port Angeles airport terminal building.

The dark car's driver pulled into one of the handicap slots directly in front of the entrance. Hawk pulled the truck into an open spot some distance down the line from the main door. He waited for the occupants to exit the car, but the doors did not open. *Damn it. If he's hurting her, I'll kill him!* The thought of Caite being roughed up by that goon made his heart tight as he clenched and unclenched his hands.

After several minutes of torturous waiting, Hawk tugged his cap down tight and prepared to move. Just as he reached to open his truck door, he saw the driver's side door of the SUV swing open. The man, Wong, walked quickly around to the passenger side and opened the door. Relief flooded Hawk when he saw Caite step out, her hands unbound. She held her arms tightly in front of her with her left hand grasping her right triceps, while the right arm swung loosely. She looked pale and tense, but appeared to be unharmed. Her unwanted companion quickly stepped next to her and placed his arm behind her along her waist. Folded across his wrist lay a light coat. Underneath that, Hawk suspected, he held a gun. They entered the terminal building.

It didn't take Hawk more than a few seconds to exit the truck and enter the black SUV. Fortunately, Wong had been too busy with his captive to worry about locking the vehicle. Hawk molded himself into the space behind the driver's seat and thanked providence for the tinted windows and the overcast skies. He hoped he wouldn't have to wait long in this uncomfortable, contorted position.

Several minutes later, the front car doors opened again. Apparently Wong had turned off the automatic door lights, as the interior of the vehicle remained unlit. The driver started the engine, backed out quickly, and exited the parking area with a squeal of tires. If Wong drove back to the shipping company's office, Hawk would take care of him then. If not, Hawk would have to improvise his plan of attack. He noted that the driver turned west out of the airport instead of the east direction that would have taken them back toward Marine Drive. He figured they were traveling on one of the wooded country roads that bordered the airport, located at the south edge out of town.

The occupants did not speak, but the tension hung thick in the air. Finally, Wong broke the silence. "You were wise to do exactly what I told you. Zis way no one else gets hurt."

Caite replied, "What are you going to do now?"

"I have one more piece of business to take care of."

Hawk, crouched behind the driver, could almost hear the anticipation in the man's voice. He tensed in readiness for whatever shape the "business" might take. Hearing Caite gasp suddenly, Hawk dared a peek over the seat back and saw Wong pointing a gun at Caite's head, with the barrel of the revolver resting against her cheek.

He had to act now. With silent deadliness, he reached around the seat back, wrapped his hands around Wong's neck and squeezed hard.

The car swerved wildly as the driver automatically let go of the steering wheel and clawed at Hawk's hands in desperation. The revolver in Wong's hand dropped to the seat and bounced down below his feet. As Wong's body twisted and stretched to be free of the life-draining fingers, his feet kicked out, randomly pressing against the vehicle's pedals. The car accelerated, careening wildly. Hawk called out to Caite to grab the steering wheel. Caite, already in motion, grasped the wheel with her left hand and counter-steered the skidding vehicle. It lurched left and right in gradually lessening extremes until she had the directional control managed. Wong's continued struggle for survival caused his kicking foot to impact the gas pedal erratically. They lurched and jerked forward. They were going too fast to maintain control for long.

"Open his door!" yelled Hawk. Caite hesitated for just a minute, then grabbed the wheel with her right hand and reached across the struggling man to pull the door handle open with her left hand. Wong freed one hand from clawing at Hawk's fingers to swipe at Caite's right hand on the wheel. She yelped in pain and let go of the wheel. They were careening again, but the driver's door swung open. Caite reached again for the steering wheel with her left hand and worked to get the car back under control. A loud horn blared. Coming from the opposite direction, a fully-loaded logging truck approached at breakneck speed.

"We've got to get control of the pedals," Hawk shouted, "you're going to have to kick him out!" Caite froze for a moment and Hawk continued, talking her through it. "Take the wheel with your right hand, lean back toward your door and curl your feet up tight for the kick.

On the count of three, let go of the wheel and kick with all your might. I'll do the rest from here." Caite did as he instructed. Hawk counted to three and they kicked and heaved the nearly-expired Wong from the vehicle. Again the logging truck horn blared, this time closer and louder. Wong's body rolled across the road in front of the huge truck as it passed. Caite turned her head away from the impending impact, and passed out.

    Hawk leaped over the seat back into the still-warm driver's seat. He quickly got the vehicle under control, counter-steering and braking until, finally, it rested on the shoulder of the road. He turned to see Caite unconscious, lying half on the floor, half on the seat. Her right arm was splayed behind her back with the elbow bent to the inside. He could see the bone end, on the hyper-extended joint, poking out oddly under the skin. The whole arm was starting to turn purple and swell.

    He remembered Stone had said he'd wait to hear from Wong before taking any action with Maria. He hoped he still had time. He turned the car around and punched the gas pedal, heading for Olympic Memorial Hospital. Hawk carried Caite into the hospital and deposited her with an emergency room nurse who quickly supplied a transport gurney at the sight of the unconscious woman. He then turned and walked back out the door, with the nurse calling out after him, "Wait, what's your name?"

***

After a long silence, Reina heard Maria's voice through the closet wall. "Peter, what are we waiting for?" After several minutes, Maria inquired again, somewhat timidly, "Peter?"

"We're waiting for word from Wong that he retrieved the DVDs." After a pause, Peter continued, "You know you never should have taken those, Maria."

"I know." Reina heard Maria's soft response. "I never meant to hurt you, Peter."

"Maria, my love, you know this has all just been a big mistake," Peter said cajolingly. "You've been confused and emotionally worn down. I know you'll get better with the help of our good God and your loving husband. You know God has called us to do great things. But His ways are mysterious and they sometimes require us to suffer, as Jesus suffered for us. You must bear your cross more bravely, for you know the rewards in heaven are great for those who put aside their personal needs for the greater needs of Christ's body."

"That's why this is so hard," Maria admitted pitifully.

"It's not hard at all," he countered. "It's very simple. Confess your sins, repent of your transgressions, and promise once again to follow God's word, which He speaks through me. If you do these things, I'll make sure all charges are dropped against you. We'll call it a terrible misunderstanding and we'll go on as we have before. You must remember, Maria, it's not about you, it's about God's will."

"You're right, Peter. It's not about me and it's not about my needs. It never has been. God knows I've set aside my wants and needs for years and done your bidding so that you could do God's great work. But I can't do it anymore. I can't!" Reina heard the sound of a sob. Not surprisingly, Maria was crying.

"Of course you can. Don't you want to continue saving lives and healing people? Aren't we doing what we always talked about?" After a pause, Peter added with feigned sincerity, "Maria, I can't stand the thought of you spending eternity in hell, twisting and tortured in the horrible flames, and tormented by devils and demons just because you couldn't see clearly to follow God's plan."

Through the thin closet wall, Reina could almost sense Maria blanch at the vision Peter described to her. Reina knew how the fear of damnation had been used through the centuries to manipulate and control people. She suspected the threat of hell's horrible tortures had been used quite effectively on Maria for many years.

"That's it," Peter said. Reina heard a shuffling noise. Was he pulling her into his arms? She could hear the confidence in his voice as he continued. "Like I said, we'll make sure all charges get dropped and we'll get you home. Then we'll get back to God's business of saving lives. Just remember," he finished, "God wants you to focus on His priorities, not yours. Remember, you must always be thinking of what is best for all of God's children."

Again Reina heard a shuffle and a loud thunk right next to her ear, as if an elbow or head had impacted the adjacent wall. *Are they embracing? Did she push him away? Did he hit her? Should I do something? I feel like I'm watching a movie blind, and in a damned uncomfortable position, too.* She wiggled her legs and toes to keep them from going numb.

She suddenly heard Maria's voice, raised in volume and pitch now, as she cried out, in a voice full of emotion, "No, Peter! No! I already told you it's not about me! It IS about God's children. It IS! I AM thinking about the children, about Lin, and about Jimmy Lai, Peter, Jimmy Lai!"

"Jimmy Lai?" Peter replied in surprise. "Who the hell is Jimmy Lai?"

"Jimmy Lai!" Maria repeated. "Jimmy Lai! The boy you sold to Samson Taylor."

There was a long silence then Reina heard Maria cry out in a soft, broken voice, "How could you, Peter? You of all people, after all you lived through yourself?"

Suddenly, Peter's voice boomed out, venomous and angry. "You're crazy. You've been crazy for years and I've put up with it, but now your delusions have gone too far."

"No!" Maria cried. "No! I know what you have done. I know the boys you've sold to Taylor. I know about the three *unknown* Asian boys discovered dead in his state. An unsolved crime. It IS a crime! It IS! It IS! And I know it! And I know about the others, the untraceable adoptions that followed large donations from the group in Portland. Did you know I went down to visit some of the adopted boys in Portland, but their addresses were deserted warehouses and strip malls? And I know about the boy found raped and murdered in the river there. I know what you have done. I know! And so does God, Peter, so does God!" Maria shouted and sobbed in hysteria.

Reina heard scuffling noises and then a crash. Her call to action had finally arrived. Flexing her stiff muscles, she pushed open the closet door and lunged out, still wearing the oversized rubber boots. Her eyes squinted in the sudden light, then she saw Peter and Maria on the floor. Peter Stone straddled his wife in a death embrace, his hands encircling her neck. His arms shook and Reina heard Maria's head banging against the floor as her husband slowly choked the life out of her. Without time for thought, Reina grasped the barrel of the heavy revolver in her hand and swung the butt end of it down hard on the back of Stone's head. Stone collapsed on top of Maria.

Reina grabbed Stone's arm and hauled with all her might to roll him off of Maria. The narrow cabin alley made maneuvering for leverage difficult, but eventually she got Stone's dead weight off his wife. She chafed Maria's hands and cheeks to revive her.

After several minutes, Maria's eyes fluttered open. They looked at first without recognition at Reina, then Maria smiled faintly and said, "Oh! I thought you were an angel."

Reina helped Maria up and got her seated on the bench. After verifying Stone was unconscious but not dead, she went and sat in the captain's chair. She surveyed the engine instruments on the panel. Well, it can't be that much different than flying a plane, she told herself, it just moves through water instead of air. Happy to see the key still in the ignition, she found the throttle controls and started up the engine. Fortunately, she could still see land faintly in the distance, so she turned the wheel in the direction of shore and pushed the throttle forward. With the sun setting on the horizon, she wanted to get this thing docked somewhere soon.

As Reina peered forward across the bow to try and discern the best direction in which to head, she heard a noise behind her. Turning to look, she saw Stone, apparently revived, attacking Maria again. This time, one good punch from his fist knocked his wife out. Stone turned menacingly toward Reina. Reina stood and fell backward in a panic against the boat's control panel as she scrambled to pull the revolver out of her pocket. Her backward fall landed directly on the throttle controls and the boat lurched forward, throwing Stone off his balance toward the rear of the cabin. Reina pulled out the pistol and pointed it at Stone. She clicked off what she hoped was the safety latch and said in a surprisingly steady voice, "Stop right there!"

Stone hesitated for only a moment. "Ha!" he said. "You don't have the guts to shoot me. I've never yet met a woman who had enough guts to stop me." He lunged toward Reina.

Reina felt every muscle tense as she pulled the trigger. As Stone fell, she said to him, "Well, you've never met me."

Before going to check his pulse, she turned her attention to the boat, which now raced ahead in nearly-dark conditions. She brought the throttle to idle to allow her time to get her bearings. She saw a light slightly to her left. As she looked more closely, it appeared to be a lighthouse, with its revolving beacon streaming out into the dimness. Confident they couldn't have gone too far, she figured it must be either New Dungeness or Ediz Hook Lighthouse. Although both lighthouses were at the end of long sand spits, at least it would be solid ground. She turned the boat in the direction of the light and advanced the throttle gently. With the boat slowly moving forward now, she turned to check on Stone. She saw a pool of red spreading out from under his body. Upon closer inspection, she observed, with just a tiny bit of pride, that the bullet had been rather well-placed. Directly into his chest, in fact. A check of his pulse verified that he was dead, stone dead. Glancing up to see where the bullet exited, she saw that it had gone clean through the boat, shattering the back window as it continued its journey out to sea.

 As Reina rose from Stone's body, she saw Maria sitting up, stiff and still. Her face a ghastly white, Maria looked straight ahead with horror, as if she had just seen a ghost. When Reina turned in the direction of Maria's stare, she realized Maria saw, apparently for the first time, the little handcuffs attached above each of the little bunks. Reina sat down for a moment and wrapped Maria in her arms.

 After a long silence, Maria turned to Reina and said, "I told you he needed to die."

Chapter 31

After dropping Caite at the hospital, Hawk sped toward Peninsula Shipping. As he approached the now-deserted compound, he tried the car's built-in garage door opener. The big bay door rolled open, eliminating the need to wade through the water again. He called Reina's cell phone, but no answer. For the second time that evening, he felt his heart constrict, now at the thought of someone roughing up Reina. With Caite safe, he needed to go find her daughter.

Hawk ran to the dock to see if the fishing boat had returned. In the near darkness, he could make out the large trawler, the runabouts, and the cigarette boat, but no fishing rig. He climbed aboard the sleek cigarette boat and searched for a key. Unable to locate the key on the dash or in the ashtray, he crouched under the ignition deck and, within a few minutes, had hotwired the boat. He quickly untied the mooring lines. Not knowing where to begin looking for the errant fishing craft, he took a moment to power on the navigation instruments. As he churned slowly away, beside the long dock, he felt a thud in the back of the boat. Looking over his shoulder, he was astonished to see Wong rolling to his feet.

"Holy shit!" Hawk yelled. "You don't die easily do you?"

Wong smiled evilly and lunged at Hawk. Hawk surged forward to meet him. At the last minute he caught the glint of metal in Wong's hand and feinted to the right to avoid the long blade. As Hawk's shoulder grazed Wong's side, Hawk threw out his left elbow catching his opponent just under the chin. Wong's head snapped back, but he twirled lithely and swung his knife at Hawk, just grazing his side. Hawk felt the sting of pain, which only served to fuel his anger and adrenalin. The two adversaries lunged again at each other, the accuracy of their punches significantly eroded by the lurching motion of the boat. With a fake jab followed by a well-aimed kick, Hawk managed to send Wong's blade soaring into the air and out across the water.

Hawk now sensed his advantage, as the smaller man began to tire. A couple more punches, then a full head butt and Wong was spinning backward. Off-balance and exhausted, Wong couldn't keep his feet as he was thrown against the back transom. Almost in slow motion, Hawk saw Wong topple backward over the edge of the boat, his arms flailing wildly for something to grasp. Hawk instinctively reached out to grab him, but it was too late. He was gone.

With the boat racing into darkness, Hawk didn't waste any thoughts of attempting a humane rescue. His priority was to find that fishing boat and make sure Reina and Maria were safe.

Hawk turned his attention to the boat panel. The expensive luxury craft had every instrument and piece of equipment a rich man's whims could buy, including a sophisticated radar system. Hawk tuned in the radar to sweep the waters ahead, but saw nothing. If Stone had taken the fishing boat out into the strait, they could be anywhere from here to Canada. He powered on toward the east, out of the protected bay but staying within visibility of the coastline. Still nothing. He worked his way toward the light ahead, the New Dungeness Lighthouse, shining its beacon in the dark for lost mariners. Drawing closer, he saw a radar blip on his screen, something close to the shore. He headed in its direction. Approaching cautiously, he could see the fishing boat bobbing gently along the high tide line of the Dungeness Spit. Hawk hunched down at the wheel. If Stone was armed, he would need the element of surprise on his side.

Chapter 32

Reina saw the long cigarette boat approaching slowly from the west. It was dark, and she couldn't see anyone at the helm. She waited until it was within shooting range, then emerged from the cabin with the revolver clenched between both hands, arms pointed straight out toward the boat. She braced her legs widely and called out, "Put your hands in the air." Waving the gun left and right, she added with bravado, "I'm not afraid to shoot!"

Hawk stood tall with hands held high. "I give up," he called out with a broad grin.

"Oh, thank God. Thank God it's you." Reina said, dropping her hands to her side. "Although I would've shot you," she added, raising her chin mulishly.

"Oh, I don't doubt it," laughed Hawk. "Are you all okay?"

"Well, Maria and I are fine. Stone didn't fare so well, I'm afraid." With the one sentence, Reina dismissed Stone from her mind. With her breath catching slightly in her throat, she asked Hawk the question that tormented her, the question to which she dreaded the answer. "Where's my mom?"

"She's fine. She broke her arm, but she'll be fine. You'll see her soon."

Reina sat down abruptly, light-headed, on a pile of rope, blinking her eyes to clear the sudden drops of moisture from them. Hawk tied the two boats together, climbed aboard, and came over to her, pulling her into his arms. She rested her head against his chest briefly, then looked up into his clear, deep eyes and wanted nothing more at that moment than to stay there, protected and safe. But wiping her finger across her damp lashes, she stood and led him into the cabin, where Stone lay glassy-eyed on the floor boards.

"He's dead," she said.

"I see that. Well, we'd better call the Coast Guard and get them to tow him in."

"No!" Maria spoke from the bench. "No! No one must know."

Reina sat down on the seat next to Maria. Hawk closed Stone's eyelids over his vacant stare before joining them on the bench.

"Maria," Reina said gently, "we can't just leave him here."

"You don't understand," Maria replied, her voice a faint whisper. "This is not about you, or me, or him. This is about something much bigger. This is about beliefs and trust and faith and eternal salvation. This is about thousands of people across the country and the world who have changed their lives because of the good *words* of Peter Stone. People who stopped cheating and lying and stealing and killing because they believed what Peter told them of a good and loving God. These people discovered hope through him. They cannot, they must not, find out his words were a lie. I cannot let that happen. I cannot let the salvation of so many be jeopardized by the discovery of Peter's human weaknesses." Maria held her hands out in front of her in emphasis, as if to physically stop this travesty from occurring. Reina could see her palms were bleeding, probably from the struggle with Stone.

"Maria," Reina replied softly, "Peter's crimes must be brought to justice."

Maria hung her head and mumbled, "Poor Peter. He had his own demons to deal with from his childhood. After what he suffered, how could he inflict the same on those boys." She dropped her head in her hands, shaking it sadly back and forth. When she finally looked up at Reina and Hawk, a jagged stain of blood, from her dripping palms, criss-crossed along her forehead. She looked a tragic sight.

Suddenly Maria grabbed the revolver off the table and stood up, holding it to her side. "Don't you see? I was willing to go to jail. I was willing to give up my life, *and his*, to save God's children. And I still am." She clicked back the gun's hammer and pressed the gun into her side.

Reina and Hawk looked at each other as Maria said firmly, "All the evidence must be destroyed."

Chapter 33

It didn't take long for them to make the necessary preparations on the boat. While Reina found a screwdriver and removed the handcuffs from the bunk walls, Hawk dragged Peter's body out to rest against the rear engine block. Alongside the body, he propped the two extra gas cans and the propane tank he removed from the gas barbecue on the deck of Stone's pleasure boat.

Reina and Maria climbed into the cigarette boat. Hawk joined them to hotwire the starter again, then turned it around, quickly showing Reina the basics of how to drive it. He then returned to the fishing boat, turned it around as well, and started to throttle out toward Canada, into the Strait of Juan de Fuca. Reina adjusted the power to keep the cigarette boat running alongside the fishing boat. After they'd gone some distance, Hawk came out of the cabin and climbed on to the back rail of the boat, holding on to the cabin wall for balance, with the fishing boat continuing to chug steadily out toward Canadian waters. He waved Reina in closer. Bouncing along in the rough water at a good clip, she tried several times to close in on the fishing boat, only to pull away when a rogue wave caused her to lose her careful position. Finally, she managed to get the sleek boat close enough, and to hold it steady so that Hawk could manage a leap across the water from the rail of the fishing rig to the floor of the cigarette boat. After Hawk was aboard, she gradually widened her distance from the fishing boat, keeping abreast of it and slightly behind.

Hawk braced his legs wide apart and leaned his thighs for support against the starboard rail of the cigarette boat. Holding his pistol out at arms' length, he sighted carefully on the propane tank in the rear of the forward-propelling fishing boat. He fired a quick succession of shots.

The explosion was immediate. With every nerve stretched taut, Reina felt herself jump about a foot at the burst of sound and fire, even though it had been anticipated. As the flames leapt into the sky, Reina saw Hawk nod his head at her. She turned the boat and headed full throttle for the bay.

Hawk watched his handiwork for a moment as it receded into the distance, then moved to the boat's wheel and offered to take over the driving for Reina. "I don't think we need to worry about there being much evidence remaining after that explosion," he said to her with satisfaction.

Reina gratefully yielded the controls to him and turned to tend to Maria who leaned limply against the side rail of the boat. To Reina's surprise, Maria was dry-eyed. She did not turn to watch the burning boat as it, and her husband, were consumed by flames. Instead, she gazed forward quietly, almost peacefully, into the darkness ahead. As Reina sat down next to her, she saw Maria's lips

Cate Mighell

moving, as if in silent prayer, as she dropped the tiny handcuffs, one by one, into the dark waters below.

Chapter 34

"Oh my God, where's Maria?" Caite asked in alarm as Hawk and Reina entered her hospital room.

"Not to worry," Reina answered. "She's okay - exhausted both physically and emotionally, but otherwise intact. I remembered your friend Steve had a sister in town and I called him to see if maybe Maria could sleep there for the night. They're fantastic people. So warm and generous. I didn't feel good about leaving her alone, but she needed rest, desperately."

"She must be in shock."

"Yeah. The only thing she would say was, 'It is finished.'"

As Reina spoke, she moved to her mother's bedside and gingerly sat down on the edge of her bed. "How are you, Mom?" She bent over to kiss her on her left cheek, grimacing at the ugly bruise that was forming on her mother's right cheek from Wong's slap.

"I'm fine, dear. The doctors say it was a nasty break, but eminently repairable. Thank God for modern medicine." Caite glanced at her arm, encased in a large cast and shoulder sling.

"Tell us what happened," Hawk and Reina said in unison, smiling at each other at the exact match of words.

"Well, as you know, that Wong person took me off to retrieve the DVDs. On the way to the car, he got a little fresh with me and when I tried to slap him, he batted my arm aside like he was going for a home run. I could hear the bone crack. He just laughed and shoved me into the car."

"So that explains why you were holding your right arm so oddly when you got out of the car at the airport terminal," Hawk exclaimed. "Grabbing the steering wheel with your broken arm to kick our friend Wong out of the car must have hurt like hell. I thought he broke it when he whacked at you during that last struggle."

"No, it was already broken, I'm afraid. That second whack just cinched the deal. Multiple fractures, the doctor said."

"Oh, Mom, I'm so sorry to drag you into this." Reina leaned over to give her a careful hug.

"Nonsense, dear, it was my choice, and I wouldn't do it any differently. My physical wounds will heal. I'm more worried about Maria. What's going to happen now with her and Stone?"

Hawk and Reina looked at each other again. They had agreed no one but the four of them would know all the details of tonight's actions. Together, they described to Caite the final outcome of the evening.

As Hawk recounted his battle with Wong on the cigarette boat, Reina had a sudden sense of *deja vu*, as if Hawk's tale was one she already knew, from something she had once seen or been told. She tried to remember, but it receded like a dream fading in the light of day. When

Hawk described kicking Wong's weapon overboard, Reina's eyes widened and she exclaimed, "You didn't tell me about all this."

"Well, you didn't ask," he replied with a grin. Reina suddenly noticed his torn shirt, caked in dried blood.

"What happened there?" she pointed. "Are you injured?"

Hawk glanced down at his belly, lifting the torn shirt flap to reveal a ragged surface wound on his side.

"That looks like it hurts," Reina said with concern, her stomach lurching unexpectedly with desire at the sight of his muscled abdomen. *Really! Back off lust girl!*

Hawk grimaced a little as he let the shirt flap fall, "Ah, it's nothing." He downplayed the cut, adding nonchalantly, "Pain is just weakness leaving the body, you know."

Caite laughed. "I'll have to remember that."

Reina described to them both her adventures in the boat closet and how she'd stormed out in the borrowed rubber boots and knocked Stone out cold. She then relayed to them the conversation between Maria and Peter. It seemed Stone had used his massive enterprise and international connections to traffic in the child sex trade. Using *The Rock* to showcase the available boys in the choir to the more discriminating purchasers, he then sold the untraceable orphan boys to the highest bidder, receiving the funds as "donations" to his non-profit entity. And when the boys disappeared into the dark, vast underworld of sex slavery, no one was there to notice, or to care. Except finally, Maria.

Her mom's eyes were closed as Reina laid out the details of the sordid affair. For a moment, Reina thought perhaps she had fallen asleep, until she saw one big tear roll slowly down her cheek and drip from her chin. They all three sat quietly, each lost in their own review of the bizarre turns of this last week. It suddenly dawned on Reina that the discussion in court of how Maria organized files in the office had broken the case open. Going through the files, alone in the office at night, Maria must have discovered the link between donations and lost boys. That explained why it triggered her tears that day.

Reina took her mom's good hand in her own when she told her about Peter Stone's demise, not completely sure how her mother would react to the knowledge her daughter had killed someone. Caite's general philosophy led her to go through life causing no harm and doing no damage. To Reina's relief, her mother took it in good stride.

"Well," she said sensibly, "a girl's gotta do what a girl's gotta do. I kicked Wong out without tormenting myself too much about killing him. Although, as it turns out, that honor fell to you," she turned to Hawk.

"Well, let's hope so," said Hawk wryly, "but last time we thought him dead we were wrong, so I'm not making any assumptions."

"I was so relieved when I realized it was you in that boat and not him," confided Reina, "although I was prepared to shoot, if need be. And I wouldn't have needed to fire four times either to hit him," Reina continued, smiling sideways at Hawk to tease him about his multiple boat-to-boat shots.

Hawk just looked at her for a long moment, his dark brows raised to points over his intense blue eyes. "One shot was for the propane tank, one for each of the two gas cans, and one for the engine. I wasted no shots." He spoke as if explaining rudimentary facts to a raw newbie.

"Oh," she felt her face flush slightly underneath his suddenly haughty look.

"And I don't miss," he added with a warm smile that reassured Reina she had not offended him. Or at least he had already forgiven her.

When Reina described the last scene, with the bleeding Maria taking the gun to herself, she was surprised to see her mom smile slightly.

"So, Maria has found both her voice and her inner strength. She has become the author of her own story."

"You know," Reina nodded, "I think it took a tremendous amount of inner strength to put up with what she's suffered for so many years. What a difficult situation! No way to go public, without causing what she considered unacceptable damage. And she was willing to sacrifice everything, including her good name and *her own life*, to save the innocent victims of this whole mess. I guess, in her quiet way, she's as strong as any woman I know. Certainly strong enough to follow through on her threat to put a hole in her side."

"Oh, I don't doubt it," her mom agreed. "Somehow, I don't think anyone will ever take the right of self-determination from Maria again." After a moment she added, "Will you be able to explain it all to the judge?"

"I'm not sure . . . still working that one out. It will have to be done very carefully to achieve the desired ending."

"Well, one thing is for sure. It looks like the prophetic words of the Reverend Peter Stone have come true."

Reina and Hawk looked at Caite in question.

"As he always said would happen, unrepentant sinners do indeed end up perishing in flames."

Chapter 35

The sun was edging west toward the treeline as Reina saw Maria walk around the corner of True Blue Aviation to the runway-side patio. Reina had gathered her friends in celebration of Hawk's student Ruthie, soloing an aircraft for the first time today. After Reina made introductions, Ditch, recovered from the vet and in residence at Reina's feet, barked once, clearly upset he'd been excluded. Reina looked down at him sternly and said, "You pitiful little mongrel, please don't be rude." He barked again and furiously wagged his scraggy excuse of a tail. Unable to ignore someone who so clearly adored her, Reina sighed in exasperation, "Yes, Mutt, you too. Maria, this is Ditch. Named for where I found him and where I should undoubtedly have left him." Ditch yelped and licked Reina's shoe.

Maria bent over to pet him, saying, "Hello you sweet thing." Looking up at Reina she added, "He's, um, he's . . . ." As she searched for a word to describe the ugly, scrappy creature, everybody laughed.

"Yes, I know," replied Reina in resignation, "but apparently I've been adopted by the little gnome." She looked down at Ditch, whose head now lay upon her foot in blissful ecstasy.

"Did you invite that prosecutor person here today?" Maria asked Reina.

"Who, Jerry?" Reina replied in surprise. "Definitely not. Why?"

"Oh, I could swear I passed him as I entered the parking lot here."

"Really? How weird." Reina raised her eyebrows in surprise for a moment, then shrugged it off. One of these days, she would figure out what was so creepy about him. She turned to scan the skies again.

The days were noticeably shorter now and the cool nip in the air warned that the loveliness of fall would soon give way to the harsh cold winter of the Pacific Northwest. Reina shielded her eyes against the low sun, watching the horizon for a sign of the small plane. Caite handed Maria a mug of steaming, hot coffee. Maria accepted it with a grateful smile, then turned to wave to Hawk who had glanced back from his waiting point out on the taxi way bordering the runway.

Reina understood Hawk's confidence and slight anxiety over his young student's ability. Although Ruthie had the makings of a fine pilot, the first flight alone always proved a little nerve wracking for both student and instructor. Reina watched Hawk, perhaps longer than absolutely necessary, standing with his legs spread wide and holding the portable radio close to his ear, listening for his student's return to the airport pattern area.

Looking over at her mother, Reina said with a smile, "Thank God the layer of autumn fog finally burned off this morning."

"Yes, I know. Ruthie would have been terribly disappointed to have to postpone her big day due to weather. Not that it matters," her mom added, "but it really is the ultimate badge of cool to actually solo an airplane on your 16th birthday."

"It is indeed," said Reina. "I remember it well." She gave her mom a quick hug, being careful of the arm that had just gotten out of its hard plaster cast and into a softer canvas arm support. "Does Jean-Pierre still have his Cap 10?" Reina inquired about the aerobatic aircraft in which she'd learned to fly while living with her mother in the south of France.

"As far as I know. We really need to go visit him one of these days soon."

"I would love to visit. It's been way too long." Reina remembered those carefree days of youth fondly. Although she'd not seen Jean-Pierre in a couple of years, she still considered him her adopted father. She had even legally changed her last name to his when they lived together like a family.

"I'll go, too," Liz chimed in. "French men are so hot!"

Reina laughed. Liz's boyfriend, Rob, rolled his eyes then leaned over and kissed Liz long and hard in front of everyone.

Liz looked at her long-suffering beau adoringly, and assured him, "Not that I'm looking, of course."

"Of course not!" Reina and Getta said in unison, supportive to the end of their fickle, faithful friend.

Reina smiled at her two best friends and said, "I think we should plan a trip to Europe in the very near future. Liz can handle the British, I'll handle the French, and Getta, we'll leave the Spanish up to you."

"I'm down," Getta replied. "Next summer. Let's do it."

Ditch barked in enthusiasm. When Reina said firmly, "Not you, Brutus," he hung his head in disappointment.

Turning to Maria, Reina asked, "So, how is the women's shelter plan evolving?"

It had been six weeks since Peter Stone disappeared, presumed dead, in the devastating boat fire seen far off the Sequim shoreline one evening in early September. Unfortunately, by the time the Coast Guard arrived at the scene of the fire, nothing remained from the blazing flames but a few charred remnants of wood.

Stone had been reported missing by his staff and further investigation revealed the missing fishing boat from the dock at Peninsula Shipping. Two and two were put together to eventually declare Stone perished in the flames, although his devoted congregation continued to pray for a miraculous survival. At first, the uncertainty around Stone's assumed death raised eyebrows in Maria's direction, but Reina swore, truthfully, that Maria had been with her at all times. There was no way to connect her to the incident.

Suspicion eventually fell on Wong, who apparently disappeared the same night as Stone. Speculation flew as to whether he too had fallen victim to the fire or, perhaps, he had created the fire itself out of some vendetta against Stone. It turned out no one liked or trusted Wong. There was a universal willingness to consider him the villain in this case.

Upon returning to Seattle, Reina had engaged in a long discussion with Judge Takahashi and opposing counsel, revealing some of the details she could safely share about Maria's circumstances. The State dropped all charges against Maria. Jerry, of course, was clearly disappointed to lose his opportunity for glory and public recognition.

After the joint meeting, Reina had gathered up her notes and headed to her office to file away the now-closed case. In the deserted hallway, Judge Takahashi appeared to be waiting for her, stepping up as Reina neared and blocking the young attorney's path. From under her craggy brows, the diminutive elderly woman looked searchingly at Reina for a long moment. She finally spoke, somewhat cryptically. "Law has nothing to do with Justice," she said, her eyes narrowing to laser points. Pursing her thin lips and staring piercingly at Reina for an uncomfortably lengthy pause, she added, "And sometimes, Justice has nothing to do with the Law." As she turned and walked away, she added sourly, "Except, of course, when you are in my courtroom. And I'll expect to see you there again soon." Reina had the uncanny feeling Judge Takahashi knew a lot more than she was saying. *But how could she?* Reina knew full well she could be disbarred for her actions that night out on the dark waters of the Strait of Juan de Fuca. She knew taking the law into your own hands was bad enough, but destroying evidence was never acceptable. Never, that is, until one day when it suddenly seemed like the only way to finally stem the egregious injustices inflicted by an unjust man. But she knew not everyone - maybe not many - would agree with her.

Despite Jerry's deep disappointment at missing his opportunity to grandstand the high-visibility case, he had continued his attempt to ingratiate himself with all of mankind for the Prosecutor's office. The evening following the judicial conference and dismissal of charges, Jerry approached Reina as she sat sharing a glass of wine with Ned at The Gavel. He stood alongside their table for several minutes, making small talk and trying to look down Reina's blouse.

"What is it about him that seems so creepy?" Ned asked as Jerry walked on to the next table, glad-handing and pumping the flesh with everyone in sight.

Reina laughed, "I've asked myself the same question. There is definitely something unsavory about him, isn't there?"

Upon regaining her freedom and her good name, Maria had lost no time in closing down *The Rock* and relieving most of the staff of their employment. Reina had no doubt she'd instigated a thorough cleaning-out of the buildings and businesses of Stone Kingdom Enterprises. A couple of weeks ago, Maria excitedly called Reina to inform her she had taken over direct management of the adoption agency and was working, herself, on adopting a set of young Taiwanese twin boys. And here she was today, glowing and vibrant, abloom with the possibilities of life.

"It's going well," Maria replied, smiling shyly as she responded to the question about her new pet project, the shelter for battered and homeless women. "There is such a huge need for women to have a nice place to go when they are alone or desperate, or maybe even scared for their lives. Do you remember me telling you about the woman, Rita, whom I met in jail? The one who got caught breaking into a convenience store?"

Reina nodded.

"Well," Maria continued, "she knows what it's like to live out of a car and to have to steal to feed her kids. But she's really smart, and kind, too. So, I made her my program manager."

Maria's enthusiasm for her new mission shone brightly in her clear, gray eyes. Reina thought for a moment of the sad shell of a woman she'd sat next to in jail not so long ago. The woman who couldn't, or wouldn't, speak. She'd seemed so dead, and now was so very alive.

Caite, standing at Reina's elbow, leaned in and whispered in her ear, "Yes, I agree. She has now stepped fully into the fairytale of her own life and is busy scribbling on every page. It is like she has risen from the dead."

Reina looked at her mother in surprise. Had she spoken aloud? For that matter, she wasn't sure her mother had spoken aloud. She smiled at her mom and her mother smiled calmly back. Sometimes, they didn't seem to need words.

Maria was still talking, "I wish you'd all come see what I've done to the Stone Kingdom building down on Fifth Avenue. My friend Heather from Montana – I think you met her – spent two weeks with me and my new vice president, Markus Pratt, helping us get everything set up for our new operations. I modernized the kitchen, too, so no one could ever get *accidentally* stuck in the refrigerator there."

Everyone laughed.

"I, for one, am happy to hear that," said Getta with a shiver.

Just then, the radio crackled and a girl's voice came over the frequency saying with authority, "Wayward Traffic, Skyhawk 735 Tango Uniform, on the forty-five for runway 34, touch and go."

All eyes turned to the northwest to watch the small speck in the sky grow larger as it entered the airport pattern. Ruthie made all the correct radio calls and executed her first landing. Although a little long and a little firm, the landing was perfectly acceptable. The crowd applauded as she powered up the engine for another take off.

As Ruthie completed her second pattern, Franco came over with the coffee pot to see if Reina wanted a warm-up. He looked handsome today in his off-duty attire of faded jeans and a long-sleeved, fitted, crew-neck shirt. Reina smiled up at him, into the brown eyes that could be so soft one minute, then hard as granite the next when faced with a law-breaker. Reina shuddered internally to think of how he would treat her differently if he knew how she had broken the trust. Even though she knew in her heart what she did was right that night on the water, she hoped she would never have to convince her peers of it. Franco, blessed with a much more black-and-white view of the world, would not condone her actions.

Reina asked him about the arrests that had been made in the big sex trafficking case. Franco and his partner had broken the sex ring wide open in the last month after receiving an anonymous tip with some key names. He assured her with grim satisfaction that the dragnet swept far and wide. The FBI, he said, was working with local jurisdictions to nail the perps from coast to coast. He swore the best lawyer in the South couldn't get Senator Samson Taylor off on the charges being levied against him for the rape and murder of three boys. In fact, evidence was mounting that the old bastard had been at his perverted practice for a long, long time. Reina remembered Maria's comment that night on the boat, that Peter himself had suffered some sort of abuse as a child growing up in the South. *Wouldn't that be ironic....* She felt a tingle up her spine at the thought.

Franco told her, too, about the Portland group that had taken a hard hit from local law enforcement. He expressed confidence that several key players in the Northwest had already been apprehended. Although, he acknowledged, they still didn't know the name of the big cheese, or cheeses, behind it all. There were rumors of Mafia connections, or perhaps a Chinese Ganglord involvement.

As Reina watched the new pilot execute her second landing and takeoff, she silently assured herself, again, that she had taken the correct action that night. Even more than she believed in the law, she believed in justice, and it appeared justice was being fairly meted out to all the right parties in this case. She looked up at Franco with gratitude and admiration, thanking him with her eyes. Even the nasty emails from the wife of the convicted police officer had ceased, thanks to Franco's straight talk with the woman.

Ruthie's third landing squeaked on the runway in gentle perfection. Clearly pleased with his pupil's performance, Hawk made his way back from the tarmac's edge to join the waiting crowd. Reina took a minute to introduce Hawk to Franco and Jomar. Although Hawk smiled and they all shook hands, Reina could almost see the hairs bristle on Franco's neck. Of course, she reasoned, Franco probably considered Hawk's ponytail to be highly unprofessional. She could think of no other reason Franco would instantly dislike the flight instructor. She turned to watch as the aircraft taxied toward the hangar where the new pilot's fans awaited.

Ruthie shut down the engine and exited the aircraft. Her ear-to-ear grin grew even bigger when everyone cheered and clapped and surrounded her and her amazing flying machine. As Ditch raced around the airplane in a furry frenzy, Reina took a picture of Hawk cutting off the back side of Ruthie's T-shirt. This old tradition indicated that a pilot could now fly solo, without an instructor tugging on her shirttails with directions. Today would indeed be a day Ruthie would never forget.

As they walked back to the patio, Reina put her arm around Ruthie's shoulders and said, "You sounded just like a professional up there on the radio."

Ruthie smiled and said, "Well, I had some good role models." She hugged Reina's side and smiled at Hawk and Caite. "You guys are awesome. That is the most amazing thing I have ever done!"

Caite smiled back, "Well, we helped with a little training, but in the end, it was all up to you. And you did it. You took charge, not only of your success, but today you were in charge of your very survival. That's a pretty powerful thing."

Maria added, "Yeah, if you ever want a job, I'd love to have you help at my women's shelter. We need capable young women like you for strong role models."

Ruthie beamed at the idea of being a powerful role model and Ditch barked in approval.

"Quiet, tramp," Reina said sternly. Ditch leaned against Reina's leg and gazed up with soft brown eyes under bushy eyebrows. "Don't try to plead innocence," she scolded. "I'm on to your trickery. I'm not falling for those sad-dog eyes again." Ditch barked happily and she couldn't help but laugh, reaching down to scratch him behind his one good ear.

Ruthie's mom, who had been too nervous to join the audience on the patio, now approached and gave her young daughter an awkward hug and a brief congratulations. Not a demonstrative family, Reina guessed, recalling that the mother had feared her husband's wrath at Ruthie's bold actions. Scurrying away, she busied herself by serving up cake and fresh coffee to the crowd.

Jomar picked up the camera from the table and snapped a picture of Ruthie with Reina and Caite on either side. Caite then insisted he take a shot of Reina and Hawk with Ruthie in the middle.

As they lined up by the plane and Hawk's hand reached out across Ruthie's shoulders, his fingers accidently brushed across Reina's face, sparking a jolt of electricity between them. Reina felt a strange sensation of twirling and buzzing, as though the prop scar on her temple had just been powered up. She blinked in dizziness and looked over to find him looking at her with his curious half-smile.

Reina caught her breath, wondering if he could feel the energy, too, if he could sense the way his eyes called her, like the summer twilight sky calling to come fly. Resisting the crazy urge to lick his finger, she turned her face to the camera and smiled widely.

Better keep your distance, this one is dangerous.

THE END

Silent Sky

Cate Mighell is a Seattle native and world traveler, having lived in countries in four different continents. As a one-time language teacher, she is well-versed in all the romance languages, particularly French.

Cate is an instrument-rated commercial pilot, and enjoys all sky activities, including aerobatic flying, skydiving, and just cloud watching. She has owned multiple businesses, including a successful flight school, somewhere north of Seattle *(really, the name similarity is just a coincidence!)*

The future adventures of Cate's heroine, Reina Dessiner, will take her to some of the places Cate knows, including France, Australia, and Africa.

You may contact Cate with questions or comments at cjmighell@gmail.com. She would love to hear from you, particularly if you noticed some of the symbolism and connections underlying this light-hearted tale.

To follow her blog, sign up at www.outoftheblueaviation.com

Cate Mighell